DEVIL'S RUN

BEVERLEY OAKLEY

AUTHOR'S NOTE

I hope you enjoy **Devil's Run**, Book 3 in the *Scandalous Miss Brightwell* series.

It follows **Rake's Honour** and **Rogue's Kiss**, and was a lot of fun to write.

Unlike the very steamy **Rake's Honour, Devil's Run** is more sensual. Eliza and Rufus are two very good, brave and honourable people who deserve each other, but have a lot standing in the way of their love.

I hope you enjoy reading their trials and tribulations and will be invested in reading the next story in the series, which centres around high spirited Katherine—Fanny Brightwell's daughter—and young Jack, the foundling child who played such an important role in **Devil's Run**.

If you want to read the first book in the series, **Rake's Honour**, you can do so by signing up to my mailing list and getting a free download (together with **Her Gilded Prison**, the first of my *Daughters of Sin* series) here.

Enjoy!

DEVIL'S RUN

CHAPTER 1

"And there's nothing else you'd like, my dear? No?" George Bramley found it an effort to keep the syrup in his tone as he straightened up after receiving the polite rebuff.

His bride-to-be had not even looked at him as she'd declined the piece of marchpane he'd been certain would win him at least a smile.

Hovering at her side, he weighed up the advantages of a gentle rebuke, then decided against it. Until yesterday, he'd thought her quiet demeanour suggested a charmingly pliant nature. Now, he was not so sure. In fact, suddenly, he was not sure of anything.

"A glass of lemonade perhaps, my angel? Or a gentle stroll?"

"I would prefer to be left alone." Miss Montrose waved a languid hand, while she continued to gaze at the still lake beside which their picnic party had situated itself.

George blinked and tried to mute his anger. The languid hand wave had not even been accompanied by a demure *thank you* as subtle acknowledgement of her gratitude, that not only had Mr Bramley, heir to a viscountcy, stepped in to rescue Miss Eliza

Montrose from impoverishment, he was prepared to treat her publicly as if she were as fine a catch as he *could* have made.

A soft titter brought his head round sharply, but the ladies behind him, bent over the latest *Ackerman's Repository,* appeared occupied with their own gossip as they lounged on cushions beneath the canopy that had been erected to protect them from the sun.

Awkwardly, he looked for occupation as he continued to eye his intended with a mixture of irritation and desire—both lustful desire, and the desire to put her in her place.

The idea of the latter made him harden. She was beautiful, this quiet, apparently retiring, young woman who said so little, but whose eyes spoke such volumes. The afternoon sun added a rich gloss to her hair and imbued her porcelain skin with a warm glow. The skin that he could see at any rate.

He pushed back his shoulders. On their wedding night in three weeks, when he'd at last taken possession of her, he'd rip that modesty to shreds. The skin she was so at pains to hide would be his, not only to see, but to caress and taste. When she was his wife, the beautiful, distant Miss Eliza Montrose would no longer get away with paying George Bramley so little attention. No, he'd have her screaming and writhing at his command. He would make her like the things he did to her, or at least show him she did if she enjoyed harmony as much as she appeared to. None of this languid reclining like a half-drugged princess in his presence. He'd keep her on her toes, ready to leap to his bidding at the sound of his footstep. She'd learn to be grateful.

Feeling ignored and superfluous, he turned to his uncle's detestable wife, Lady Quamby, and said with a smile, "Perhaps you and Miss Montrose would like to accompany me to the turret. Since you appear to have enjoyed this new novel, *Northanger Abbey,* so much, you might be interested to know there is an excellent view of the ruined monastery not far from here."

He was just priding himself on being so attuned to the feminine inclination for pleasure, when Lady Quamby half turned and sent him a desultory smile. "Oh, I think Miss Montrose looks perfectly comfortable, and Fanny and I are having such a lovely little coze." As if imitating Miss Montrose, she waved a languid hand in his general direction. "Why don't you take Mr Patmore off to see it? The two of you can tell us all about it when you return."

The fact that Miss Montrose didn't deign to even speak for herself, much less glance in his direction, sent the blood surging to Bramley's brain. By God, when he was married to Eliza Montrose, the limpid look of love so lacking now would be pasted onto her face every time he crossed her line of vision. She'd soon learn what was good for her.

He inclined his head, hiding his fury, and was on the point of leaving when Lady Quamby's sister, Fanny—for he'd be damned if he'd accord the little strumpet the title of Lady Fenton—leapt up from her chair. She'd been poring over the latest fashions, but now she smiled brightly up at him.

"I'll come with you, Cousin George. We'll have an excellent view from the battlements of the children learning to row. I told Nanny Brown and the nursemaid they could take them in the two boats if the children had been good."

Bramley fixed her with a dampening look. In fact, he was about to give up the idea of going up to the battlements altogether when his other guest, Rufus Patmore, suddenly rose and joined Fanny's side with a late and unexpected show of enthusiasm.

"Capital idea!" declared Rufus.

George flashed them both a dispassionate look. He'd chosen to invite his betrothed, Miss Montrose—whose chaperone was currently tucked up in the green bedchamber nursing a head cold —to be his guest at his uncle's estate, Quamby House, after receiving intelligence that Ladies Quamby and Fenton would be safely in London with their husbands and children. Instead, the brazen Brightwell sisters—as they'd infamously been called when he'd first made their acquaintance—had altered their plans, and were now in dogged attendance, reminding him as they always had, of some awful tenacious climbing plant, determined to find a foothold wherever they could in order to rise in the world.

Rufus, a last minute addition and acquaintance from his club, Boodles, was here because he'd purchased a horse from Bramley the night before. Now, Rufus was gazing at Lady Fenton with the same dewy-eyed fondness George was used to seeing reflected in the eyes of his uncle, the Earl of Quamby, who called the Bright-well sisters his precious rosebuds. To George, they were common dandelions! And now they had overridden Quamby House, the rambling Queen Anne manor house and estate that would have passed to George the moment his uncle quit this mortal coil, were it not for the snotty-nosed infant Lady Quamby had borne far too early in her marriage to George's uncle.

George shook his head. He'd changed his mind. Only, there was Rufus already ten yards away, striding across the lawn with Fanny at his side, and George didn't want to be seen as petulant for having offered the suggestion in the first place. Or have his snubbed and ignored status so much on parade, since the two remaining ladies—Miss Montrose and Lady Quamby—now had their heads bent together in deep discussion, with no apparent interest in seeking his company.

By God, he thought, clenching his fists as he set off after the other two at a brisk trot, they'd all rue the day they showed George Bramley so little respect.

Doing his best to hide his bubbling rage, he trailed them across the lawn, breathless when he reached the bottom of the spiral staircase that led to the battlements, while the pair in front chattered the whole way. The pert outline of Fanny's shapely bottom, at eye level as she climbed the stairs in front of him, was a taunting reminder of what he'd failed to secure for himself so many years before, and had Rufus not been there, George might have done something to assuage the dull ache that frequently erupted into blind fury when he recalled the scathing manner with which Fanny had rejected him. George did not forgive easily.

Now, Cousin Fanny's presence at Quamby House was a

constant reminder of how poorly George had been treated. Seven years ago, he'd been prepared to rescue not only Fanny from scandal and disgrace, but also her insufferable sister and deplorable mother after the girls' father had sucked on the barrel of a gun, leaving the remaining impecunious Brightwells flailing in the River Tick.

Stopping to catch his breath, he watched Fanny and Rufus, now at the top, put their heads together and laugh at some little joke, and the bile burned the back of his throat. He'd hoped to get his revenge through Fanny's younger sister, Antoinette. Lord knew, the girl had been willing enough, though he was always in two minds as to whether the former Miss Antoinette Brightwell was the most featherbrained peagoose, or the most dangerous cuckold he'd ever had the misfortune to lure into his bed.

"George, you're looking very red, and you're panting very loudly. Why don't you turn around and go back. Mr Patmore and I are quite happy here on our own."

George was damned if he'd meekly acquiesce to Fanny's barbish attempt to rid herself of his company. He could match her stamina, breath for breath, and one day he intended doing just that—on a featherbed like the one he'd taken her sister just nine months before Antoinette had given birth to the squalling infant, whom his uncle—who had never intended marrying, for he had no interest in women—happily claimed as his own. The so-called heir that had ousted the rightful heir, George.

To add insult to injury, Miss Antoinette Brightwell—who'd been saved from carrying the lifelong shame of becoming a fallen woman and an unwed mother had, after she'd giggled her way down the aisle to assume her title as the new Duchess Quamby, insisted the child was named George. Young George.

"I'm enjoying the exercise," rasped George, forcing his mouth to turn up at the corners, though his vision clouded with rage and his eyes watered as he stared past her into the orange, limned sunset once he'd collapsed onto the parapet beside them.

What could he do? Hope Young George disappeared down a

well, and Antoinette had produced no further heir to replace the dweedlenap, meaning George was again set to inherit? George would be happy if Antoinette and the bastard were erased from the face of the earth, though doing anything about it, himself, was a step too far.

"What a lovely girl your betrothed, Miss Montrose, is," Fanny gushed as she leaned over the battlements, flanked now by the two gentlemen. George wished the battlements were just a little lower, and that Fanny would lean just a little too far. It would be preferable to see her lose her footing and hurtle through space, breaking her head on the cobblestones below, than knowing she'd never be his.

Fanny turned and slanted him a knowing look from beneath her lashes. "She looked positively in transports at the prospect of becoming your bride, Cousin George."

The fact that Miss Montrose had barely addressed anyone all weekend, and had gone so far as to publicly avoid George, would not have gone unnoticed.

When he didn't answer, she went on sweetly, "I think it very noble of you, Cousin George, to want to rescue Miss Montrose from her penniless state, but I can't help but wonder if there's another reason you would wish to wed her, for all that she's very lovely to look at."

Now Rufus was looking at him expectantly, but there was no way on God's earth George would admit to anything beyond the fact that Miss Eliza Montrose was a beauty, and that if she inherited her aunt's estate, not only would George's comfort be assured, he'd be married to a diamond of the first water. He'd been prepared to take a wife of great beauty and no fortune when he'd offered for the social climbing Miss Fanny Brightwell, now laughing gaily beside him at some inane remark Rufus had just made, but she had destroyed his illusions about women. George intended having a wife of great beauty *and* fortune, and Miss Montrose would soon have George to thank for her aunt choosing to favour her with her worldly goods.

Yes, Miss Montrose would have a lot for which she would learn she must be grateful.

"Indeed, Miss Montrose is very lovely," agreed Rufus, adding thoughtfully, "though perhaps a trifle retiring, if you don't mind my saying so. I've not heard her murmur more than two words together."

Somehow, it pleased George to hear Rufus put a dampener on Fanny's endorsement of the young woman, who'd publicly snubbed him not minutes before.

He bowed in acknowledgement of this observation. "It's true that her conversation is limited, though after we are married, her ability to make conversation will be even more inconsequential, I daresay. I've chosen her to be my wife, regardless of her short-comings."

He grinned, challenging them to share the humour of his double entendre. Instead, Rufus appeared to consider the matter. "I must say, I like the idea of a wife who can entertain me with lively conversation. Yes, a woman of beauty, kindness, and virtue is what I'm after. I want to grow old with a helpmate who displays intelligence and spirit, not a porcelain doll."

"Indeed?" For some reason, George didn't like the fact that his friend Rufus sounded so...modern, though what did it matter? Rufus wasn't really a friend. He'd simply evinced an interest in buying a horse at their club one evening, and George had been keen to boast the merits of those in his uncle's fine stable, which George managed.

Certainly, the ladies seemed to admire the pleasantly agreeable Rufus Patmore, and George had been more than happy with the sum Rufus had handed over for a feisty stallion named Carnaby; a sum very different from the amount George intended to declare to his Uncle Quamby.

But while George had done well out of the transaction, he resented the attention Rufus garnered, which the fellow just took for granted. Just as Rufus took for granted the rest of his good fortune. Rufus Patmore knew nothing of hardship, unlike George who had been unfairly treated his whole life.

George glanced up from contemplation of his Hessians and the reflection that Rufus also enjoyed a more conscientious valet than he, judging by the shine on their respective footwear. Perhaps the time had come to dispense with the services of Timkins, he thought idly, before noticing that Fanny's sharp-eyed gaze remained unwaveringly upon him.

"It doesn't have anything to do with the fact that Miss Montrose's aunt is weighing up which of her two nieces should inherit her considerable fortune?" she asked. "I'm talking about your nuptials, George, in case you've lost the thread of the conversation."

God, he hated the way she talked to him. And the way she could read him. Stiffly, he responded. "Of course not, though I'd stake my money on Miss Montrose. She's a far better fish than her cousin."

Fanny looked admiringly at him. "What a betting man you are, George. I didn't know you knew anything about her cousin. Or perhaps yours is in fact a true love match?" She put her hand to her heart and her expression softened, before her eyes gleamed with mocking humour. "I'm curious, though, as to whether you'd still be prepared to go ahead with the marriage if Miss Montrose *doesn't* inherit her aunt's fabulous fortune?"

"We would contest the will. I didn't offer for her without consulting a lawyer, who said I'd have a good claim. Or rather, Miss Montrose would. She's lucky to have me to look out for her interests."

"Lucky, indeed," Fanny murmured, again leaning over the battlements.

"Yes, indeed," corroborated Rufus, leaning over the battlements also, and appearing to lose interest in what George was saying.

A flare of anger skittered through George at the boredom in Rufus's voice. He hated the way people dismissed him. Well, Miss

Montrose—Eliza—never would. To reclaim their attention, he said, "She is beautiful, and kind, and that is enough for me. Have you noticed how she achieves stillness like an art form?"

They both looked at him in some surprise. Yes, they were well-crafted words, George decided, and they were true. The latter part, anyway. He pointed at the tiny figure that was Miss Montrose, still reclining in her chair exactly as they'd left her. Indeed, she could have been a statue, for Antoinette had left her side and was returning to the house, already some distance up the sweeping slope that greened the hill between the manor and the lake.

In front of Miss Montrose was the broad expanse of water, a small island in the middle, two rowing boats bobbing in between. Fanny and Antoinette's children—Young George and Katherine—were in one, pulling at the oars with the straight-backed figure of Nanny Brown at the helm. In the other, sat the nursemaid who was being rowed by the urchin from the foundling home who often visited his uncle's estate.

"I hope Eliza hasn't bored them," George muttered, not sure at this stage whether it would add more to his consequence to build up the supposed assets of his bride-to-be, or to highlight her deficiencies.

"It's true; she doesn't say much,' Fanny conceded. 'Still, she is very lovely to look at, and I'm sure you'll make it your life's mission to bring a smile to her countenance, George." She shaded her eyes. "Poor Nanny Brown. Do you think I should go down now and rescue her? She does hate the water, and Katherine does love to torment her."

Rufus grinned as he pointed. "She's doing it now. Look, there's a veritable water fight going on. I meant to ask earlier, who is that fair-haired lad in the other boat. Oh look, your Katherine is trying to climb over to join him."

"I do wish she wouldn't," Fanny murmured anxiously. "She's utterly besotted by him. That's Jack from the foundling home. He comes three days a week to play with Young George, who was becoming so sulky and difficult without a playmate to keep him in check. Lately, however, Katherine seems to want exclusive rights to his company and Young George is forever in tears since *he* wants exclusive rights to Katherine, it would seem." She sighed. "Still, having a foundling lad was a good idea for young Albert, Grayling's son."

"Good Lord, do you mean that gypsy boy who left with the Graylings was young Albert Grayling's companion? And the two boys are from the foundling home? I thought that gypsy lad was the bootboy." Rufus looked surprised, though not scandalised as George was by the liberal goings-on in his uncle's home.

Unexpectedly, Fanny flashed a smile at George, and his heart ratcheted up a notch before he cursed himself. She'd done it on purpose, he was sure. Yes, she'd deliberately brought into the conversation mention of her cousin, Miss Thea Brightwell—now married and the mother of the aforementioned young Albert Grayling—reminding George that his attempts to blight the marital aspirations of another unworthy Brightwell had been inferior to Fanny and Antoinette's efforts to effect for their Cousin Thea a fine matchmaking outcome.

Fanny brushed her hand lightly across the back of Rufus's where it rested on the battlement, and George felt a surge of jealous rage. It only intensified as he registered the flare of unmistakeable interest in Rufus's eyes before she said, "I must tell you the story of how Jack comes to be spending three days a week at Quamby House, Mr Patmore. It's most diverting. Would you care to hear it?"

"Indeed, I would."

Fanny then launched into a tale of the afternoon Fanny's cousin, the penniless Miss Thea Brightwell as she was then, had been travelling in her carriage when her coachman had knocked over a young woman running across the road. In her arms was a bundle, a young boy of about three months with, Thea noticed, a tiny sixth finger on his left hand.

"Anyway," Fanny went on, "after Grayling and Thea's darling

Albert was five, they decided he needed a playmate, and it would be a fine thing to choose one from the foundling home en route for a five-day visit to Quamby House. Well, when she was there, Thea discovered Jack, whom she knew must be the infant her coachman nearly killed, because of his sixth finger. His mother had obviously been trying to put her unwanted child into the basket near the gates of the home when she'd been knocked over."

"What a coincidence," Rufus remarked, clearly invested in the story.

"Indeed it was! Cousin Thea is so softhearted, she couldn't bear to leave Jack behind. Nor could she resist taking another child, the big, strong gypsy boy whom she thought would be the ideal playmate for Young George, since Antoinette was forever wailing that he needed putting in his place if he weren't to grow up a puling, whining creature."

George turned his head away from the quick look Fanny darted at him, and pretended he wasn't listening as she went on.

"Unfortunately, the gypsy lad, Rafe, was forever getting into scraps with Young George, while Jack was the consummate diplomat. Rafe and Albert seemed to like playing together and are today as thick as thieves. Meanwhile, Fenton and I decided that after five days of peace and calm and no fights between Katherine and Young George, we should have Jack here on a regular basis."

"And Lord Quamby allows this?"

"He agrees to anything if it'll make Antoinette happy and his life easier."

George had to bite his tongue as he knew any interjection would only further encourage Fanny, who went on, "It's not as if these orphans are being brought up to expect the privileges of their playmates. The foundling home boys come only three days every week. They share Katherine and George's lessons so that, with a little rudimentary education, they will not disgrace their noble playmates. It's all rather a novelty, really. My Katherine, and Antoinette's George are brought up to understand that they are superior, but that they're not to take advantage. Thea and

Grayling live some distance away, but they have a similar arrangement."

Rufus laughed. "How novel and modern. I must say, I did think Young George rather an unprepossessing ninnyhammer compared to your spirited Katherine, and Grayling's bold young Albert, not to mention Jack, who seemed a lively, intelligent lad."

George pushed his shoulders back and his chin forward. Cousin Fanny was secretly taunting him, while encouraging Rufus to deride the boy. Well! His detractors would be singing a different story when Devil's Run made him a fortune, and became the lauded champion of the East Anglia Cup, in less than two weeks' time.

He cleared his throat. "If Young George is to be criticised, then might I say that I think your Katherine could do with a little less spirit." Young Katherine was far too much like her mother and in decided need of a set-down, he thought. "Most gentlemen like their wives pliant. I certainly do, which is one of the reasons I'm happy to wed Miss Montrose."

Fanny raised an eyebrow and offered him a smile he did not like. However, she was prevented from saying more by a piercing scream from the direction of the lake, which had them all jerking their heads around, and shading their eyes to see if the children's high jinks had progressed to downright naughtiness that Nanny Brown was unable to suppress.

It was far worse than that.

"Dear God, one of the boats has overturned!' Fanny screamed, hiking up her skirts and flying down the slippery stone steps that wound to the bottom. Her precious Katherine was barely six and unable to swim.

With a cry of pain as her ankle turned, Fanny had to stop on the second level and support herself against the wall by the archers' slits while the two men passed her on the stairs. Her heart pounded against her rib cage as she stared through the narrow window, searching vainly for more timely assistance that might be rendered the vulnerable children, then screamed again when, in the distance, she caught sight of Katherine's dark head as the little girl floundered in the murky water, her white cambric dress bubbling up about her.

Despite her pain, Fanny continued to the bottom of the staircase to the lawn, her breath rasping as she saw Antoinette far away by the manor house, her sister only turning now and becoming aware something was wrong as Mr Patmore pounded down the slope.

Fanny tore after him, scanning the far distance before she saw the most incredible sight. The previously marble-like Miss Eliza Montrose had left her sanctuary and was at the water's edge, as fleeting as a hare. Now she was plunging into the lake, and with strong, expert strokes had almost reached Nanny Brown, who was clinging to the side of the non-upturned boat. The two children and their nursemaid in the other boat surged over to the side, hands wildly clawing for Katherine, who mercifully gripped the older woman's hand, and Fanny was just thanking God her precious child was safe, when that boat suddenly flipped, plunging the others—including Young George and Jack—into the water.

"Dear God, no!" In all her life, Fanny had never felt so helpless, so frightened, and so at the mercy of the gods. Her ankle be damned! Her feet barely touched the ground as she flew across the lawns, praying for forgiveness for all the terrible things she'd done, though she hadn't been *so* bad, surely? Fanny's many past detractors had warned her she'd one day be called to account for her sins, but what god would punish an innocent child? Besides, Fanny's transgressions had been done in the name of self-preservation.

Jaw clenched, eyes trained ahead, she could see in her peripheral vision that her sister was now tearing down the slope—screaming. Meanwhile, Miss Montrose had reached one of the upturned boats, but there was too much flailing and splashing for Fanny to deduce what was happening.

Then—dear Lord! Miss Montrose disappeared beneath the water. Did she no longer have the energy to save them? Were they all to be consigned to a watery grave?

"Save them! Oh, please save them!" she shrieked, placing all her hopes now in Mr Patmore, who had just torn off his jacket to plunge into the water.

But it was Miss Montrose who came up triumphant, emerging at the water's edge, staggering out of the shallows with two bedraggled children, one under each arm. Fanny arrived the moment she dropped them ashore, before she wordlessly turned back, wading through the water, her expression dogged, her breath coming in short bursts.

Mr Patmore, who had since disappeared in a spray of water, rose from the shallows after righting one of the boats and tossing the nursemaid into it. Bedraggled Nanny Brown was too heavy, so clung to the side as he towed the boat back to shore.

Fanny was just heaving a sigh of relief when Antoinette arrived at her side, slipping on the wet grass, barely coherent as she cried, "Where's George? Dear God, the children are all accounted for except Young George!"

The sisters shaded their eyes to gaze across the lake, glittering beneath the high sun, Fanny turning to George Bramley who was standing, dry-footed, at the lake's edge. "Find Young George!" She gripped his lapels and shook him. "He must be under the water still! Go!" She had to push the odious creature into the murky depths to find his own son, realising with a jolt of horror that she was forcing him to save the life of the one creature who stood between him and inheriting his uncle's title and estate.

There was no time to see how far reluctance would have stood in the way of decency and duty, for at that moment, Miss Montrose rose from the depths clutching the collar of the bedraggled young George, who sucked in a huge breath and began to splutter and then cry as he was deposited on the shore by the other children.

The three youngsters, nanny, and nursemaid had all been saved from drowning through the efforts of Mr Patmore, and, perhaps more remarkably, Miss Montrose—who stood staring down at them as if she too couldn't quite believe what had happened.

Antoinette was weeping, crouched over Young George, while Jack the foundling lad looked as he'd just had a wonderful adventure, and Katherine was just fine, dancing about the others, taunting Young George for being a crybaby. She didn't need her mother. But then, she never had, Fanny thought a touch sadly. Miss Independence was her Katherine.

Fanny moved forward to thank Miss Montrose, but Mr Patmore cut across her, putting his hand on Miss Montrose's shoulder.

His voice was full of wonder. "Miss Montrose, you were remarkable. Where did you learn to be so…fleet of foot and…like a fish in the water?"

She blinked as if coming out of a daze. Then she smiled, and because the young woman had never smiled, Fanny noticed she was suddenly transformed into a beauty. "I grew up by a river. My brother and I swam in it all the time." She began to shiver, and Mr Patmore called out. "We need a blanket. Miss Montrose is in shock. Hurry!"

A servant was soon running down the grassy slope with a blue woollen blanket which Mr Patmore wrapped around Miss Montrose, rubbing her vigorously at first, before turning her in his arms to look down into her face. And Fanny, who was about to take Katherine in her own arms, caught a fleeting glimpse of the look that passed between Mr Patmore and Miss Montrose, and was most intrigued.

CHAPTER 2

Eliza had forgotten what it felt like to enjoy a man's attention. Mr Patmore had started to dry her in a vigorous attempt to warm her, but then his touch gentled, and he simply stared down at her.

The wonder in his eyes as he murmured words of praise was a rare sensation. Embarrassed, she turned away. Yes, turned away because she could not afford to be so obviously disquieted by another man when she was affianced to George Bramley, who stood a few feet away from her. Mr Bramley was also staring, but there was no softness in *his* countenance.

Hoping to avoid any more gestures of admiration or kindness from Mr Patmore, Eliza politely extricated herself and put her hand out to arrest the progress of the foundling home lad whom Nanny Brown was pursuing with a piece of dry linen.

His impish grin reminded her of young Miss Katherine's, Lady Fenton's daughter. Clearly, the two had had a great adventure, unlike Young George, who was lying on his stomach upon the grass, shaking with sobs.

"Did you drink a lot of water, Young George?" Eliza asked, looking down at the crying boy, but he ignored her.

"I *said* we shouldn't go out! I *said*!" He pounded his fists on the ground. "No one ever listens to what I say!"

Eliza shared a wry smile with the rather lovely Mr Patmore. He was still staring at her and, disconcertingly, looked about to approach her again. To deflect him, she knelt to address the foundling boy. Eliza would not have Mr Bramley—or anyone else— accuse her of encouraging the attentions of a man not her betrothed.

"Jack—that's your name, isn't it? Well, you'll have something to tell them back at the foundling home." She'd seen him only from a distance and now, mud bespattered and with his hair matted over his forehead, it was difficult to make out his features, though she knew from various anecdotes that young Jack distinguished himself for keeping Miss Katherine's wilfulness in check, and peace between Katherine and her cousin, Young George.

Jack stood obediently before her as he started to wring out his threadbare shirt. "Nah, I'm fine, m'lady," he said, glancing up to reveal a pair of small white teeth in a freckled face. "But thanks for savin' me, an' all."

Eliza was about to let him go. Releasing her grip a second later might have changed the course of her life, she thought that evening, and perhaps it would have been better if she had. Why repeat the trauma she'd already experienced?

But for now, she was acting on instinct, and instead of letting him go when it would have seemed natural, her grip on his wrist tightened while the air in her lungs disappeared, and she had to open and close her eyes three times before she was ready to believe what she saw.

"Gideon?" There seemed still no air to say his name. A great pressure was building in her head. Finally, she was able to gasp in a breath, forcing herself to resist the urge to draw him into her embrace and wail her joy.

How many other boys of seven years sported a tiny extra claw on their left hand? Or had been thrust into the cold, unloving world of the foundling home, she thought bitterly.

He stopped what he was doing to look at her uncomprehendingly, and she added faintly, "Though that's not what they call you, of course."

An amused look crossed his face, making him seem older and wiser than his seven years. Nearby, the weeping and wailing George was a puling infant. Smiling at her was a little man.

He pushed out his chest and said in a tone that was neither boastful nor self-pitying, "There's some 'at call me Devil's Cub, or bastard, but at the manor here they call me Jack."

Devil's Cub? The sixth finger accounted for the nickname, of course.

"Miss Montrose?" In the distance, Lady Fenton was calling her. Eliza was suddenly shaking like one suffering the ague. "Jack," she repeated in a whisper, still staring at him as she clenched her own fists. Was the child tormented by his deformity? Eliza couldn't remember how many times she'd been told the sixth finger was God's punishment upon her bastard babe, but he seemed unfazed.

"Miss Montrose! Come away! Susan is waiting in the house with a warm bath and blankets. You must be chilled to the bone!"

Vaguely, she could hear the sounds of concern all around her, but all Eliza could focus on was the impish face before her—that of her lost child.

She tried to pull herself away from an unseemly and unhelpful display of emotion, but as the past rushed up to meet her, her knees seemed suddenly to have no substance, and she would have collapsed over the boy had not Mr Patmore, who appeared to have been watching her all this time, put his arm about her shoulders to steady her.

"You're wet through; the ladies are calling you, and the sun has gone behind a cloud." She must be more helpless than she'd thought for his arms tightened about her as he supported her weight. "Let me help you to the house."

Eliza was barely conscious of him—other than that he offered her, in a general manner, a warmth and comfort she was unused to —as she stared at her child.

Then Katherine called out, and Jack sprang to attention in answer to his little friend's imperious beckoning, an impish lad leaping over Young George, who still lay curled, foetus-like on the ground, while Nanny Brown tried unsuccessfully to soothe his hysterics.

"Please, Miss Montrose; you can lean on me. We must get you warm again."

Eliza didn't think to question why it should be Mr Patmore taking charge and not her betrothed, though Mr Bramley, it was true, wove about her pretending concern.

Yes, pretending to have her best interests at heart like he always did, and as he would after he married her. Pretending he was a good prospect and would be a good husband. Eliza had only accepted because there had been no other marriage offers during the past seven years and, yes, despite everything, she did still yearn for the one thing that could not be granted her outside of lawful wedlock—a child.

Her time at Quamby House was a world away from the privations she endured living with her aunt, but after this weekend, she'd thought to cry off. George Bramley seemed to grow less appealing a prospect the more she got to know him.

"Yes, warm," she repeated, not knowing what she was saying, while before her eyes danced images of the infant who'd been with her long enough for her to remember every loving embrace, every babyish smile. The pain of what she'd been forced to give up had never lessened. Now she was face to face with the very being she'd shredded her soul to be reunited with. Her own Gideon. Only, he wasn't Gideon. What did they call him?

"Come here and let's clean you up, Jack." Nanny Brown seized the boy's arm and hauled him across her lap, roughly drying him while Katherine danced about the two of them. "Naughty Jack, it was your fault we all tumbled in, but it was fun, wasn't it?"

"We'll get the details in good time!" Nanny Brown grumbled, sending her mischievous charge a severe look. "Like as not it was you, Miss Katherine, behind it, only young Jack will take the blame like he willingly does, if only to get you out of a scrape and your just punishment."

So, her boy was a true gentleman? Eliza experienced a little spurt of pride before Nanny Brown's next words quashed her lifted spirits.

"We'll have to find you a dry set of clothes before we send you back to the foundling home, eh Jack? And Cook will give you a nice bit of sausage as a treat, eh, considering the nasty fright you've had."

Foundling home? They were going to send him back to the terrible place tonight? After all that had happened?

Guilt tore through her, and she had to resist the urge to step forward and claim him as her own.

But how could she, surrounded as she was by her betrothed and the society to which she needed to belong if she were to secure his future?

So, her Gideon still lived in that cold, cruel place to which she'd consigned him as an infant, without love and tenderness, knowing only the most rudimentary of both here? She thought she would cry. Her aunt had told her Gideon had been adopted by a loving family. A childless farmer and his wife. She'd even shown Eliza a letter to prove it.

But really, he was just where she'd left him. It was almost impossible to fathom. Yes, he was rewarded with regular visits to Quamby House to play with aristocratic children, but what compensation was it to get a taste for the good life if it only reinforced what he was missing out on?

Her mind raced as she was aided up the slope. Aided by whom? She glanced up to see Mr Patmore's profile, a determined look on his face as he stared ahead, though his fine, handsome features softened each time he glanced down at her. He had the face of a thoughtful man, she decided. In stark contrast to Mr Bramley. Her betrothed walked on her other side, but other than offering her his arm, he made no attempt to touch her.

She was aware of someone speaking, and saw it was kind Mr

Patmore. "Please don't cry, Miss Montrose." He squeezed her hand. "It's shock, I know, and you were so brave and collected as you plunged into the lake. I've never admired someone more."

She hadn't known she'd been crying, and his words sounded curiously intimate as he lowered his head to comfort her.

She hoped Mr Bramley couldn't hear, and found herself smiling gratefully at Mr Patmore before berating herself. No! She wasn't that kind of woman. She would give no man false encouragement.

"Lords Quamby and Fenton and their wives will forever have you in their debt." His hand was squeezing hers again, and with shocked awareness, she jerked her head up to look at him. Was it a sign of sympathy? Of solidarity or respect? Eliza no longer knew what physical gestures meant. After her lapse, she'd not received kindness. It had been forbidden, it seemed.

The look Mr Patmore sent her was that of a man who wanted to do much more than just squeeze her hand. He murmured, "Lady Fenton said just now she didn't think she could ever repay you.'

"I did only what I had to."

"Risked your life to leap fully clothed into the river?"

"Anyone else would have done the same." They'd stopped at the bottom of the portico steps, and now Eliza turned and looked over her shoulder, back down to the lake. The children were up and running around. Except Young George. Eliza closed her eyes, wondering how she could leave.

"Somehow I don't believe that." There it was again. The admiration in Mr Patmore's voice that was so...unfamiliar.

"I was the only one in a position to render assistance," Eliza replied, forcing distance into her tone. And then, with irony, "Besides, it was no hardship to throw myself into the lake." She'd often thought of throwing herself into a lake. Or a river. Or off the castle battlements.

Not now, though. Not now she'd found Gideon. She just needed to devise a plan so she could protect him. Nurture and protect him and safeguard his future.

Which meant safeguarding her own, she thought with a pang, as she glanced at Mr Bramley.

"Remember, you are among friends, Miss Montrose." Mr Patmore was still supporting her, encouraging her to lean upon him as they took the steps, for she was shaking now. The cold had seeped through to her very bones. She appreciated Mr Patmore's kindness and gentle concern. Finally, Mr Bramley pushed in to offer the necessary assistance, and she felt again the discord he always occasioned; the slight prickling at the back of her neck, and steeled herself as usual to accept his caress.

"Thank you, Mr Bramley." She injected her words with a qualified gratitude. And she'd be grateful now, like she'd not been before because, in a twist of irony, Mr Bramley truly did offer her her heart's desire.

When she moved into his apartments here, he guaranteed that children would be part of her life. Most importantly, Gideon—Jack —who was all but a fixture here, would play in the gardens and she'd watch over him. Just as she did in her dreams.

Really, it was a dream come true.

"And thank you, Mr Patmore." She inclined her head in dismissal, while she accepted her betrothed's offer of an arm to escort her the remaining few steps towards the house. The front doors had been thrown open, and the servants were murmuring their awe, nodding their heads as the ladies and gentlemen made their progress through the earl's palatial reception hall and then to the staircase, arriving in the corridor above where Eliza was met by her chaperone old Mrs Mayberry who appeared, briefly, with a compress pressed against her the side of her face before she disappeared back into her bedchamber.

Eliza arrived at her own bedchamber door, turning upon the threshold to see Lady Fenton hurrying up the corridor. Almost running, Eliza would have called it except that aristocratic ladies didn't run. That said, Lady Fenton's behaviour didn't always accord with what Eliza considered would pass muster in the set to which she belonged, although in the twenty-four hours Eliza had spent under this palatial roof, she could see that Lady Fenton would be excused almost any transgression by her adoring husband.

"Miss Montrose, I didn't thank you properly."

Eliza offered her a faint smile. "You said all that was needed down by the lake. And, of course, you've been attending to your Katherine." She hesitated. "Dinner is at the usual time?"

"Perhaps you would like to come into the drawing room earlier than that." Lady Fenton looked almost anxious. "It would be pleasant to...spend time in conversation before we're joined by the gentlemen."

Eliza was surprised. Lady Fenton had shown no desire to further her acquaintance with her earlier. In fact, Lady Fenton had said barely a word to her. Eliza knew she considered her dull, and the truth was that Eliza had not felt it worthwhile making an effort. She rarely did.

"If you wish."

"I do."

To her surprise, Lady Fenton clasped her hand, her smile warm and genuine. Most odd.

"I shall rest now." Eliza withdrew her hand as courteously as she could. She felt it incumbent to offer another smile, though it was hard when she so wanted to be alone, bursting with excitement as she was about her new discovery. Hesitating before she closed the door, she asked, "I trust I will see the children?"

"Katherine and George are generally brought down by Nanny Brown before we repair to the dining room."

"I mean the other boy. The foundling home boy."

Lady Fenton seemed to consider this. "He may already have been taken home, as is the usual arrangement, but it's true, he's had a great shock. And it would be appropriate that he say a personal thanks to you."

"I should like that very much."

With her heart pounding with joy, Eliza closed the door

between them. It was bliss to sink into her bed and to have something to look forward to.

Finally, she had a reason to wake up each morning. Here, under this roof with Mr Bramley, she would discover the love that had been denied her so long.

CHAPTER 3

Eliza arrived in the drawing room earlier than arranged, to find Lady Fenton waiting for her. She wasn't going to miss a single precious moment in case the children were already downstairs.

They weren't, but they arrived shortly afterwards looking clean and tidy as they followed Nanny Brown across the carpet.

Eliza returned the smile flashed her by the exuberant Miss Katherine who bounced ahead of the boys, darting back to give Young George a poke in the back, before innocently clasping her hands and looking demurely above her head when George wailed at the outrage.

Gideon looked askance at the young miss, but said nothing and Eliza's heart contracted. A true diplomat. Was this, however, part of his nature, or was he subdued or in delayed shock by this afternoon's events?

She was careful not to make a mistake. "Hello, Jack," she said, extending her hand. He looked surprised as he shook it before taking a seat between George and Katherine on the sofa opposite. Not an honour generally accorded him, it would appear, judging by his look of surprise before the renewed urging to "sit up straight, now, like a young gentleman and mind your manners."

"Are you feeling perfectly well now, Jack?" she asked. "Are you children completely recovered?"

They nodded dutifully.

"And so you will go back to the foundling home now, Jack? Do you like it there?" she asked, wanting to draw him out, but Lady Fenton interjected with a wave of her hand. "Of course he does! You can't imagine the boy would be mistreated when it's known how fond we are of him. Do take a seat next to me, Miss Montrose. I was so looking forward to enjoying a pleasant chat with you before George and the others arrive."

"And what will...become of young Jack?" Asking the question brought home afresh how vulnerable her child was, and how helpless Eliza was to aid him. She could barely push out the words as, reluctantly, she took a seat upon the blue velvet seat beside her hostess. "Afterwards? When he is...no longer a child?"

"He'll be trained in something suitable." Lady Fenton looked surprised. "Fenton was worried we'd be giving the boy ideas above his station if we indulged him too much, but I think the lines are clear enough at this stage. Jack is a quick lad and has on occasion shared the children's lessons, but I'm afraid he's always besting Young George who doesn't take too kindly to it." Lady Fenton looked fondly at the fair-haired, handsome lad, tall for his age. "I don't think he'd make much of a servant. Of course, he'll be trained to serve, but I wouldn't wonder if, given a bit of an advantage from the connections he makes here, he might not become something more." She glanced over her shoulder to see who might be listening before saying to Eliza, "I know, it's very wrong to imagine these foundling boys could aspire to something more, and yet...I have observed many admirable traits, even though he is so young. I would not see him leave here merely to become a bootblack."

"So how do you think Gid...I mean, Jack, might be given advantage?" Feverishly Eliza's brain went over every possibility as to how she could see her son rising beyond a footman—a servant. Ironically, Eliza's status was little higher. She was unlikely to ever be her own mistress, and had played servant to her Aunt Montrose for more than seven years. But Jack—she must start to call him that in her mind or she'd make mistakes—deserved the opportunities of any well-born young man. It would be so wrong for him to be denied a future just because his mother had...

She cut the thought off at the root, and besides, Lady Fenton answered thoughtfully, "Jack is quite charming when he's not being a scallywag, which I think is something Young George brings out in him since George can be so very vexing. However, when George isn't about, Jack is very studious. There's something very deep about young Jack. I'll be interested to see how he turns out."

"Yet his birth doesn't favour him. Valet or blacksmith is likely the most to which he can aspire."

Lady Fenton must have heard the bitterness in Eliza's tone, for she raised her eyebrows before changing the subject. "And what of you, Miss Montrose? What is to become of you since you've evinced interest in that topic with regard to the boy?"

"Why...I'm to be married." What a curious question.

"Yes, to Mr George Bramley. You surely don't imagine you'll be happy."

Eliza stared at her. The impertinence. She drew back her shoulders and hoped her look was quelling. "That depends on how one qualifies happiness. I am no longer in the first flush of youth, Lady Fenton, and it is my desire that I don't remain a spinster."

"So, George Bramley was the only gentleman who has ever offered for you?"

"That is correct."

Lady Fenton gasped. "How can that be? You are quite lovely."

"And quite penniless...that is until my aunt hinted that I may become her beneficiary."

"Which is when Cousin George made you an offer."

"That's of no account to me." Eliza hesitated, wondering whether to say more. But then, perhaps if she were perfectly transparent, Lady Fenton would stop asking impertinent questions. "I'm taking a gamble; he's taking a gamble. If I have children and can be left in relative peace, I shall be happy. By the same token, I've gained the impression Mr Bramley would be quite happy to be left to his own devices also, and simply to enjoy the benefits of a wife on his terms and when he chooses. I can live with those terms."

To her astonishment, Lady Fenton put down her glass of Madeira, leaned across the space between them, and clasped her hands in entreaty. "Do not, Miss Montrose, I implore you, be satisfied with such slender pickings when you could have so much...so much joy."

Joy? A strange word to use. Eliza allowed a smile as Lady Fenton, realising, of course, they had company, waved Nanny Brown away, exhorting her to take the children to the far end of the drawing room. Hoping to turn the tables on her hostess, Eliza said, "The match between you and Lord Fenton is quite unusual. A love match that had all London talking. I would not expect such a thing for me."

"Not so unusual? Why, look at my cousin Thea and her husband, Mr Grayling, whom you met when you first arrived. They are equally devoted. We all went out on a limb to marry for love. There was opposition, but it was worth all the effort and striving, believe me."

Eliza would not be drawn, despite the fact Lady Fenton seemed quite passionate about the subject. She wanted to be kind, for clearly Lady Fenton had her best interests at heart. She wouldn't know it was too late for Eliza; that her mind was made up.

"Lady Fenton," she said, full of patience, levelling her warmest smile at her though it was brief. "It is delightful to hear a proponent of the love match wax lyrical on its merits so many years after your marriage was contracted. But what suits one person doesn't necessarily suit another."

Lady Fenton seemed lost for words, which was very unusual for her. Finally, she said, "You don't *wish* to marry for love?"

Eliza frowned as she puzzled it out. "I would not see my fruitful years disappear in the hopes of finding a love that is perhaps not just elusive, but never forthcoming."

Lady Fenton looked despairing. "Miss Montrose, I admit that when I first met you, I did not take to you at all. I thought you were cold and distant and could have nothing in common with me."

Eliza smiled again. "I *am* cold and distant, and I believe that, indeed, we do have nothing in common. Yet that doesn't mean we can't be civil, even friendly, as inevitably we grow more sociable. I am, after all, marrying into your family. Is that your objection?"

"Not at all! Indeed, you entirely misunderstand me if that's what you believe."

The sound of shoe leather ringing over the flagstones in the hall made her glance up and, in a rush, Lady Fenton whispered, "You don't know Mr Bramley properly, and if you did you would certainly not wish to marry him. He is a self-centred, even a cruel man—"

"You will not put me off, Lady Fenton."

"Afternoon, ladies." Lord Fenton bowed with a flourish while Mr Bramley and Mr Patmore brought up the rear, also bowing as they arrived upon the threshold. Fanny smiled at her husband, and Eliza rose to allow him to sit beside his wife and went to another chair beside which she had her workbasket. Inclining her head at all three gentlemen, she picked up her tatting and absorbed herself in her creation.

Lady Fenton's pleasure at seeing her husband reminded Eliza of emotions she'd once felt. But that had been a long time ago.

She no longer felt an interest in the opposite sex—and, no, Mr Patmore didn't count. She'd come on this weekend visit to Quamby House as the guest of Mr Bramley, whose marriage offer she'd accepted at an Assembly Ball several months earlier.

Of course, her reason for accepting Mr Bramley had been because marriage offered her the chance to have children. Now, her life had been turned upside down. The discovery that Jack was a regular visitor to Quamby House where she'd be living as Mr Bramley's wife made it imperative that she follow through.

She just wished her heart would stop making these silly little leaps every time Mr Patmore looked at her. No, love wasn't going to visit her a second time, and it certainly wouldn't stay around if the truth of her wicked past were made known.

As her fingers nimbly worked the stitches, she covertly watched the scene at the end of the room where Jack was playing with Nanny Brown and the other two children.

It took a moment before she realised she was being addressed. And by her own betrothed.

"I beg your pardon; what did you say, Mr Bramley?"

His mouth turned down, and his expression was sour as he lowered himself into a seat beside her. "I said, my dear, that you are quite the heroine of Quamby House. I do hope you haven't caught a chill."

Eliza stared at him and was disconcerted by the revulsion she felt. No, she certainly would not be marrying for love, but marriage to Mr Bramley was the price she would pay for her past sins and to ensure Jack had someone to watch over him.

Dutifully, she smiled. "I'm quite well, thank you."

"A wonder, is it not, that we shall be married before three weeks is up?"

"Indeed it is, Mr Bramley."

"I'm willing to be generous in the matter of wedding attire, my dear." He put his hand on her knee. "I know your aunt has provided only the smallest clothing allowance, but I would not wish to be judged a cheeseparing husband for allowing you to walk up the aisle in something that is not in the first stare. Indeed, I would be *severely* judged."

Eliza looked down at her evening gown, which had been fashionable three seasons ago before her cousin, Susana, had offered it to her.

"That is very generous of you, Mr Bramley."

"Anything to bring happiness to the heroine of the day."

Happiness? Eliza had squandered her brief chance at happiness seven years ago and no, she didn't expect, or seek, a second chance at it.

But if she could do something to advance her boy's happiness, no sacrifice would be too great.

Still smiling, and trying for warmth, she queried, "Heroine? I am not a heroine simply through doing what any decent human being would have done."

Lady Fenton arrived to stand between them. "You are too modest, and we must repay you, Miss Montrose."

Eliza wished Lady Fenton wouldn't make such a fuss. The young matron was far too vibrant and joyful with her lot to be a comfortable companion.

"Indeed, we must!" As her betrothed continued speaking, she no longer heard his words. She was too concerned with the fact that it appeared Jack was being ushered towards the door, about to be despatched. Rather peremptorily, she interrupted Mr Bramley's rambling monologue and rose. "I must say goodbye to young Jack. And young George and Katherine, of course," she added quickly. "They've all had such a shock today."

Nanny Brown duly brought Jack over to Eliza en route to the door, and Eliza did her best to curb her excitement—such a rare feeling.

Of course, she was a stranger to her boy, and she couldn't behave in too familiar a fashion, but his sweet face with its baby-blue eyes, so reminiscent of his father's, made her clutch her heart.

Mr Patmore came round and put his hands on Jack's shoulders, commenting that he was a bright one after the boy duly recited his alphabet at Eliza's instigation.

"He is, and what a shame his quick memory and wits will be wasted in the foundling home," Eliza said, colouring at the surprise levelled upon her.

"Well then, we shall have to please Miss Montrose, won't we, and see that Jack's talents are stretched." Mr Bramley puffed out his chest as if he would be the one to grant her every wish. He turned to Antoinette. "I've long worried that the rivalry between my...nephew...George and young Jack is only exacerbated by three days here a week. What do you say, Lady Quamby, if we increase it to five? That way, Jack might learn faster who is master. It seems, also, that such an arrangement would please our heroine of the day, Miss Montrose, when she lives permanently at Quamby House?"

Eliza felt her cheeks burn. It was more than she could have hoped for. If Jack really were able to spend five days—even part of five days—in the company of Mr Bramley's nephew, and Eliza were living in apartments at Quamby House, why, her impending marriage to Mr Bramley had suddenly acquired a gloss of pure thrilling joy.

Antoinette wrinkled her nose. "Really, I don't know that Young George needs to be so much in the company of—"

"Oh, please!" Immediately embarrassed, Eliza dropped her gaze and murmured, "I do so love to see an opportunity go to those who are disadvantaged by birth, but who have wit and brains that would see them go far."

"Quite the philanthropist." She thought she detected something condescending in Mr Patmore's tone, but when she glanced up, she found he was smiling at her as if he found her quite enchanting. She blushed, surprised by the warmth of his expression.

Lady Quamby shrugged. "I suppose it'll only be for a few hours a day when Young George would otherwise be alone. And Jack is a lovely chap. Yes, I'll see that it's organised."

Eliza's shoulders sagged with joy. She didn't even feel the usual revulsion occasioned by Mr Bramley's closeness.

"I have pleased you, my dear Eliza?" he murmured once she was back in her chair. The others were chatting at the other end of the room now the children had been removed by Nanny Brown, and Jack had been taken home in the dogcart by one of the servants.

"Very much, Mr Bramley." She thought he looked like a toad with his smug self-satisfaction, and wondered how much of a priority pleasing her would be after they were married.

He picked up her hand, forcing her to drop her handiwork, and kissed the back of her wrist. "I look forward to our nuptials, my dear. You've made me very happy."

"And will make you even happier should my aunt choose me as her beneficiary."

"I've no doubt you are hoping for the same."

Eliza shrugged. "Whatever I possess becomes yours once we're married. It will make little difference to me during our life together."

"But a great deal of difference should you become a widow, and for our children." Mr Bramley chuckled. "I don't think I've ever met a woman who speaks the bald truth as you do."

"Better the truth than a gilded lie. And now, if you'll excuse me, I will repair to my bedchamber." Eliza rose, smiling over her shoulder as she started for the door, knowing she would never renege on this marriage. "I'll see you at the dinner table."

"And you'd better not be late," he told her, pointedly.

With a nod, Eliza escaped, and two minutes later was lying joyfully on her bed, blissfully alone, her arms thrown wide as joy filled her lungs.

Lord, she'd not expected great happiness from her marriage to Mr Bramley, but if it were to reunite her with her beloved Gideon, she'd sacrifice her soul to ensure the union went ahead.

๑๋๑

FANNY FLUNG AROUND TO HER SISTER ONCE DINNER WAS finished and they were alone, though Fenton lounged in the shadows. He'd returned to join the ladies in the drawing room once the gentlemen had retired for the night, and now sat quietly at the escritoire poring over some correspondence.

"She can't possibly marry George!" cried Fanny. He doesn't deserve her! He doesn't deserve someone with half her bravery and her—"

"Don't say 'wit' because Miss Montrose really is very dry and not witty at all, though she is very lovely to look at," Antoinette interrupted. "She's penniless, though," she added as she examined the lovely moons of her nails.

Fanny was used to her sister's preoccupation with her bounteous assets but knew that beneath the venality was a passionate nature and, essentially, a kind heart, though Fanny would never publicly vouchsafe the latter. Both girls knew there was safety in being considered a heartless beauty, and that sentiment was hardly an asset in the competitive, sometimes vicious, climb to safety and security. No doubt that's what Miss Montrose had come to realise, too.

"Well, she can't possibly marry Cousin George," Fanny repeated. "Not after today revealed her *true* nature and" she added thoughtfully, "the possibilities that might be nurtured between her and Mr Patmore—"

"Who needs a wife with at least a thousand a year, and that's if he's prepared to be penny-pinching," Antoinette said, having now transferred her attention to the decoration on her fashionable pink-and-white striped silk gown. "Oh dear, but I do hope Nanny Brown wipes Young George's nose before she brings him to see me tomorrow, for I have plans." She sent Fanny a meaningful look, then sighed. "For all that your Katherine is such a hoyden, she is never less than immaculate. I don't know how she manages it."

"I'm impressed too by Katherine's ability to remain pristine, whereas your Young George, who doesn't like to get his hands dirty, always looks as if he's been rolling in mud," Fanny remarked, ready to enjoy her sister's reaction.

Antoinette threw up her hands, prepared to forgo a mother's instinct to defend her cub. "Exactly! But we were talking about Miss Montrose."

"And Mr Patmore. I can't imagine why Miss Montrose agreed to marry Cousin George, or even persists when I was quite open about what she was letting herself into." Fanny stood up and began to pace, nibbling on her little finger. "It's almost as if she's punishing herself for something." She stopped before the window and put her head on one side. "Do you suppose there's been someone in her past whom she once loved, but when she couldn't have him, she's decided she must live either like a nun or with a man she knows she can't love?"

"Well, to know George Bramley is to know one cannot love him." Antoinette sniffed. "One would certainly want to live like a nun if one were married to him, but I don't think that would go down very well."

Fanny slid her sister a narrow-eyed look. "Pity you didn't deduce these important facts about him before it was too late, Antoinette."

Not surprisingly, Antoinette bridled in her usual decorative way. "I'd say it was just as well I *did;* otherwise I'd never be married to darling Quamby."

From her post at the window, Fanny sent her an arch look. "You forget, dearest, that Quamby offered for me first!"

"Yes, of course, and that's finally when *your* darling Fenton decided you were sufficiently up to the mark to make you his wife, when before he was quite happy to have made you his mistress," said Antoinette, all innocence. "Oh, sorry, Fenton; I forgot you were lurking in the shadows over there."

"No offence taken," came his disembodied voice, and when Fanny turned, she saw her husband was now scanning a newssheet from a large armchair in the shadows at the other end of the room. He caught her eye, and immediately her insides responded to the desire she heard in his voice as he growled, "However, I do think, sister-in-law, that we've listened to you long enough, and it's time I marched my irresistible wife off to bed before she makes any more wild speculations about poor Miss Montrose. I really don't think I can stomach a repeat of the matchmaking that nearly ended in disaster for poor Cousin Thea."

Fanny let out of a hoot of laughter at the memory. "Disaster? I'd say it was a hugely successful outcome, though not for dreadful old Aunt Brightwell, who looked likely to go to the moon in that hot-air balloon, leg-shackled to Cousin George, as a result of brother Bertram's wrong-footedness!" With a flick of her flounced skirts, she crossed the room to her husband and draped herself across his lap, curling a languid arm about his neck and bringing his head down for a kiss. "A good thing Bertram has gone to the West Indies to make his fortune instead of coming up with any hare-brained ideas with regard to Miss Montrose's future," she remarked when she came up for air.

Antoinette, who was used to such open affection in the drawing room they shared during her sister's frequent visits to their country estate, plucked at the folds of her gown and ignored them. "Indeed! Cousin Thea owes her happiness to the clever *Miss* Brightwells and admits it too. She'd be handmaiden to Aunt Brightwell this very day, rubbing her swollen legs with smelly unguents, if we hadn't intervened."

"Precisely." Fanny, now resting her cheek against her husband's, sent Antoinette an approving look. "I'm glad you agree, sister, that the time has come to intervene now in the case of—as you so touchingly put it—*poor* Miss Montrose." She rose, inclining her head as her husband gallantly caged her hand upon his coat sleeve and started to lead her to the door. "But first we must discover what painful event in Miss Montrose's past has so reduced her to the cool, detached, and emotionless maiden prepared to sacrifice her future as Cousin George's bride. If there *is* a gentleman who has broken her heart, we must find him, and he must be made to atone."

Antoinette straightened, shaking her head. "Oh no, Fanny, you are entirely wrong if that is how you propose to secure Miss Montrose's future, or at least prevent her from marrying Cousin George."

Fanny stopped on the threshold and sent Antoinette an enquiring look. "Wrong? When have I ever been wrong? Fenton, can you think of an occasion when I've ever been wrong?"

"None springs to mind, my dear," murmured her loyal husband with a lively look in his eyes. "Admittedly though, I wouldn't test my memory overmuch at this *very* moment, considering I have a mind to my future prospects which, in this case, extends only so far as the end of the corridor and up the stairs."

Antoinette ignored the banter in order to press her point. "No, Fanny! The past is the past and what is happening *now* is what's important. We must encourage *Mr Patmore* to see Miss Montrose as more than a penniless young woman in need of a husband. We must make him fall in love with her."

Fanny smiled as Fenton drew her into the shadows. "Too late, Antoinette dearest." She gripped the door frame, putting her head around to deliver her final words. "I saw the very moment it happened. For both of them. They just don't know it yet."

CHAPTER 4

The following morning, Rufus Patmore had returned to the battlements of the ruined castle from where he'd observed the prior day's dramatic events. A fresh wind sliced his cheeks, and as far as the eye could see, the picturesque grounds of the Earl of Quamby's residence stretched from manicured park to patchwork fields, disappearing over the horizon.

All that interested him at this moment, however, was the couple strolling by the edge of the dam—the rather thuggish George Bramley, and the magnificent and fascinatingly self-effacing Miss Montrose.

Bramley, of course, wasn't in his sights as anything other than the unworthy recipient of Miss Montrose's charms.

Miss Montrose was an entirely different kettle of fish; a refreshing, delightful creature unlike any he'd met. At first, he'd mistaken her silence for timidity, but when she spoke, she seemed to say exactly what she thought. Refreshing, indeed! Yes, Miss Montrose was fearless, which she'd have to be if she were going to marry George Bramley.

He squinted, trying to see if there were any sign of discord. He'd heard rumours that Bramley was hedging his bets on the fact

Miss Montrose's ageing aunt was going to make her niece her beneficiary. Could Miss Montrose really have agreed to such a thing?

If she were penniless, she had nothing to lose...but what did she really know of Bramley?

The pair had stopped to feed the ducks. From this distance, they looked companionable, and he felt a strange note of disquiet tug inside his chest.

Did Miss Montrose have any idea of the kind of man she was marrying? Bramley was well known at the Club for qualifying for the status of gentleman only on account of his birthright.

Squinting a little more closely now that the couple was heading in his direction and he could make out Miss Montrose's facial expressions, he tried to puzzle it out. Miss Montrose was not in love with Mr Bramley. He felt he could confidently make such an assertion.

In fact, Miss Montrose didn't seem to be a young woman who desired to have her heart engaged.

Mr Patmore hadn't set out to have his heart engaged either, though he'd dutifully attended a great number of Assembly Balls at the urging of his sisters, and while there'd been a great many pretty girls in attendance, none had taken his fancy.

But Miss Montrose, now...

He tried to puzzle out his feelings as he descended the winding staircase to the grassy tussocks that spread out before him at ground level.

Pretending surprise when he met the pair walking, he could discern nothing in their manner to suggest he was intruding. In fact, they seemed to have been walking in silence for some time.

Bramley asked how he liked his new purchase.

"A fine animal," Rufus responded. "I look forward to taking Carnaby for a gallop this afternoon. He's just what I'm looking for in terms of speed. My faithful Barnabus back home is slowing down a bit."

"Carnaby is lovely, but I do miss my little grey mare." Miss

Montrose glanced up at Bramley. "I'm so glad you like horses. I'm looking forward to getting to know each one in your stable."

"Can't stand the creatures, to tell the truth." Bramley gave a mirthless laugh. "That's unless they come up trumps with good odds. You're welcome to exercise any of them that take your fancy."

Rufus saw his opportunity. "Perhaps you'd both care to join me on my ride this afternoon," he suggested, and was delighted when Bramley said he had matters to attend to, and somewhat dispirited by Miss Montrose's obvious indifference towards the companion with whom she was now saddled.

"If you wish for company, then, of course I'm happy to join you, Mr Patmore," she said, "however, I do like to give my horse its head. I like the solitude of a long, lonely ride."

"I promise not to bother you with too much small talk in that case." Rufus suspected Bramley would be happy to have him out of the way and occupied with Miss Montrose as he attended to these unnamed 'matters,' which no doubt involved a bet or wager involving horses and the turning of a coin.

He tipped his hat to the pretty young woman. "I shall meet you at the stables at three o' clock if that suits."

She hesitated, still not evincing much more than reluctance at the idea. "What time do the children get presented to their parents, Mr Bramley?"

Bramley shrugged. "No idea, though you should get your gallop in beforehand. Don't know why you're so interested in the dirty creatures, but you could always visit the schoolroom, I daresay."

Rufus noticed that her pleasure at such a suggestion outstripped any she'd evinced at going riding with him. Still, he intended to ensure she gained maximum enjoyment from her hour galloping hell for leather over dales and downs, if that's how she really liked to spend an afternoon. Indeed, Rufus was determined that he'd do such a fine job diverting her with his conversation, she'd not spare a thought about smiling at snotty-nosed brats.

༕

ELIZA COULDN'T BELIEVE HER HOSTESS'S GENEROSITY. WHEN Lady Fenton learned she was going riding with Mr Patmore, she insisted she borrow a lovely, dove-grey riding habit. Not only was it in the first stare, but it fitted like a glove. It was rare Eliza regarded her reflection with such pleasure.

In this happy mood, she descended the stairway of Quamby House after she'd looked in on her chaperone who was still in the throes of her terrible head cold. When she passed Mr Bramley in the hallway, he raised his eyebrows as he took in her ensemble and looked as if he were about to whistle his appreciation, but then he merely nodded and continued walking towards the library, saying over his shoulder, "You cut a fine figure, Miss Montrose. I'm sorry I can't accompany you, but I'm sure Mr Patmore will be agreeable company. I've instructed my groom to ensure your safety for the afternoon."

"That was good of you, Mr Bramley." She was grateful for the chaperonage. The look in Mr Patmore's eyes had been a little too appreciative for her liking.

The moment she was astride Brownie, a sweet, relatively docile animal the groom considered suitable, Eliza forgot all other considerations.

"Race you to the hedgerows!" she cried to Mr Patmore, urging Brownie forward and laughing as they picked up pace more rapidly than she'd expected, and the wind whipped her face. She couldn't remember feeling so carefree. Of course, that was because Gideon —no, she would call him Jack from hereon—was playing in the nursery, and she'd been promised he'd still be there when she returned.

Furthermore, she was free of her aunt. Really free! For three days, she'd been away from the constant sniping of her crotchety relative and her aunt's elderly neighbour who'd been sent along to chaperone her. Eliza couldn't remember the last time she'd enjoyed such latitude.

Now, in the warmth of this lovely September afternoon, she could ride in silence and dwell on those past events that had led to this. Falling in love at seventeen had caused her great pain and had led to Jack's existence, but she'd experienced true passion, and she'd not take that back. It might be the only love she'd ever know.

Soon, Jack would be part of her life again. She would not dwell on past mistakes, nor would she make another. She was about to embark upon a carefully calculated path—marriage. She knew what was involved, physically, and accepted her body would never again thrill to the touch of a caring lover. As a wife, she would submit and do her duty, just as women had been doing since time immemorial. Marriage for love was a new notion for her generation, and rare for those of her grandparents' time. She must remember that if she needed to feel any better.

"Whoa there, Miss Montrose!"

Eliza brought her mount around and sent Mr Patmore a questioning look.

He indicated the hedge at the bottom of the hill and the stream beyond. "You don't know the area. I was afraid you might try something foolhardy.'

"And try to jump across them both?" She felt the blood tingling in her veins, pulsing at her fingertips. She felt alive. "And what of it? I'm game if you are!" She pulled her horse's head around and pointed its nose in the direction from which Mr Patmore had feared danger before galloping hell for leather towards it. Mud splattered her face and the wind whipped her cheeks while the ground tore past at a tremendous pace. When was the last time she'd felt so exhilarated? Yes, the hedge was high, but the mount she'd thought docile was up for the challenge. Giving it the command, she clung to the pommel, head down, and felt herself soaring. The last occasion she'd ridden like this was when she was a bold and reckless schoolgirl.

Light gleamed through the trees ahead, beckoning her forward. She felt gifted in all senses. Gifted with new courage, and with a new life also. Gifted with the return of her son.

"Bravo!" she cried as her mare's hooves pounded into the soft earth on the other side, having cleared the hedge by a good margin. "Good girl!" It was self-congratulation for herself as much as for her horse.

Panting, she edged Brownie across the stream and turned to wait for Mr Patmore. He wasn't far behind her, an impressive figure in his buff riding breeches and well-cut jacket. Even from here she could see the set determination in his eyes, the square chin above the broad shoulders, a face that was handsome if one liked interesting angles. Not a question for herself to consider.

He raised his head a moment just before his horse took off into the air, and for a split second, they locked glances. There was the shared jubilation of conquering danger, a rare camaraderie.

His horse came down on the other side hard as it reached the stream, seeming to right itself before its right fetlock rolled. It seemed it encountered something loose and unsteady beneath the shallow water's surface. A rock perhaps. Or a stone. And as Carnaby went down, whinnying in panic, Mr Patmore disappeared into the water beneath the full weight of his horse.

Eliza saw it happening in slow motion, it seemed, long before the inevitable; her scream echoing in the air before she knew she'd opened her mouth. Flinging herself from the saddle she splashed into the shallow depths, exhorting her groom who'd just appeared on the other side of the hedge, to ride for help.

Mr Patmore was only partly visible beneath the flailing animal, but her seeking hands found the lapel of his jacket, and she pulled with all her might. Nothing budged, neither he nor the horse, until she felt a thrashing against her thigh in the murky depths, and a spear of relief his neck hadn't been snapped by the impact.

Plunging her hands once more beneath the water she felt for his face, just at the moment Carnaby made a supreme effort to raise himself.

The water was deep here, and one more step had her almost losing her footing. The terrible whinnies of the agonised animal tore at her eardrums and her heart, but her focus was on saving Mr Patmore's life. She only had seconds.

Mercifully, the broken horse managed one final thrust, which enabled Eliza to snatch at the gentleman's arm with both her hands. Dragging his body with all her might, she was able to free him so that he emerged, gasping, breathing in life-giving air.

"Dear God, I thought that was the end of me." Mr Patmore, waist-deep in water like Eliza, struggled to his feet, and was only able to keep his balance with the help of Eliza's steadying form. He leaned on her, limping to the side of the stream, shaking his head as he stared at the wounded animal whose heart-wrenching noises tore at Eliza's heart.

"What can we do to ease his pain?" she asked, putting her hands to her ears before wading back into the water to see if she could do anything.

"Poor wretched creature." Mr Patmore limped over and crouched beside them to stroke Carnaby's muzzle. The sweet bay gelding gazed up at them with pain-filled eyes, and Eliza had to turn away.

"Carnaby here, and I, had not had time to become acquainted, and Lord knows, I couldn't have borne it if it had been my faithful steed, Barnabus, back home, but I'm a cad for pushing him to do something so risky before I knew he was up to the task."

"You were trying to keep up with me. Any gentleman would have done the same." Eliza felt the tears burn her throat before looking about them—green fields bordered by hedgerows and not a soul in sight. "I hope help comes soon."

"And that the groom thinks to bring a pistol to put poor Carnaby out of his pain."

"No!" cried Eliza. "You don't know that he won't survive. He mightn't be up for what you bought him for, speed, but he deserves a chance." She felt as if her heart would break.

Mr Patmore stroked the animal's muzzle and nodded. "Of course, I'll see the best is done for him. Now, do you think you can help me negotiate the incline? I think we're both getting chilled."

The current was strong, and to reach the riverbank required quite a step up. Mr Patmore winced in pain as Eliza helped him to his feet once more. "Lean on my shoulder," she said, "and you can apply what pressure you need to climb out of the river. I assure you; I'm stronger than I look."

"After your Amazonian efforts yesterday—and just now—I don't need to be told." He nodded. "Thank you, Miss Montrose, I fear I shall have to put you to the test."

"No need to feel guilt if I buckle. But we have nothing else to try."

With painful effort, they got Mr Patmore out of the river, and Eliza helped to settle him against a fallen log.

She stared dubiously at the deserted fields. "I hope we won't have to wait too long until the groom returns with some strong men, and hopefully the doctor."

"And bandages for Carnaby."

Eliza turned her gaze upon his ankle. "Let me help you get your boot off before the swelling makes it difficult."

He stretched out his leg to give her access and closed his eyes, tipping his head up to the sky. Eliza could see the sheen of sweat on his face—not water—though he was dripping wet. So was she. Glancing around, she reassured herself that her little mare was doing what she ought. The well-behaved creature was quietly cropping the grass nearby, and Eliza was grateful for its obedience.

"How are you bearing up, Mr Patmore?" She felt anxious.

"I'll just have to endure, won't I, Miss Montrose?" He didn't open his eyes, and he spoke through gritted teeth as Eliza began to tug at his right Hessian. Wincing, he added, "Perhaps you'd amuse me with your conversation to help me take my mind off the pain."

Now that the urgency was passed, Eliza felt calm. Calm and able to be herself. Which is why she meant it when she said, briskly, and with no self-pity, "I'll talk to you, but I can't promise to amuse you, Mr Patmore. There's nothing amusing or entertaining about me. I've been told so on more than one occasion. I'm a spinster soon to be married, and one day I shall die. Like most women, my life will be unremarked upon, but I'm sure I can be content with this lot as any other."

"Good Lord, what a dreary speech! You don't even *aspire* to happiness?"

She paused as she'd made only slight inroads into her task. "Well, of course it wouldn't be natural to wish to be *un*happy. But why torture myself with unattainable aspirations? I'd rather surprise myself by discovering unexpected happiness than be disappointed in my hopes for something else."

His eyelids fluttered as he worked to regulate his breathing against the pain, while Eliza struggled to gain another couple of inches of loosened foot from the boot. When he began to shake, she rose with the sudden idea of retrieving the blanket from beneath the saddle to keep him warm.

"Do you have siblings, Miss Montrose?" he asked, watching her as she loosened the leather straps before pulling the blanket free.

"I had a brother once," she said, draping it over him.

"Once?"

"Killed in a duel. He taught me to swim." *Introduced me to the man I loved also, then died for it. Honour was a curse.*

"I am sorry."

"So was I." She forced a smile. Forced herself also to ask no questions of him. He was kind. Most women, she supposed, would consider him handsome. But she didn't need the complication of developing an interest in him. She hoped Mr Bramley wasn't the jealous kind. Mercifully, he'd evinced little interest in her as a woman, but still, she was all but his property, and a man guarded his property with care. Again, it was a matter of honour.

So she stared out across the hill, hoping help would come soon, cutting into Mr Patmore's conversation when it appeared he wished to quiz her further, this time with a question of her own. "And how is it you and Mr Bramley are friends?" She wasn't interested, she told herself. This was only to deflect him from invading her privacy further.

"A shared love of horseflesh."

"Mr Bramley said he detested horses."

"Riding them, yes. However, he loves to race them. He has high hopes for one of his two-year-olds, *Devil's Run*."

"Lovely animal. I wanted to ride him this afternoon but was warned against it. Dangerous? I hardly think so."

"He'll be yours to ride any time you wish, after a fortnight."

Quietly, she murmured, "Thank you for reminding me." Yes, it was true. That would be another bright spot in the routine of her daily life. Eliza would have access to all the horses in Lord Quamby's stables.

"Right at this moment, he's bartering on his next hope in the East Anglia Cup. That's my guess. Or else he's proposing a swap."

Eliza digested this for a moment. "He wants to swap something from his own stable for something he thinks will perform better? Mr Bramley does enjoy horse trading." Their nuptials weren't so different. She wished, though, she'd not made a remark that invited more questions.

He looked at her sharply, moved slightly, then winced again. Eliza glanced at the darkening clouds then at his pallor and was concerned. "Lady Fenton will, I'm sure, have had the foresight to call for the physician while someone else comes to help you."

"Oh, I've suffered worse than this. Left for dead on a battlefield throughout a rainy night. Was sure the cold was going to get to me before the bayonet wound."

"Goodness! How brave."

"I'm not blowing my own trumpet."

"I know, but I'm impressed. I should have discerned the army man in you. Something about your bearing, perhaps."

"You're very lovely, Miss Montrose." He shifted, wincing again. "I wish you weren't going to marry Mr Bramley."

Eliza gasped and he looked embarrassed, as if the words had been spoken unguardedly and he realised their inappropriateness.

Trying not to sound stiff, she said, "We have an understanding. There are advantages for both of us. I went in with my eyes wide open. No one in my family is a proponent of a love match and, to be frank, neither am I. Pragmatism is my mantra." She hadn't meant to sound so hot under the collar. She looked away. *Please make help come soon.* Eliza didn't want to know more about this man or his thoughts and feelings. The unsettling interest in his grey-eyed gaze was not helping her cause. Not now that she had more reason than ever to marry Mr Bramley.

"Look! They're coming!" She didn't care if he heard the jubilation in her voice, and that he might rightly interpret it as relief she'd no longer be alone with him. "They mightn't find us unless I alert them. Excuse me, Mr Patmore." Cutting off his next question she returned to the stream, hitching up her skirts to negotiate the deep middle before she reached the smooth upwards slope to hail the oncoming riders.

She wished she'd not caught the flash of disappointment in his eyes as she'd turned. Nor the hint of something that spelled interest. A deepening interest. Interest spelled curiosity, and the last thing Eliza needed right now was a handsome, eligible man becoming curious.

Not when her course was set in stone.

CHAPTER 5

"Poor Mr Patmore," Fanny soothed as she swept into the grand, high-ceilinged bedchamber where he'd been settled. His leg was now bandaged, and the physician was bleeding him. "What a terrible tumble. So lucky you didn't break your neck."

"So lucky Miss Montrose was on hand to save me from drowning, but I feel for that poor animal."

Fanny, a devoted horsewoman, was glad to see his contrition was genuine. She sat down on a chair by his side. "No doubt Mr Bramley is highly relieved you paid him for Carnaby last night, and it was kind of you to consider the animal worth saving, even though he'll never race again. But yes, it sounds as if Miss Montrose is to be commended for her quick acting. Miss Montrose *is* unusual." She pretended to puzzle it out, while darting him a look to ascertain whether her words evinced more than a spark of interest. They did. "And not just with regard to her heroism, it must be noted."

His frown was wiped away by a beatific smile. "Indeed, she is not the usual miss by any standards. She might appear a shrinking violet, but she certainly speaks her mind."

"I can't imagine why she would want to marry Mr Bramley." There, Fanny would get straight to the point. "They have nothing in common. I don't think she even particularly likes him."

He sat up straighter, his look more interested. "I gained the same impression."

"Did you, Mr Patmore?" Fanny pretended astonishment. She leant in closer. "Might I confess something to you?"

He looked highly gratified as he nodded. "It will go no further."

"Mr Bramley is a cruel and selfish man. I will be transparent." Oh, she'd tell the whole world if she could. "Some years ago, he tried to mire me in scandal so that Lord Fenton would have no desire to wed me." She raised her eyes to the ornate plaster ceiling. "Of course, the bonds that bound my darling husband and myself were too strong to be broken. Bramley failed in his miserable quest. But I fear that his malevolent streak will make the woman he weds deeply unhappy. I would so wish to find someone else who could turn her head. Do you know of anyone, Mr Patmore?"

"Know of anyone?" he repeated, somewhat stupidly, she thought.

"Yes, someone who you think might find her strange and reticent ways appealing. To be perfectly honest, she isn't likely to take the average gentleman's fancy. She appears distant, yet it's clear there are hidden depths of passion just waiting to be tapped." Fanny rose. This was a good thought on which to leave him to dwell.

With a final smile, she went to the door. "Ah well, I just looked in to see how the patient was faring, Mr Patmore. I'm so glad you're on the mend. Fenton and I shall be returning to London shortly, and I wanted to reassure myself you were going to live. Cousin George insists you must remain here until your ankle is quite healed. Very generous of him. I really didn't mean to be so uncharitable earlier." She sighed. "I'm sure he's quite enchanted with Miss Montrose and has every intention of being the man to tap her hidden depths. You know him better than I do, after all, through your shared love of horses."

৩৯৩

"I LOVE TO RIDE THEM, AND BRAMLEY LOVES TO BET ON THEM," Rufus answered the second Miss Brightwell—or rather, Duchess of Quamby—when she bounced into his room a little later with a question on whether his other friends shared his equine interests. Naturally, he couldn't call her Antoinette as she'd invited him to do, and, naturally, he couldn't respond with a liveliness or flirtatiousness that matched hers. Granted she was lovely, but her seductive manner made him uncomfortable. He got the impression she was sizing him up. Whether as a potential lover or for something else, he couldn't ascertain. But sticking to the topic of horses seemed safe enough.

She fired another question at him as she settled herself on the seat which her sister had recently vacated. "What kind of horse does Miss Montrose prefer? Like you, she loves horses. Loves riding them, that is! And darling Quamby and I were just discussing how we'd love to make her a gift of one of the mounts from Quamby's stables. You know, to thank her as a reward for yesterday's great act of heroism in rescuing my darling Young George and the other children."

"And rescuing me, don't forget, Lady Quamby."

"No, you wouldn't forget that in a hurry, I'd wager, Mr Patmore."

Rufus's mind wandered as he considered her question and suddenly an idea popped into his head. A very wicked idea that had the potential to go awfully wrong and yet could have quite delightful ramifications.

"She showed a great deal of partiality for Devil's Run."

"Lord, Devil's Run is a brute. Well, that's what Cousin George says."

"Exactly what the groom told Miss Montrose. Yet she protested. Said she was an excellent horsewoman, and if she could have the pick of any of the mounts in Lord Quamby's stable, it would be Devil's Run."

Lady Quamby clapped her hands. "Then she shall have Devil's Run. It's what my darling Quamby would want as a sign of his appreciation."

Sudden doubt made Rufus cautious and, despite his earlier devilry, he wondered if he'd been too cavalier. "Perhaps you should consult Mr Bramley first."

Lady Quamby stared at him a moment, a faint frown creasing her brow before her expression cleared. "Indeed, I shall do no such thing. Devil's Run belongs to my husband, and if I wish for him to give the horse to Miss Montrose, he will happily accede."

Rufus shifted beneath the bedcovers and imagined the fine figure Miss Montrose would cut when seated high upon Devil's Run's back. "Perhaps she can take the horse with her when she leaves tomorrow. I know she laments the fact she'll have no diversion in the interim leading up to her nuptials."

Lady Quamby rose. "Good idea! I shall see to it! It'll be just a little thing to find stabling for a couple of weeks before Devil's Run returns here."

"Here?" Rufus raised an enquiring brow. "So it is true that Mr Bramley and his new wife will take up residence on a permanent basis?"

"Yes, in a set of apartments at Quamby House that I helped decorate myself." Lady Quamby hesitated on the threshold, apparently in two minds as to whether to make him a confidant. He could see the way her eyes danced and the turn-up of her rosebud lips. Lowering her voice, she said conspiratorially, "Lord Quamby believes his nephew, Mr Bramley, should be ready to run the estate in the event that Young George isn't old enough to take the reins should that terrible day come earlier than anticipated. However, the real truth is that Quamby agreed to have George Bramley in residence as a favour to his sister, who clings to the vain hope her son can be made a man. Not very likely, I say. Nevertheless, Quamby is quite firm on acceding to what he considers his sister's dying wish."

"It sounds like you know Mr Bramley well." Rufus was

intrigued to hear more about the relationship between Bramley and the Brightwell sisters in view of Lady Fenton's earlier transparency.

"Too well, I'm afraid, Mr Patmore." Lady Quamby looked sorrowful. "Quamby is too softhearted for his own good, so he will do as his sister wishes. However, he knows, too, that his nephew is completely irredeemable. I do wonder that you and he could be such friends."

Friends? Oh, they weren't friends, Rufus reflected when she'd gone. He wished he'd never become involved with the fellow if the truth be told.

If Miss Montrose took immediate possession of Devil's Run so that the horse would not be available to Bramley for the East Anglia Cup, it would suit Rufus very well. He didn't mind winning but he was not a cheat.

He also couldn't deny he'd enjoy spending a little more time with the enigmatic Miss Montrose if he had to delay his time beneath the same roof. Too bad she was marrying Mr Bramley, was his last thought before drifting into a marvellously dreamless stupor thanks to the healing cordial beside his bed.

❦

It was perhaps fortunate Rufus wasn't around when Bramley returned from his visit to a horse dealer in Kentish Town to discover that not only had his bride-to-be left the estate, but so had his favourite horse. Well, his most needed horse.

Furiously, he confronted his uncle to demand why, loathing the fact that his uncle's wife happened to put her head into the room just as George raised his voice to demand the meaning for giving Devil's Run to Miss Montrose without consulting him.

Quamby, who was propped up with lots of cushions in front of the fire, wearing his favourite gold and purple silk dressing gown with matching tasselled fez, and nursing a gouty foot upon an ottoman, shot him a look of displeasure as he put down his teacup.

"Devil's Run is not your horse, I might remind you."

"But I have care of all the horses. You can't just give one away. Not like that."

Antoinette sidled over and put her hands on her husband's shoulders. The gesture was supposed to look protective, he was sure, though he knew it was just so she could gloat. He glared at her, waiting for her to say her piece, which she naturally did in the most innocent of tones.

"You won't have time to miss Devil's Run, Cousin George, not that I ever saw you ride him after he threw you last year. In fact, I was quite convinced you were terrified of him. You certainly said at the time you'd never climb on his back again. But that aside, Devil's Run will be back in your tender, loving care in less than two weeks upon the happy event of your marriage." She reached over her husband's shoulder to pat George's arm as if she truly felt sympathy.

With an effort, George tried not to show he was needled, as this was clearly the intention of the trumped-up little baggage. God, she was beautiful though, he thought, trying not to let his gaze stray to the dimples in her peaches and cream cheeks; which instantly reminded him of the dimples of her shapely buttocks. This then led to thoughts of the most astonishingly debauched, and insanely satisfying, lust-filled five days he'd enjoyed with this woman, who then presented George's Uncle Quamby with the result as his legal wife nine months later. And it wasn't as if it were a secret. Quamby *knew* Young George was the son of George Bramley. And if George didn't know better, he'd say his uncle even gloated over the fact that the squalling infant had cut George out of his inheritance.

Ignoring Antoinette, he went to pains to make it clear to his uncle that he was not pleased for very valid and important reasons, not just pique. "I'm afraid I need Devil's Run long *before* two weeks is up. I need him in ten days, in fact. This is just not acceptable."

"And what plans do you have for Devil's Run that you have thought not important enough to mention to me when in fact the horse is mine?" Two spots of colour appeared on his uncle's cheeks, and George recognised the signs that he was sailing close to the wind. It wasn't often Quamby let off steam, but there were occasions when he'd made his nephew feel the sting of more than just his irritation.

He heard Lady Quamby's gasp, and caught a glimpse of her excited smile as if she were hoping to witness an altercation between them.

George tried to breathe evenly as he chose his words with care. "He is to race, Uncle, that's why."

"Then race one of my other horses. Devil's Run was mine to give away, and since Miss Montrose through her bravery has ensured my heir still lives, I thought gifting her a horse she took a fancy to was the least I could do."

George wasn't about to say that this was doubly galling. "Devil's Run is the only horse up for the course. Ten miles over the dales. He's fast, and he has stamina. I'm set to win a fortune."

"Using my horse," his uncle reminded him. He leaned back in his chair and patted his wife's hand which still rested on his shoulder, casting George a dismissive look as if the topic bored him. "Well, perhaps you can persuade your bride-to-be to bring back the wretched horse and earn herself some of your good favour before she condemns herself to becoming yours forevermore." The petulant tone suggested George would be wise to keep his response measured.

Lady Quamby piped up, "Aren't you supposed to be going north for some more horse business tomorrow, Cousin George? I don't see how you can manage the time to do that *and* see Miss Montrose to beg her to return Devil's Run to you. Perhaps I should pay her a visit and let her know how matters lie."

George glared. Oh, he knew exactly what she'd say. She'd tell the girl lies, dress up the whole business in a cloak of skulduggery, and he would never see his horse again. Lady Quamby would encourage Miss Montrose to sell the beast while she still could, before the marriage that would immediately see all her assets become his.

George felt like weeping. How could he manage to do all he had to do up north, which was to effectively set up this whole damned horse race, as well as visit Miss Montrose at her aunt's cottage so he could persuade her to part with Devil's Run?

The silence was deafening as he pondered his next words, before his uncle let out a peevish sigh. "Give Mr Patmore a letter to hand to your young lady when he departs the day after tomorrow, all being well with his ankle," Lord Quamby said with a dismissive wave of his hand. "If it means that much to you."

"Oh, I wouldn't entrust it to Mr Patmore," Lady Quamby said. "I'll do it. It'll be a nice excuse to get away for a few days."

This decided George. "You will not," he muttered. "I'll do as my uncle says—give it to Mr Patmore to despatch." Yes, he thought. That would do nicely. After all, Mr Patmore would be as motivated as he was to ensure that Devil's Run ran the race once he knew how matters were to be organised.

⚜

RUFUS WAS ASTONISHED WHEN GEORGE BRAMLEY ENTERED HIS patient's room that evening, sat on a chair and said without preamble, "I'm going to north to see about a horse, and you're going to get Devil's Run back from Miss Montrose. He's running a race in ten days, and I have everything invested in it."

Rufus wriggled up straighter in bed and stared. "But my ankle..." He wanted to go, of course, but he didn't want to appear too eager. "Besides, I thought you were going to run the horse you bought last month. Lucifer is just as fleet of foot. No need for you to send me halfway round the country. You made no mention of running Devil's Run before."

"I've changed my mind." Bramley fiddled with his waistcoat button and glowered. "I don't have time to chase after a wretched horse which my uncle had no right to gift to someone else."

"The horse will be yours before too long." Rufus was surprised at how uncomfortable he felt saying those words. He didn't like the idea of Miss Montrose becoming this thug's property. Especially after what the Brightwell sisters had told him. Still, there was nothing Rufus could do about it. "I thought Devil's Run belonged to the Earl of Quamby, and that he had every right to gift him to Miss Montrose."

"I am in charge of his stables. I make the decisions regarding the horses. What do you want for your trouble?"

"Oh, it'll be no trouble trying to persuade the lovely Miss Montrose." Rufus grinned. "You don't seem to appreciate the rare gem you're about to wed."

Bramley shrugged. "The contract suits both of us. She showed unusual bravery for a woman, though I trust she won't crow about being such a heroine."

"I doubt she will." Rufus reflected on her intriguing stillness; her serenity as the sun had burnished her crown of shining hair before she'd leapt out of her chair to save the children from the lake. Not to mention saving Rufus's life. She'd been truly magnificent, and he didn't care that his admiration was transparent. Bramley needed reminding of the extraordinary qualities of his future bride. So he added, "I should very much like to spend an afternoon in the company of the young lady, without whose quick thinking I probably wouldn't be here, though, like any man, I like to think I'd have wrestled my way out from under Carnaby's dead weight in time."

"Hmph! And now Carnaby is no good to anyone. I can't imagine why you didn't just have the animal shot. Will your foot be mended enough to ride Devil back here in three days' time?"

Rufus sent the bulk beneath the blanket a dubious look. "I might have to take a groom with me. Obviously, I can't go before tomorrow. Still an invalid under your roof, as you know." He grinned. He was enjoying the attention he'd lately garnered. Lady Quamby and Lady Fenton liked to look in on him regularly. And to take a seat and chat. Not only were they exquisitely beautiful in their very different ways, but they were vastly entertaining and each possessed of a wicked, or at least, playful, sense of humour.

And indeed, not an hour after Bramley had skulked out of the room, the two sisters swept in, each taking a seat on chairs which they arranged at the side of the bed so he could see them both.

"You're going to visit Miss Montrose?" Lady Quamby clasped her hands, and her eyes shone as if she were soliciting the greatest, most secret information.

In a measured tone which belied the slight ratcheting up of his heartbeat, Rufus replied, "I'm going to ask her if she'd be so gracious as to allow her betrothed to race Devil's Run in the East Anglia Cup which is what Mr Bramley has so set his heart on, apparently."

Lady Fenton looked surprised. Lord but she was a beauty, Rufus reflected, her glossy dark hair and elegance in complete juxtaposition to her sister's riot of blonde curls and impish smile. "Devil's Run is not as fleet of foot as he looks. To be sure, he's a sturdy mount, but I can hardly imagine Cousin George winning his fortune on him."

Lady Fenton was a shrewd piece. And a fine horsewoman to boot. He wondered if he should allow a hint of his suspicions to pass his lips. Miss Montrose might also pry deeper than she ought to; the truth was, Rufus was in two minds as to whether he should even try to persuade her to return Devil's Run.

At the moment, he had no confirmation of his suspicions regarding Bramley's intentions, though he felt he knew Bramley well enough to confidently say he was up to something. Rufus could claim ignorance and possibly earn a great deal of money. But the morality—or lack of—troubled him. So did the fact he'd be lying to Miss Montrose though he couldn't deny that the idea of visiting her, alone, was very tempting. Where did she live? How would she conduct herself on her own turf, so to speak? What kind of welcome would she extend him?

Deciding that the best course, for now, was to play ignorant, he adopted a look of mild curiosity and asked, "When did you last ride him?"

"About six months ago," Lady Fenton replied after a considered pause.

Rufus thought quickly. All right, for the moment he'd play Devil's Advocate and play George's hand if only to see where that led. "Then you wouldn't believe his form now," he said. "Bramley has been training him with this one goal in mind. Miss Montrose certainly can't be so churlish as to deny him the beast for this crucial week."

"I don't know why he kept all this such a secret from my husband," Lady Quamby complained.

But already, Lady Fenton was saying hotly, "And how could you even suggest Miss Montrose would be churlish about this, much less anything else? Miss Montrose doesn't have it in her to be churlish. I wonder why Cousin George isn't champing at the bit to go west and persuade her? Isn't that what lovers are supposed to do? Anyway, do you like Miss Montrose better now that you've not seen her for all these hours, and the gratitude you owe her for saving your life must still be fresh in your mind?" Lady Quamby's question should hardly have surprised him, and yet he felt the heat beneath his skin. He hoped he didn't give himself away when he said offhandedly, "As I said before, I'm very grateful. And I certainly admire her."

"I won't if she marries Cousin George." Lady Quamby's tone was uncompromising. "I don't know why she'd marry Cousin George when she could marry someone like you—if you only asked her. Will you, Mr Patmore? Ask her to marry you if you find you like her even more than you'd expected?"

"And what if my affections are elsewhere engaged?"

To his surprise, Lady Fenton asked, quite seriously, "Are they?"

He had to be quite honest and admit they weren't, but that he had only the briefest of acquaintance with Miss Montrose.

Lady Fenton nodded, equable for the first time. "And she is, by her own admission, distant and undesirous of making people warm to her."

"A rather surprising admission." Few young ladies, whatever their marital ambitions, surely confessed to such attributes. The thought made him feel better, for she'd been clearly disinterested in pursuing conversation between them when they'd been forced to keep one another company. He'd decided she found him unattractive and was surprisingly piqued by this, for he liked to think he could turn heads when he expended the effort.

Rufus sighed. "I'm not looking for a bride, and if I were, I can't put matters of the heart entirely before pecuniary considerations."

Lady Quamby shifted forward on her chair. "Mr Bramley is even more cheeseparing in his attitude than that, but he's prepared to take a gamble on the fact that her aunt will make Miss Montrose her benefactor."

"I hardly consider myself cheeseparing—"

"And you've probably never had your heart engaged to the extent you've had to weigh up the advantages of eternal domestic happiness over a meagre portion. I completely understand you. No need to justify anything to my sister, who is the first to consider financial gain above anything else. But you are to visit Miss Montrose, for which I'm glad, as you would be easing my concern for her greatly if you could only persuade her to renege on her marriage to Mr Bramley. For all that she would make a very agreeable cousin-in-marriage, I can't help but feel her life would be one of complete misery."

Lady Quamby, who'd not seemed at all offended by her sister's assessment of her priorities, sighed. "I don't believe you can change her mind though, Mr Patmore. Miss Montrose has had her heart broken, and that's why she doesn't care that she's throwing herself away on Mr Bramley."

"Throwing herself away on Mr Bramley?" Rufus repeated her words, asking with a wicked smile, "Please remind me as to why you have such an aversion to Mr Bramley, Lady Quamby, if I am to discharge your request?"

Lady Quamby, seated demurely on a Chippendale chair, looked the picture of feminine disapproval as she began to list his defects.

"His selfishness?" he countered, interrupting her after the third item on what he anticipated would be a very long list. "Why, Mr Bramley is noted for the great care he takes of the winning cockerels who've earned him a pretty penny. And you know his love of horses! I've not heard a whisper suggesting he stints on their good care."

"Mr Bramley cares only for things that can benefit himself," Lady Fenton declared.

"Surely, Mr Montrose, you are not rushing off to petition Miss Montrose to give up her beloved horse *only* to satisfy Mr Bramley?" Lady Quamby asked. "Not after our recent discussion!"

"We have a shared interest in horses, and I shall enjoy the diversion." He had to quash their hopes. "That is all, Lady Fenton."

"When shall you leave?" she asked.

"Tomorrow. I think my ankle is merely bruised, so although it's still tender, I shall soon be walking on it."

"I realize you are charged with encouraging her to return Devil's Run but would you be so good as to discharge *our* request, Mr Patmore? Would you at least try to persuade Miss Montrose against going ahead with this ridiculous marriage, even if you have no vested interest?"

"I don't know why you think I might be any more successful than either of you ladies who, I believe, have both tried to dissuade her."

"That is true, but she may believe we simply dislike Cousin George, so will question our motivations. You, on the other hand, are a very attractive man and it's quite clear she is not averse to you."

Rufus blinked at Lady Quamby and decided he liked the bewitching wench even more. "You flatter me, but as I said, I can't promise I'll have any more success than either of you."

Lady Quamby put her beautiful, blonde head closer to his, mesmerizing him with the exotic scent of lily of the valley. "Maybe you could discover if there's some deep, dark secret at the bottom of all this. Maybe Cousin George is holding her to a promise.- Maybe she'll confess to you the real reason she insists on going ahead with this marriage. For it certainly isn't because she wants to."

CHAPTER 6

At midday the following day, after a three-hour ride, Rufus was shown into the drawing room of the surprisingly humble cottage occupied by Miss Montrose and her aunt. To his surprise, there was no enquiry by Miss Montrose regarding the health of her intended, only a thoughtful, "So, Mr Bramley considers Devil's Run a sure bet for the East Anglia Cup? He never mentioned it to me; otherwise I'm sure I'd not have accepted the unexpected and greatly appreciated gift from Lord Quamby."

Rufus had been waved to a dangerously spindly chair near the window opposite Miss Montrose, while the onyx-eyed aunt regarded him from the corner. After she'd fired a few sharp-edged questions at him regarding his mission, she picked up her knitting so that the resulting quiet was punctuated by the rhythmic click of the needles.

Suddenly, Miss Montrose gave a short laugh. It was completely unexpected, but what Rufus found most surprising was the transformation of her features. He hadn't realised quite what a beauty she was.

"So, Mr Bramley *really* thinks Devil can win the Cup?" She lowered her voice, though it appeared the old lady was now sleeping, her knitting balanced precariously on her lap. "I must tell you that my aunt was horrified that I'd returned with a horse. Unfortunately, she disapproves of most things, and as she's saddled with a dependant as unsatisfactory as I am, she'd no doubt regale you with a litany of complaints if she got the chance." Miss Montrose's concern over her aunt's attitude was suddenly swept away as she said, brightly, "However, I've found stabling for Devil, and I've done what I have to in order to pay for his keep during the next two weeks. While it *would* spare me some expense to release the darling horse back into Mr Bramley's tender loving care, I'm not convinced I wish to do that." She put her head on one side and regarded him with an impish smile. "Devil's Run is not a horse I would imagine Mr Bramley would pin his hopes on. It's not that his racing days are behind him, but I just don't think he's particularly fast or exceptional in any way. I wonder if you have any thoughts on why Mr Bramley considers Devil ripe for contention."

"I have never ridden the animal, Miss Montrose."

"So you knew nothing before about Mr Bramley's desire to race Devil's Run in the Cup? Do you not think it curious?"

"Curious, Miss Montrose?"

"That Mr Bramley is so desirous to get the horse back when he's most unlikely to win the Cup."

Rufus tried to laugh. He didn't want his suspicions that Bramley was up to no good to be true and he didn't want to be compromised, either. In fact, he was about to do a volte face and advise Miss Montrose to stand to her guns and refuse to return her horse when a derisive snort from the corner made them turn. The old aunt had woken, hitched herself up in her chair and was glaring at her niece. "For Lord's sake, Eliza, just give Mr Bramley back his horse. There's always some objection from you, isn't there?"

Rufus wasn't sure who was more surprised or indignant. Miss Montrose's mouth dropped open, and he was surprised to see real hurt in her eyes before she managed, with a pointed lack of emotion, "But I always do my duty in the end, don't I, Aunt? And so, Mr Patmore can take Devil back with him this afternoon, if he chooses."

"Tsk, tsk, a girl who does her duty should not spend the next seven years reminding all and sundry how reluctant she *is* to discharge that duty. The only reason you stay to tend an old woman is because you hope I'll leave my fortune to you." The elder Miss Montrose focused her beady eyes on her niece. "Maybe I will and maybe I won't. That Susanna only ever visits when she thinks there might be something in it for her. I don't care for her, but while she might be a vain, flighty gold-grubbing piece, she's as much my niece as you, and she isn't a sinner."

"Well, if that's what you want to do, Aunt, then why not call the solicitor now and ensure that all your wishes are put in writing."

"Ha! And have you leave this house before the ink is dry? What kind of addlepate do you take me for?"

Rufus was surprised at the malevolence in the old woman's tone. So here was the reason Miss Montrose was taking a chance on Mr Bramley. It was uncomfortable enough being a visitor in the home of old Miss Montrose, but he imagined that living with such daily taunts must be exhausting.

Apparently tiring of the conversation, Miss Eliza Montrose rose suddenly with a cursory nod at her aunt. "Devil is in the top paddock without a blanket, and the sun is going down. I really think I should excuse myself and take him to the stable if I'm to be back in time to get your dinner, Aunt. Mr Patmore can take him in the morning."

She hadn't invited him to accompany her, but Rufus neither intended prolonging his visit if the old termagant in the corner happened to suggest it, or to return to his lodgings. "I'll assist you."

She shook her head. "I'm perfectly capable, thank you, Mr Patmore. You go back to the inn, and I'll bring Devil to you in the morning."

Her short, clipped sentences made clear her aversion to his company. Rufus shrugged. "There's still plenty of daylight, and it's less than two hours' ride to Quamby House so, if you're agreeable to relinquishing him, I'll take him back now. It'll save you the trouble of tending to him."

Miss Montrose stopped abruptly in the doorway and turned her large, luminous gaze upon him. To his astonishment, he saw the tears that were so close to falling. She gritted her teeth and stepped into the passage, muttering, "It's no trouble to spend a few more hours in the company of an animal that asks nothing of me. Allow me this comfort, at least, Mr Patmore. I'm sorry to hold you up when you'd much rather be on your way than having to decamp at the local inn, but...please let me keep Devil's Run until tomorrow."

Rufus lengthened his stride to keep up with her as she hurried up the passage. On the path outside the front door of the cottage, he touched her arm to make her stop and attend to him. "He's your horse to keep for as long as you choose," he reminded her. "I'm in no position to demand that you return him, and nor is George Bramley."

She was standing beside a hollyhock nearly as tall as she was as she gave him the vestige of a smile. "Mr Bramley is to marry me within the fortnight. Only a foolish woman would dig in her heels over a request like this."

They walked in silence through the garden to the bridle path which meandered through the surrounding paddocks to the small wooden stable where Miss Montrose had agisted him, and which she pointed out from the top of a hill. The weather was warm but dark clouds had appeared on the horizon.

"There are candidates other than Mr Bramley." Rufus wouldn't have felt so emboldened except that the Brightwell sisters had made clear that he was their emissary and not just a disconnected bystander. If he were to report to them the emotion-charged encounter between the two Misses Montrose, he'd need to reassure them he'd done his part to remind Miss Eliza Montrose she had alternatives. It also made him feel rather noble, as if he could help direct her to future happiness. It certainly wasn't that he was developing any greater tenderness for her—he told himself sternly.

"In seven, years that hasn't proven to be the case," Miss Montrose said, continuing to walk briskly and not looking at him. "You see what it is like, living with my aunt. I've chosen to swap my current detestable situation with one where I might hope to exercise a little more autonomy."

"You've lived with her for seven years? You must be a saint."

"A sinner in her eyes, didn't you hear? I've heard it every day since I took up residence. But at twenty-five years old, I'm long past my first flush of youth. I do not get marriage offers every day. Mr Bramley's was the first."

Rufus found this hard to believe. The girl was a beauty.

They'd reached the paddock now and Devil's Run, hearing them, ambled over and nuzzled his mistress's arm. To Rufus's surprise, Miss Montrose produced a carrot from the pocket of the apron she'd taken from a hook by the door as they'd left the cottage.

"I imagine a woman as beautiful as you would receive many marriage offers if you were allowed to meet more gentlemen."

She'd put her face up to the horse's, almost nuzzling it, smiling as she stroked it. There was a softness in her eyes that Rufus hadn't seen before, and as she relinquished the carrot she stepped back, turning to Rufus and asking, "I beg your pardon; I didn't hear what you said."

A lady who didn't hang out for every compliment was a novelty. Instead of answering though, he said, "Forgive me for speaking so plainly, Miss Montrose, but you must surely suspect that Mr Bramley's interest in marrying you is solely on account of the inheritance that might pass to you on your aunt's death."

"Of course I know that. Just as he knows that my acceptance is predicated on the knowledge that an offer from him is preferable to spending another six or more years with my aunt."

"So you admit that neither of you has any affection for the

other." He was truly surprised that she was so forthcoming about this.

Miss Montrose shook her head as she fondled the horse's ears and rested her face against its muzzle, breathing in its horsey scent. She looked happier than he'd seen her.

"But...what if you received another marriage offer? One that wasn't from Mr Bramley?"

A curiously evasive look that Rufus couldn't quite interpret crossed her face. Then she said, "I told you, I haven't received any others, so the question is irrelevant."

"If you went about more in society, I'm sure you'd be surprised at the interest you'd garner, even if it were known you..."

"Were penniless?" She laughed. "Goodness, Mr Patmore, I didn't expect to be having this conversation with you."

"I've never had such a frank conversation with anyone." He was trying hard now, his concern genuine. The girl was lovely. He couldn't bear to see her throw herself away. "I just don't believe you would be happy marrying Mr Bramley. Indeed, in good conscience, I cannot take Devil's Run from you tomorrow if I'd not spoken up about my concerns regarding a match between you and that gentleman, for all that he is, purportedly, my friend. Ladies Fenton and Quamby—"

She raised her hand to silence him. "They have been even more frank than you in detailing every reason—good and bad—for why I should cry off; indeed, why I should have rejected Mr Bramley out of hand in the first place. So you have done your duty, and I thank you for your concern, Mr Patmore." Her expression became stern. "You offered to help me, so perhaps you'd be so good as to fetch my sidesaddle from over there." She flashed him a smile before moving around Devil as she waited.

Rufus was uncertain what to say. "You'll need help to get that off when you come back from your ride." He indicated the heavy leather saddle he'd just thrown onto Devil's back and which she was now adjusting.

"It's easier to get it off than on, though I can do both alone, I assure you."

Rufus watched her work. She looked content enough, absorbed in the practicalities. Undoubtedly, she was stubborn, and he wondered how that would go down with Bramley. "Tell me where the farmer lives so I can settle the account without troubling you further, Miss Montrose."

She stopped her work to send him a sharp look, her brow furrowing as if she was surprised at his attitude. "I think I've offended you, Mr Patmore. I'm sorry." She went round to him and put a conciliatory hand on his sleeve, smiling into his face with genuine contrition. "My aunt's sharp ways must have rubbed onto me more than I'd realised." She shrugged. "I suppose seven years will do that to one."

Without thinking, Mr Patmore placed his hand over hers and gave it a squeeze. "I know I have no place saying it, but Ladies Fenton and Quamby were quite explicit that I do all in my power to persuade you against this marriage." His short laugh echoed the amusement he saw in her eyes, and he realised she'd not withdrawn her hand, and nor had he.

She tilted her head, her mouth a perfect rosebud. "So, I should offer you a few words, a sentiment perhaps, for you to take back to those two good ladies at Quamby House. Something that will ease the conscience of everyone who knows Mr Bramley, and who fears they were derelict in their duty if they hadn't thoroughly warned me of what lies ahead if I marry him."

"Very perspicacious, Miss Montrose. I would greatly appreciate that."

He was disappointed when she withdrew her hand. "You are not unintelligent, yet you can't begin to imagine what it is to have utterly no means of support. Have I not already told you in the plainest terms why I will not be dissuaded? Faced with the choice of continued tenure with my aunt—which may last a decade or more—or a life with Mr Bramley that offers me a modicum of independence as a married woman and the possibility of children, I have chosen the latter."

⚜

SHE FAREWELLED HIM WITH JUST A FEW WORDS AFTER THAT. She'd rejected his offer to accompany her back to her aunt's cottage, although she'd have enjoyed the companionableness of it —for she liked Mr Patmore more than she liked most men. But she wanted to be alone with Devil. It had been such a long time since she'd enjoyed companionship that required nothing of her. No need to justify her actions, her decisions, or account for her absence. Devil's Run truly was the ideal companion.

And when she really thought about it—as she did after she'd made herself comfortable on a bale of hay and was watching Devil chew rhythmically in the corner of his stall—Mr Patmore's company *was* unsettling. She couldn't remember when she'd last been with a gentleman who took notice of her, responded to her remarks as if they were more than inanities or irrelevant, or whose eyes held genuine interest and admiration.

Once, at an Assembly Ball a few years before, there had been a gentleman whose obvious interest she'd returned. She'd been disappointed to hear Mr Morley had left the district without a word, and when her aunt had teased out the reason for Eliza's long face, had told her briskly that sin was like a stain, visible to *everybody*.

She wondered at the fact Mr Patmore seemed to enjoy her company.

It was amusing that *he* seemed as determined as Ladies Fenton and Quamby that she shouldn't marry Mr Bramley. Well, her mind was not going to be changed, even if Mr Bramley was revealed as Bluebeard himself, though her conversation with Mr Patmore had reminded her she'd have to mend her manner if she weren't to ruffle the acute sensibilities of her husband-to-be.

With fresh purpose, she jumped to her feet on the hay bale and mounted Devil. The handsome sidesaddle had been the last gift from her father, but she'd have ridden astride if she'd had no choice. That's why she was going to marry Mr Bramley. Because she had no choice. No choice at all if she were ever going to be happy again.

Breathing in the scent of late summer as they ambled into the yard, she raised her head and smiled at the sun filtering through the top branches of the silver birches. Soon she'd be a mother again. She could ride Devil as often as she wanted, and she'd watch her boy grow. It was almost too terrifying to contemplate how happy that thought made her, but any sacrifice would be worth it. Even marriage to Mr Bramley, and though it might not come easily, she *could* be the pliant, obedient, even admiring wife he required her to be if it meant Jack was in almost daily residence.

Flicking the reins, she put Devil into a trot, riding out through the trees and taking the bridle path that bordered the property. She wouldn't go farther afield where she might encounter anyone else and be forced to engage in idle banter. Devil was all the company she wanted right now.

Only a brisk fifteen-minute walk separated her aunt's cottage from his stabling. The farmer's daughter she'd approached had been happy to earn a few coins in return for the use of the unoccupied dwelling while she waited for her late father's property to be sold.

Eliza hoped Mr Patmore would be generous enough to pay the woman until the end of the month, as per the original arrangement, though if Mr Bramley were settling the account he'd not pay a penny more than he had to. He wasn't a generous man, and Eliza would have to work to make a union between them tolerable. After the experience she'd gained in soothing delicate sensibilities, she was certain she could rise to the task.

Besides, the incentive would be more than sufficient. George Bramley could not banish Jack if he was the favoured playmate of the earl's son.

On that wonderful thought, she closed her eyes as she recalled his sweet profile. He'd not been at Quamby House on the day she'd left—and wasn't due to return for several days—so she'd not had the farewell she'd have liked.

But soon...soon she'd be a permanent resident at Quamby House, and she'd contrive to see her son every day.

⚅⚄⚅

AFTER A LONG, MEANDERING CANTER, ELIZA BROUGHT DEVIL back to his stable. She dismounted, removed his saddle, rubbed him down and prepared to say her farewells, watching him munch contentedly on hay.

What underhand plans did George Bramley have that he was so anxious to have Devil's Run race in the East Anglia Cup, sending an emissary to all but demand his early return?

Brushing a few loose bits of hay off her skirts, she went to rest her cheek against his flank. His warmth seemed to seep through to her very marrow. With a sigh of contentment, Eliza closed her eyes again, and he brought his head down and nuzzled the top of her head. The contact made her wistful. She loved horses but hadn't owned one since her father had sent her to live with Aunt Montrose. Perhaps if she'd had one of her own, she'd not have ended up so sharp and astringent— spinsterish—as Mr Patmore clearly thought her, though what else could she be when her daily ritual was dancing attendance on a demanding old woman and parrying her barbs. There'd been no warmth or companionship from another human being for...nearly a quarter of her life, if she wanted to use hard facts and figures.

Well, didn't that make her ideally suited to being Mr Bramley's wife? She had no expectations of warmth, companionship or kindness, though, seven years ago, it's what she'd thought she'd have for a lifetime.

Unexpected tears pricked her eyelids. She hadn't cried in years, though after Gideon had been torn from her, she'd cried every night for weeks until her aunt had beaten sentiment from her with a willow switch, and finally, Eliza had learned life was easier if she simply bottled up emotion.

With another soft whinny, Devil nuzzled her cheek.

It was as if he understood and sympathised with her precarious emotional state. He was on her side. He might be the only one when she was ensconced at Quamby House, but if she only had Jack and Devil, it would be enough.

It should have been a comforting thought, but the first tears that trickled down her cheeks were rapidly joined by more, a veritable torrent which seemed to unleash a great tide from within, representing the great, aching chasm of loss she'd tried to cauterise for so long.

She took a shuddering breath as she wrapped her arms about Devil's Run's neck and exhaled on a wailing sob. It was cathartic. She could never cry like this in her aunt's home. But here she had peace, and solitude.

And an undemanding audience who continued to nuzzle the top of her head and offer her all the comfort and understanding she needed.

৩১৫৩

AFTER AN HOUR OF KNOCKING ABOUT THE VILLAGE, AND another hour loitering in the taproom of the *White Swan* where there'd been no decent company, Rufus was thoroughly bored.

If he'd persuaded Miss Montrose that his convenience was more important than her sentimental notions of having Devil's Run for another twelve hours, when she'd see the horse in less than a fortnight, Rufus could be on his way now.

Then he felt churlish for even thinking he should have talked her into letting him leave with Devil's Run this afternoon, considering the life she led with that demanding old woman.

He wondered what could account for his dismal mood. It was more than just his recklessness that had ruined Carnaby and the fact his wrist was causing him pain after the fall, though his ankle was better..

With dusk falling after a light dinner, Rufus decided he'd take a walk to where Devil's Run was being stabled and see for himself what might be the attraction the horse held for Bramley. There was little else with which to amuse himself, after all.

It was attractive countryside, if a little dull. He wandered the bridle tracks past the hedgerows that bordered neat paddocks, irritated that his thoughts frequently turned to Miss Montrose. The weather was fine and mild, and the birds seemed cheerful enough; a thought that only seemed to cast him into a more dismal frame of mind.

When he pushed open the stable door and beheld the sight within, he realised his lack of cheeriness was nothing compared with the utter tragedy that seemed to have overtaken Miss Montrose.

"What is it?" he asked, striding across the hay-strewn floor and without thought gathering her into his arms for, as the eldest brother of three sisters, this wasn't an unusual course of action. "Is it your aunt? Devil's Run?"

She shook her head, and perhaps she resisted—he wasn't sure when he thought about it afterwards—but he was renowned for his fortifying brotherly hugs, and that was what he was offering.

Well, it *was* until she raised her beautiful, tear-stained face and her eyes, brimming with tears, widened with sudden awareness.

For a moment, they simply stared at one another. Her lovely rosebud mouth parted in surprise, and her gaze seemed to seek something more from him than just his comfort. Beneath his hands, he was conscious of the gentle curve of her waist and her swan-like throat. She seemed like a glorious creature, frozen at his touch, suspended in anticipation of what would happen next; holding her breath, just as he was.

A second after that, he was acting on primal instinct alone when he brought his face down and touched his lips to hers.

Her arms went up and around his neck, and she pressed her body against his as her mouth eagerly responded.

The slow burn in his belly was soon a conflagration as he supported her over his arm and trailed kisses the length of her throat, across her décolletage, and all the way back up to her mouth.

She moaned softly, her eagerness unmistakeable.

And then Devil whinnied loudly, and the spell was broken.

With a gasp, she tore herself away.

CHAPTER 7

"What do you *really* know about Miss Montrose?" Antoinette asked the question as she idly wrapped a ringlet about one finger while reclining on a chaise longue in the drawing room. "I mean, about her past?"

Before Fanny had a chance to put down her book to answer her, Young George's latest antics had his mother throwing up her hands in frustration. "If you hit your cousin once more just because she's won at cards—*again*—I shall wallop your bottom myself, young man! Only you'd then deafen the whole household with your wails." Hauling on the bellpull, she let out a plaintive, "Nanny Brown! Nanny Brown! Take this child away! Oh, Fanny," she added when the squalling seven-year-old had been removed, and a now pliant Katherine lay on the Aubusson rug making card houses, "what have I ever done to have to bear such a cross? Young George is going to send me to Bedlam before he's ten."

"What have you ever done?" repeated Fanny, smiling over the top of her book. "Why, Antoinette, I'm the last person who should be commenting on such an ill-advised question, rhetorical though I know it was. *I'd* say you've done plenty that warranted such a cross to bear, but I'm not one to harp on past misdemeanours, and truth to say, I'm rather grateful for your multitude of wickednesses that have resulted in us enjoying such a pleasant life so far away from Mama." She focused her gaze once more upon the page, adding, "And the way things are progressing, I'd say Young George will see you in Bedlam long before he's ten. Why don't you ask one of the servants to fetch Jack from the foundling home? There's no one else who can keep your child in check and I, for one, am losing patience with you for allowing him to send you up into the boughs as often as he does."

Antoinette sighed, still playing with her hair. "I suppose so; only Jack doesn't usually come on a Tuesday."

"That's because you chose to be the coddling mother on a Tuesday—such a foolish whim, and one that's not working at all! Can you hear the boy—*still*? My, but he has a pair of lungs! Come along now, Antoinette, just have Jack fetched and be done with it! Quamby will be in a far better humour if you do. He likes Jack."

"Well, he certainly likes him for being able to keep Young George in order without resorting to his fists, unlike that gypsy boy."

Fanny considered. "Jack seems to have a knack for making Young George follow along like a puppy dog, soon perfectly engrossed in whatever game they're playing. And Katherine can't get enough of him, which is becoming a little troubling. I'm glad Miss Montrose took to Jack. I just hope she won't want to see the back of him once she has her own child, which, I gather, is her primary reason for wanting to marry Cousin George."

Antoinette contemplated a cherub on the painted ceiling and then her pointed toe, for she'd just acquired a new pair of pink satin slippers with which she was rather pleased. "My guess is that Miss Montrose lost her heart when she was very young, and believes she'll never feel love and passion again. If Mr Patmore doesn't come up to scratch, I'll know I'm right, for he is rather delicious—"

"I hope you don't intend acting on that gleam in your eyes, Antoinette!" Fanny said sharply. "Mr Patmore has lost his heart to Miss Montrose. It's as plain as the nose on his face. Now, we just have to make Miss Montrose realise she's done the same thing."

"What if he's too much a gentleman to persuade her he's a better bet than his so-called friend? I do so fear Miss Montrose will go ahead and marry George, only because he's the one man who's offered her a roof over her head and the chance of babies."

Fanny put down her book and chewed on the tip of her little finger. "I suppose *some* might think George a good catch," she conceded. "You did, at any rate. He's set for a title and an inheritance even richer than Fenton's. Who are *we* to condemn Miss Montrose for putting security above matters of the heart? Or Mr Patmore whom I believe is reasonably plump in the pocket, but really would be looking out for a wife who could bring *something* to the marriage."

"We were certainly lucky, and isn't it a marvellous thing to have security *and* to be able to follow your heart?" Antoinette turned a beaming smile upon Fanny. "Miss Montrose should be able to, also. She's not after George for his consequence, I don't believe. Not at all. As you said, he's simply the only suitor she's had. Unless there was one before? Like last season, perhaps. One who threw her over owing to a terrible misunderstanding, and now he's languishing, alone, somewhere; not knowing that the set down he received was calculated to make him return to her on his knees—with a marriage proposal. Oh, Fanny!" Antoinette clasped her hands together, her eyes shining. "That's what must have happened. I had an inkling of it, before, but that must be why she's so quiet and guarded. Her heart has been broken, and it's up to us to discover exactly who the gentleman is who broke it and bring him here to atone if we can't bring her to acknowledge her love for Mr Patmore. Don't you think our heroine deserves a second chance?"

Fanny, who'd been quite engrossed in the amorous pursuits of the heroine of her book, was ultimately more distracted by Miss Montrose's plight. "I do think Miss Montrose exhibits all the signs of someone nursing a deep sorrow. Of course, Mr Patmore is visiting her as we speak—"

"And he'll be back here within hours, and then we'll know whether he *is* in with a chance or whether we have to dig deeper and find her long-lost love," Antoinette interrupted. "And, *of course*, I won't do anything about Mr Patmore's deliciousness because I'll be seeing my darling Ambrose very soon." Unconsciously, she cupped her bosom and raised her eyes to the ceiling, then burst out, "I have a plan!"

Fanny flicked Antoinette a sardonic look. "Your plans have a tendency to be rather far-fetched, Antoinette, with rather unforeseen outcomes."

"I don't dispute that, but it's the *conclusion* that's important, and I'm very good at conclusions, even if matters don't always go according to plan along the way." Without waiting for Fanny to respond, she went on, "My darling Ambrose fancies himself quite a dab hand at ferreting out information on all manner of things. I don't believe this is beyond him."

Fanny raised an eyebrow but resisted the impulse to remark on her sister's proclivity for gentlemen of a rougher order. "So, clearly this Ambrose chap, who's been lurking in the wings and to whom you have made mention more than once, doesn't mix in our circles? It hasn't escaped me that you've been very much the doting wife, clinging to Quamby's arm at all society events, lately."

Antoinette beamed. "Quite a novelty that, isn't it? I think Quamby is getting quite tired of my devotion, to tell you the truth." She exhaled on a beatific sigh. "No, Ambrose is an actor and an awfully good one. We're currently devising an exciting and plausible persona for him, perhaps as a foreign prince, so that he can rub shoulders with the rest and best of us at Lady Devenish's soiree next week. He's very clever at slinking about in the shadows and discovering all manner of havey-cavey goings-on. In fact, I should set him the task of finding out exactly what Cousin George is up to with that ridiculous notion that Devil's Run could win the East Anglia Cup. But discovering Miss Montrose's lost love is our most important cause, don't you agree?" She ran her hands over her sprigged muslin, unconsciously contouring her curves as her smile broadened. "I'm confident that Ambrose will be assiduous in his enquiries, especially when I give him a little something to fund the project with the promise of his heart's desire—in fact, *all* of his desires—if he's successful."

CHAPTER 8

Devil's loud whinny might have been a reminder that what they were doing was very wrong, but Rufus wasn't the least bit sorry.

The shadows were long when they broke apart, stumbling back and gazing at one another in quite obvious confusion before Miss Montrose turned to pat her horse's flank, saying briskly, "It's time we both went our respective ways, I think, Mr Patmore."

Of course, that would have been the moment to say something. Apologise? Good Lord, no! He wanted to do it again. He wanted *more.*

"Miss Montrose—" he began, but she put her hand up to deflect him from whatever it was he was going to say—and for the life of him he didn't know what he *was* going to say, except that his heart was pumping wildly, he was incredibly aroused—though such an innocent must never know *that,* and he did most definitely want to talk to her about love.

"Mr Patmore, I have one request, and that's to be good to my horse. Don't ride him too hard, will you? I fear that's what Mr Bramley will do when he's training him, but perhaps I can count on you to ensure that no harm will come to Devil at the hands of my intended."

My intended. She spoke of George Bramley so blithely and still in those terms?

Through the gloom, he tried to read some clue in her expression as to what she was feeling. Gad, but he couldn't seem to rein in *his* as he searched her eyes for something to give him hope. Anything. His heart was still behaving much like Devil's would be at the end of the ten-mile race he was to run a few days hence.

Now, though, the emotion Miss Montrose had revealed when he'd unexpectedly come upon her weeping was nowhere in evidence. Had he taken advantage of her vulnerability? Was he a cad? Perhaps she was thinking so at this very moment.

But Miss Montrose was stroking Devil's flank as if nothing whatsoever out of the ordinary had occurred, when Rufus would have bet his right arm she wasn't in the habit of kissing gentlemen on limited acquaintance.

A sudden flash of a winsome smile almost winded him; she looked so lovely as she glanced up and caught his eye.

Maybe she was waiting for Rufus to question her on her feelings regarding the kiss they'd shared. His breathing was still ragged, and inside his head rioted a multitude of tumultuous feelings.

"Miss Montrose, I—" His gentlemanly instincts came to the fore at the mention of Bramley. He *was* going to allude to the passion that had just touched them both, but it seemed she intended to have none of it.

With her cheek still resting against the flank of the horse, she spoke over him. "I must return home now if my aunt isn't to be worried. And so I will bid you good night."

"You can't go alone at this late hour."

"Of course, you may accompany me, if you wish, though I've returned home at this hour on many occasions without an escort." She shrugged as if it were of no account to her, stepping away from him to go around Devil's head, and Rufus watched her final tender moment with her horse, and was ridiculously envious when a beatific happiness softened her expression. Had she looked like that when he'd kissed her? He'd had his eyes closed, and the sensation that seemed to have taken hold of both of them was, he'd thought, more of rising passion rather than beatific happiness or contentment.

Instead of saying anything, he now found himself waiting outside rather awkwardly while she insisted on seeing to a few things inside Devil's stall before securing the stable door. Still, it gave him time to devise a few artful words that went beyond his hitherto pathetic efforts to address what had just happened, and he was on the verge of speaking when she said, quickly, as she strode past, expecting him, it seemed, to match her brisk pace.

"I shall not see you again after this, but I do want to thank you for your concern. Both for Devil's Run and for myself. I know most gentlemen can't bear to see a weeping woman and would rather run for the hills, but I thank you for your comfort." Her shoulders were slightly hunched from the effort of walking so quickly, but now she slanted a glance over her shoulder from beneath her very long and beautiful lashes—now he'd seen them at such close range—adding, "And some men take advantage in such a situation, but you were the perfect gentleman. You offered just the kindness I needed."

Having delivered her little speech to let him know—what? That he was off the hook? That she didn't want him to feel beholden? That she had no interest in him from a romantic point of view? A great weight seemed to have dropped from her. Almost gaily, she swept her arm about their dusk-imbued surroundings and declared, "This has been my home for seven years, but soon I shall swap it for much more exciting vistas, don't you think? Tell me about the view from the battlements of the ruin at Quamby House?"

So he did, for she gave him no alternative, and it was her clear purpose to deflect him from what had happened until she was safely at the gate that led up the gravelled path to her aunt's cottage.

"Farewell, Mr Patmore," she said, nodding. "Enjoy your ride back to Quamby House."

He nodded, feeling strangely disappointed and empty. "I shall." Clearing his voice, he added, "And I shall pass on your regards to your betrothed."

"Naturally," she said without a hint of anything to suggest she felt either dismay or guilt at the mere idea that she had a betrothed.

So that was that. He wasn't aware he was touching his lips as if in remembrance of the sweet sensations he'd unexpectedly enjoyed so recently until at least three minutes later. That was when he was nearly at the fork in the road—for he'd walked from the village to the cottage—and he heard his name being shouted with increasing urgency.

Turning, he saw Miss Montrose running down the track, hatless, her hair escaped from its pins and hanging in delightful disarray about her face and shoulders. She looked so young and astonishingly beautiful with the flush of excitement visible on her cheeks as she neared him that he had to stifle the urge to do something spontaneous and inadvisable, given he had no idea what was sending her back to him.

Had she changed her mind? Perhaps she had a note for Mr Bramley she wanted Rufus to deliver, ending their betrothal? He swallowed, an uncomfortable confusion accompanying that thought. That would mean she expected something more from Rufus on account of their exchange.

He waited for her to close the distance, while he raced a variety of possibilities through his mind. A few minutes before, he'd been piqued that she should dismiss him so thoroughly. He liked her; no, he more than liked her. And that kiss had been a clear reminder of how different it was to kiss a woman who stirred the senses and was young and innocent. He'd had a few trysts where the kiss was a prelude to a prearranged transaction negotiated to satisfy mutual desires, but they had never stirred him as had his kiss with Miss Montrose.

His anxiety increased. What *could* he say to her? What did she expect? A marriage offer? After one kiss? Well, she wouldn't be so direct, of course, but she might imply that their kiss had led to her deciding to dissolve her arrangement with Bramley, which would place Rufus in a conundrum regarding what he'd be honour-bound to offer in consequence.

Gad, she was lovely though, he thought as she flew towards him, he now walking to meet her, still uncertain how he could put the stoppers on what she might be about to ask him.

As she drew within a few feet of him, he saw that the wildness in her eyes was panic rather than ardour.

"Please, fetch the doctor, Mr Patmore. Quickly!" she cried, stumbling but righting herself before she drew level. "My aunt is having a seizure!"

☙❧

Eliza hurried back into the cottage and, with shaking fingers, undid the fastening of Aunt Montrose's gown and loosened her stays, which was difficult since the old woman was stronger than she looked and her flapping arms and strangled cries weren't making Eliza's job easier.

"Someone is fetching the doctor. He'll see you're soon well again," Eliza soothed, unable to make out the slurred words her aunt was trying to articulate. She'd tried to lift her aunt out of her chair to get her to her bedchamber but the old woman was too heavy. That's when Eliza had run outside in the hope of hailing a passerby, finding, to her surprise, that Mr Patmore was still within sight. He must have been loitering outside the cottage for some time before he'd started to wander off. Eliza certainly hoped he'd not formed the wrong idea. She shouldn't have kissed him.

Maybe, though, he'd kissed *her* and she'd responded. Oh Lord, she thought with concern, whatever had happened, there was nothing to it, and she'd have to make that clear though, goodness, it *had* felt wonderful being in his arms for a few moments; as if her heart and soul had been transported to a different place.

And now he was still here and helping her. It wasn't often she'd been able to call on help during the difficult times in her life, but Mr Patmore seemed not only a kind man but one who could be depended upon.

With a cloth she found in the scullery, Eliza wiped away the spittle dribbling down Aunt Montrose's face as the old woman continued her efforts to speak.

"Hush now, Aunt, the doctor will be here soon. Don't waste your strength." She felt desperate and also annoyed at herself, the way she kept thinking of Mr Patmore when there were so many more matters of importance.

But her heart lurched as she heard him returning—and not only with hope on account of the gruff voice of the doctor who'd clearly conveyed them both in his carriage. No, it was more fearfully awkward than that since she couldn't deny that Mr Patmore was the cause.

When that gentleman ducked beneath the lintel to step inside, his reassuring smile was just what Eliza needed, as was his briskness as he suggested he help Eliza put on the kettle while the doctor did what he could for her aunt.

She closed her eyes on a sigh of relief. Good! He wasn't going to take advantage and allude to what had happened earlier then. He was perspicacious enough to understand how matters stood between them.

Setting a lamp upon the table, she said, feeling helpless, "I'm not sure what else I can do except offer food, Mr Patmore. "I've never seen my aunt suffer a day's sickness. Perhaps she'll be completely well after Dr Rutledge administers his medicine."

Her voice faltered, and she dropped her eyes as Mr Patmore sent her a direct look, full of sympathy. He took a step forward and gently unclasped her hands from the handle of the kettle, setting it down upon the table. She'd forgotten she was still holding it.

"I hope so, too, Miss Montrose, but regardless, you have to eat. You're shaking, so I suggest you sit down and tell me where to find things." He opened the tea caddy, talking easily as he spooned out the precious leaves. "A warm cup now, eh, rather than after, and when the doctor has done what he can, I'll help him take your aunt to her bedchamber. You'll have to offer him refreshment for I found him as he was about to sit down to his evening meal." He glanced about. "I see there is no maid in attendance, but she's clearly made something." He sniffed, appreciatively. "A pie, perhaps? Getting a meal onto the table will take your mind off what is beyond your control."

Eliza was astonished by his capability. Most men of his station had never been in a scullery much less knew how to boil a kettle. They imagined food magically appeared whenever it was wanted. "There is gammon pie in the larder. Dora comes in from the village each day. She prepares the food and sets the table before she leaves. I'll bring out everything." Eliza rose with a smile, hesitating before she went to the larder. "Thank you, Mr Patmore. You've been very kind. Please, see if the doctor needs help with anything. I'll do what I can here."

The increasing warmth of his smile in response sent strange shivers through her. Quickly, she turned away.

❧

WHILE THE MEN SAW TO AUNT MONTROSE, ELIZA WENT through her evening ritual of bringing to the table the food that Dora had cooked. Her aunt was reputed to be wealthy—some said, fabulously so—but insisted on a simple existence and detested live-in servants. Eliza's presence helped bridge the gap, for although Eliza didn't do the hard work of scrubbing floors, polishing, washing pots and pans, and skinning rabbits, she did a great many chores that enabled her eccentric aunt to enjoy the reclusive life she preferred.

When Mr Patmore reappeared upon the threshold sometime

later with the doctor, Eliza wasn't sure if she was pleased or disappointed that Dr Rutledge had accepted the offer to join them for supper. Eliza had known the taciturn physician for as long as she'd been in the village. She'd found him a cold and formal man when he'd attended her through several mild maladies, and she wondered if he knew about, or at least suspected, Eliza's sins, despite Aunt Montrose's promise all those years ago to keep her secret.

But of course, she should be glad of his chaperonage, she thought with a spurt of uncomfortable moral righteousness. Eliza didn't need any more slurs upon her name, and even her aunt's illness wasn't a reason to spend another moment alone with Mr Patmore, who made her heart do foolish things.

"Your aunt is resting peacefully, Miss Montrose, but you'll need to check on her hourly," Dr Rutledge said, as he prepared to cut into the thick pastry that encased the gammon pie on his plate. "I can't say what will be the outcome. There have been occasions when the patient, after suffering a seizure like this, makes a complete recovery. However, it's entirely possible she may be rendered incapable of movement and may live thus for years. Others linger and die after a few days."

"My aunt is very strong," Eliza said quickly, looking down at the congealed gravy on her plate, hoping her aunt's case would be in the first category. The uncertainty of her marital status should her aunt expire was almost more than she could contemplate right now.

"So she is, but that means nothing in the case of a seizure like this I'm afraid, Miss Montrose." The doctor's voice was kinder now. Eliza saw that Mr Patmore too had ceased eating and that his expression was concerned. She felt a surge of gratitude and solidarity.

"Nevertheless..." the doctor cleared his throat before he picked up his knife and fork once more "...I suggest you contemplate tonight what might become of you if your aunt fails to make it through this difficult time."

At his enquiring glance at Mr Patmore, Eliza said quickly, "I am to marry in ten days' time. Quamby House will be my new home."

"Good!" The doctor nodded, approvingly. "Being a practical man, might I then suggest you discuss with your groom the possibility of bringing forward your nuptials to mitigate the possibility of being placed in an awkward, unprotected situation."

When he glanced meaningfully at Mr Patmore, Eliza burned with embarrassment and said quickly, "Mr Patmore isn't the gentleman I'm to marry, Dr Rutledge. But I shall do as you say and discuss the matter with my intended."

Her mind was reeling as she saw the doctor out a little later, after he'd again looked in on her aunt who was sleeping soundly.

IT WAS ONLY RIGHT THAT MR PATMORE LEAVE AT THE SAME time, but when he asked, "Are you going to be all right on your own?" Eliza had the most tremendous desire that he sit with her in the dim drawing room just as a reassurance. Suddenly, the future was fraught with uncertainty.

She nodded. He could hardly stay. And there would be no reason for him to remain in the village, either. No, that would be decidedly too dangerous.

So she said, with a wave and a half smile as she turned, "I'm perfectly all right here on my own, and you need to get Devil's Run back to Mr Bramley before my future bridegroom starts champing at the bit. He's not a man who likes to be kept waiting, and I don't want to start my marriage on the wrong foot."

⚜

ELIZA HARDLY SLEPT. EACH HOUR, SHE WENT IN TO CHECK ON her aunt who continued to sleep soundly, though one side of her face seemed to have sagged even more, and her mouth drooled a steady run of spittle which had collected on the floor beside her bed.

Eliza fetched a cloth.

When dawn broke, she felt as haggard as her aunt looked in the morning light. Eliza reached over to pull the covers up to the old woman's chin before turning to stare out of the window.

So that was it. Without warning, Aunt Montrose had gone from a harping termagant who looked like she might have years of spite to unleash upon her niece, to an invalid whose life hung in the balance.

And so did Eliza's. Within days, Eliza might be penniless. The old woman had threatened just that only the night before. Oh, she'd said it so many times Eliza usually remained unaffected, but the memory of the words over an afternoon cup of tea returned to Eliza with terrifying portent. "You care nothing for me, unlike Susana, who visits me with sweet words and comfits to please an old woman." She'd leaned forward and said with her usual peevishness, "But then, who knows what I might choose to do once I know the end is nearly nigh. Mr Cuthbert (who was her solicitor) has my will, and don't you know, but that I've changed it three times in the seven years since you've lived with me. All I can say, Eliza, is that you'd do well to continue to humour your old aunt. Yes, indeed."

Fortunately, she'd not harped on about the cousin who always looked so pristine and fresh, a circumstance that was hardly surprising since Susana lived a life of comfort, and only visited her moneyed relative when it seemed timely, no doubt, to remind her of her competing claim with Eliza.

Eliza cast her gaze around the room. For seven years, she'd plumped the pillow in her aunt's favourite chair before helping the old lady into her seat. Daily, she'd read to her, sewed in silence with her, jumped up to assist her when the whim for something just out of reach took the able-bodied woman.

Eliza knew she was paying for her sins. Aunt Montrose would never forgive her, just as Miss Montrose's brother—Eliza's father— never had. And any softness Eliza's mother felt towards her remaining child had disappeared the night her husband died within hours of Eliza giving birth to the bastard who was quickly spirited away.

Mrs Montrose had not factored in her daughter's talent for cunning, or Eliza's determination to be a mother. Eliza had snatched Gideon from the foundling home one night and, for three months, had survived on charity, sleeping in barns, even working as a farmhand so that she could keep Gideon, her precious, blue-eyed, six-fingered cherub.

Then she'd been found by a man sent by her father. Not long afterwards her child had, once again, been torn from her arms, and Eliza had been sent to live with her aunt.

The joyful song of a nightingale made her smile suddenly. She should concentrate on shoring up her future, regardless of how gravely ill her aunt was. Yes, her impending liberation was terrifying. Mr Bramley wouldn't marry her if her aunt left her penniless.

But Eliza had cunning and determination. She'd demonstrated that. She'd find a way to be near Jack.

She took a seat at her aunt's side and gently stroked her hand. It was as frail as a bird's; the skin thin and papery. Not at all did she resemble the sharp, brusque, controlling woman who'd ruled Eliza's life.

Yet even in this state, she ruled it as much as she ever had.

She took a deep breath, hoping her aunt could hear her as she whispered, "Please understand, Aunt, that I don't want a large bequest. And whatever I wish for, it's not for myself." She had no idea what her aunt was worth or what Mr Bramley's expectations were. She only hoped there was some way to navigate between the two to Mr Bramley's satisfaction. "No, it's not for myself, but for an innocent child. My child, Aunt. Your nephew, and your late brother's grandson. Surely a child born out of wedlock is not born in sin if its parents felt a truly great love for one another. Surely it's *only* the parents' sin rather than the child's burden to carry through life. Your fortune was inherited from my father, whose disgust at my shame was so great that he changed his will to favour you, and he left me nothing. Would you do the same? Is that not to condemn me twice?"

She rose and again went to the window where she saw a figure on horseback silhouetted against the morning sun. Shocked, she realised it was Mr Patmore, and that he was leading another horse on a long lead—Devil's Run. She wasn't sure who she was more glad to see, though she knew her pleasure was wrong on both counts. Devil's Run should at this moment be on his way back to Mr Bramley if she weren't to incur his displeasure...which she certainly did not want to do at this delicate juncture. And as for Mr Patmore, she'd expected she'd not see him again after last night. She'd steeled herself not to want to see him, and yet, here he was, and her heart was skittering in her chest like it belonged to a foolish schoolroom girl.

"Good morning, Mr Patmore," she greeted him, careful to show nothing of what she was feeling as she opened the door while he dismounted at the gate and tethered the two horses.

"Good morning, Miss Montrose." He grinned, as if he were exceedingly pleased with himself for having brought her such a gift.

"And what will Mr Bramley say when he's without his horse another day? He'll assume I displayed intransigence." She couldn't let him see how much she liked seeing him again.

"I'll be entirely truthful, Miss Montrose," he responded, doffing his hat with a gallant bow before issuing up the path. "I'll say you were in such desperate spirits at the precarious health of your aunt, that I took it upon myself to delay my return with Devil's Run so you should enjoy one more breathtaking gallop." His expression became grave. "You know I couldn't leave you after what's happened. I saw Dr Rutledge this morning, and he said the most useful I could be was to help take your mind off your cares, and off any other assistance you can think of."

"My aunt hasn't woken, but I can't leave her."

"Of course you can. Your servant is five minutes away on the road, and she tells me the doctor is following. I've said she must pass on the message to the doctor—and your aunt, should she wake—that you'll be gone but an hour, but that you'll be back to resume your place at your aunt's bedside shortly. Now, go and change. I'll wait here."

"I can't leave for an hour! What reason did you give her?"

"None. Why should you have to account to your servant? Now, fetch your bonnet or modish feathered riding hat, or whatever it is you wear to deport yourself on horseback and come with me."

She couldn't resist, though she knew she should. The desire to be out and about on horseback, and the desire to spend some time with Mr Patmore, alone, was too irresistible.

"You are too smooth, Mr Patmore," she said, allowing the tiniest smile as she took his arm. "A dutiful niece should offer at least another five minutes' worth of objections, but then if Dora caught up, I'd let her disapproval and then Dr Rutledge's dire pronouncements weigh too heavily upon me, and of course I'd not go at all, so thank you."

It was worth it. The crisp air that slapped against her body, and tore her hair back from her face once she was mounted and galloping over the paddocks, invigorated her. She had a new appreciation of the beauty of the early-morning countryside and a strengthened hope for her future, and when she finally dismounted at the gate to her aunt's cottage only twenty minutes later, she couldn't help laughing with pure pleasure.

"You have been so very kind, Mr Patmore. I am filled with renewed courage, but now I must bid you farewell."

He also dismounted, nodding at a handsome landau tethered to a nearby railing, empty but for the muffled drive., "Your aunt has company, I see. Naturally, I would like to pay her my respects in the hope she's improved since yesterday."

Eliza hesitated, wondering if she could say no for it seemed Mr Patmore was dead set on coming in. So she shrugged and led the way towards her aunt's bedchamber where, on the threshold, she started. "Susana! I didn't know it was you. When I saw the landau outside—"

"Yes, it was high time I was conveyed about the district in something a little more up to the minute than the sad old dogcart I've been driven in forever. But really, Eliza, show some consideration," her cousin added, lowering her voice. The girl was holding their aunt's hand, and Aunt Montrose was propped up on several pillows, her eyelids fluttering, her mouth moving as she again tried ineffectually to speak.

"Aunt Montrose, you're awake!" Eliza cried, genuinely pleased.

"And we've had a lovely old coze. She's feeling far more the thing, aren't you, Aunt? But who is this?"

Eliza bit her lip as Mr Patmore appeared in the doorway. She made the introduction, and didn't miss the calculating interest in Susana's eyes as they travelled from Mr Patmore's Hessians up to his laughing grey eyes. Mr Patmore was, Eliza realised, a man of very easy spirits. Not once could she remember having seen his mouth turned down or thunder in his eyes. Not like Mr Bramley, she thought with a shudder, and was dismayed at both the dislike she felt at the thought of Susana taking an interest in Mr Patmore and the prospect of Mr Bramley for a husband.

"Miss Montrose—" Mr Patmore took a step towards Eliza as she stood at the end of the bed, and for one wonderful moment, she thought he was going to take both her hands in his. Instead, he gave an abrupt bow. "I should return Devil's Run to your intended."

Was there some deeper meaning he was trying to convey? He certainly seemed to be focusing very intently on Eliza.

"I'll see you out, Mr Patmore," said Susana gaily, jumping up from her aunt's bedside and stepping between them. "Aunt Montrose and I have been talking for simply an age, and now that Eliza's returned I'm sure she'll be glad of the change of company."

Eliza tried not to let her feelings show as she first thanked Mr Patmore for his help and bade him farewell, before lowering herself onto the chair near her aunt. She picked up a book lying on the bedside table and opened to the page marker, realising at the same time that her Aunt Montrose had slipped back into unconsciousness.

She should start reading nevertheless, if only so that she wasn't accused of eavesdropping, for through the window she could hear Susana talking in her quick, vivacious way, and Mr Patmore responding politely. Did he like her? Was he as taken by Susana's fair prettiness as most men? Susana had rejected three suitors in the past year for she was anticipating her first London season shortly. She wanted a match more illustrious than the local squire's son, and no doubt she could aspire to an earl if she inherited her aunt's wealth.

She probably would, Eliza thought with a stab of angst.

"Did you speak, Aunt?" she asked, lowering her head as she heard the jingle of harness indicate Susana's departure.

Her aunt was awake again, her eyes wide and fearful, her mouth working quickly though no intelligible sound came. She began to thrash about as if she were in the grip of another seizure, and Eliza leapt to her feet and ran to the front door, just as Mr Patmore mounted Devil's Run and started riding down the street.

She didn't think he could have heard her. She was out of earshot, but he turned as he was about to round the bend and so saw her flailing arms signalling him to return.

Eliza had intended to ask him to fetch the doctor back again, but he insisted on coming back into the cottage, telling her the doctor was attending another gravely ill patient three miles away, and perhaps there was something with which he could assist.

There wasn't, for when they reached Aunt Montrose's bedside, the old woman was trying to speak what would be her final words. Eliza thought she heard her name, but as she took her aunt's outstretched hand, it went limp and the old woman's eyes glazed over.

She looked up at Mr Patmore who shook his head.

Aunt Montrose was dead, and Eliza had no idea what the future had in store for her.

CHAPTER 9

Eliza put on an old gown that had been dyed black to mourn her father seven years before. There was so much to organize, and appearance was the least of her concerns.

She was glad of Dora's practical presence. What must happen both spiritually and physically were matters with which she needed help, to ensure the right people were notified and fetched.

The doctor arrived and wrote out a death certificate. There would be visitors, said Dora, adding that she would need help washing and dressing the body.

Aunt Montrose might have left a fortune, but she had lived like a village woman.

Eliza was sure Mr Patmore would leave at this juncture, but he didn't.

"Abandon you in your darkest hour, Miss Montrose?" he asked, raising his eyebrows as Eliza pushed up the sleeves of her gown and donned an apron in preparation of her grim and unwelcome task.

"But what about Devil's Run?"

"You mean, what about Mr Bramley?" he clarified with a sly look. "He can wait another twelve hours. The race isn't until next week. Now, burden me with something useful to do." He gave her a bolstering smile. "It won't be long before the cottage is full of mourners, and it'll fall to you to ensure their comfort, even if you've never seen most of them in your life. I have firsthand experience of this."

She was grateful for his support. He didn't offer false condolences, and he was innovative in what would be required. He seemed able to think of everything. Eliza could only think of one thing—what now?—as she attended to her aunt's cold dead body; washing the limbs that had been sources of endless complaint—her tired old legs, or her aching arms that had never offered Eliza a single comforting caress. Finally dressing the old woman in her Sunday best, she put a book under her chin to keep her mouth closed before calling Mr Patmore to help Dora lay the body out in the parlour.

Eliza admired his capability when he must come from a family that had all such practical matters attended to by servants. He admitted he'd never cooked a meal or made his own tea, so how could he anticipate her every need? A cup of tea when she was tired. A hot meal he arranged to have brought over from the White Swan.

And what must he think of her? She was little more than servant to a woman who lived like a villager, yet her aunt had a fortune in the three and four per cents. Or was that only a rumour?

Eliza tried to remain pragmatic. Since she could do nothing as regards the outcome of the will, she'd best be thinking of artful ways to make herself a valued proposition to Mr Bramley, she thought with feverish intensity as she went about her duties.

By midafternoon the next day, nearly a dozen old biddies crowded the parlour; drinking tea and eating sandwiches and plum cake. Aunt Montrose had more friends in death than she had in life. Eliza nearly said so to Mr Patmore, who had just returned from an errand fetching loaves of bread to assist Eliza in her duties of playing hostess to her aunt's mourners, five of them occupying all the available seating in the small room.

Eliza was glad they didn't seem to consider her company a requirement, but deeply offended when she overheard Miss Siddons say in clipped nasal tones, without lowering her voice, "I can't imagine Annabelle would leave a penny to that sinning girl. She ought to be grateful she had a roof over her head and lived in such comfort the past seven years, don't you think?"

A shiver ran through her. What did she know of Eliza's sins? Of course, Miss Siddons' companion agreed with clucking noises, and Eliza glanced at Mr Patmore to see if he'd heard. He made no indication as he stoked the fire. What would he make of Eliza's past? Why was he here? Out of the goodness of his heart? Surely it was more important for him to get Devil's Run back to Mr Bramley than stay here?

Her eyes followed the curve of his back as he leant over to drop a large piece of wood into the centre of the flame. She wanted to caress the elegantly curved line and feel the strength beneath; the muscle and hardness that made up the dependability he'd shown her this past day and a half.

He turned, unexpectedly, catching her eyes on him and Eliza looked away, embarrassed, before asking Miss Siddons if she'd like more tea while thinking what satisfaction it would give her to pour it down her scrawny cleavage.

The voice of Mr Patmore sounded a discordant note when the room was again bathed in silence, and the doctor had gone. She'd lost herself in conjuring up dreams of her unknown future, and she'd forgotten his presence.

"Is there anything else you need, Miss Montrose? I don't believe you've eaten a thing and now there's nothing left."

The light had dimmed, and the room looked gloomy and untidy.

She smiled. "You've been so very kind and helped me so much. I really do appreciate it."

"After what you did for me the other day, Miss Montrose, it was the least I could do."

He gripped her hand, and she was dismayed by the extent of

her disappointment when he dropped it as if realising the inappropriateness of the gesture.

"I'm reluctant to leave you here alone, Miss Montrose," he said, glancing about the room. "Yet, anything else wouldn't be appropriate."

"Since Mr Bramley sent you as his emissary, I'm sure that you remaining a little longer would be condoned under the circumstances." She nodded towards the sideboard. "Perhaps you would be so good as to find something a little stronger than lemon barley water to go with whatever I can find to put on the table. Aunt Montrose might turn in her grave—" she put her hand to her mouth before saying ruefully, "—I did not mean to sound flippant. But I do intend to raid her medicinal brandy cupboard which she kept quite well stocked."

A few minutes later, she was back with the remains of a meat pie and some cold cooked potatoes which she placed upon the table, together with cutlery and crockery.

"I'd better draw the curtains, in case we're spied upon. And if someone calls upon me to offer their condolences, it might be preferable if you took yourself off to another room. I don't mean to suggest anything untoward, Mr Patmore, but you know how tongues will wag."

FROM HIS POSITION BY THE SIDEBOARD, HE WATCHED HER closely. Her movements were unhurried and elegant. She seemed as much at home in this more humble setting with so much to do, as she had when he'd been only partly aware of her at Quamby House. Her stillness was part of her essence. She imbued calm. And yet she could act like lightning when she had to. Nor should her quiet manner be mistaken for shyness, he'd realised. She was an impressive young woman.

"I do, but you'll leave here soon enough, Miss Montrose, and I don't think you'll be sad about that. Now, there is plenty on the table. Take a seat with me and drink." He handed her a glass containing a liberal quantity of brandy. "You've had a great shock today, and your nerves need calming. I'm only sorry it's not your intended who is in my place to comfort you."

Eliza laughed at the searching look he sent her before he picked up his knife and fork and began to eat. "I don't expect Mr Bramley is the comforting kind, do you? Though that's not the reason I'm marrying him."

She speared a potato, giving a shrug at his incisive look. "Fortunately, my need for comfort has well and truly been cauterised. My aunt was perfectly horrid to me. I'm sorry she's dead, for her sake, but if her complaints were anything to go by she didn't enjoy her life very much. *I* certainly haven't enjoyed mine the many years I've had to live with her."

"And now you're free." He sent her a level look. "You don't have to marry Mr Bramley if you don't wish to. You don't have to do anything you don't want to."

"My dear Mr Patmore..." She laughed softly. *How little you understand.* She didn't say it, of course. "I am a woman. An unmarried woman without resources, as we speak. That may change, or it may not. But you came here to take Devil's Run to Mr Bramley so he can race him next week, and it isn't in my interests to irritate the man upon whom my future depends. Oh dear, I wonder who that is, now?"

The knock at the door had her swiftly picking up his plate to hide the evidence she had dined with another person. She nodded towards the room at the end of the passage, and obediently Rufus disappeared into the parlour where the old woman was laid out; a smile of smug serenity upon her marble face. Further observation of the corpse brought up no likeness between the severe features of the spare, scrawny woman in her coffin, and the lovely woman in the other room whom he could hear speaking to a well-wisher.

The candles laid out about the room cast gloomy shadows over the walls and floor. He pitied Miss Montrose having to spend the night alone with her dead aunt, though he had no doubt she was up to it. He'd not seen her self-possession falter. He appreciated that quality in a woman. He certainly would appreciate it in the one he'd someday take for his wife.

Restlessly, he moved about the room, wondering why he was feeling all at sea; reluctant to go when he should have gone long ago. Before his heart had become inconveniently involved.

He could hear Miss Montrose talking. She appeared to be soothing a rather emotional woman on the front doorstep, though she didn't invite her in.

Idly, Rufus considered the room's plain but comfortable furniture. Miss Montrose senior certainly was perplexing. She lived in far humbler surroundings than Bramley would have had him believe, considering the old woman was worth a fortune, inherited from her brother who'd made his riches in copper. Rufus assumed the brother couldn't have been Miss Eliza Montrose's father, though now that the question arose, he should find out. Miss Eliza Montrose's father was no doubt an impecunious sixth or seventh son, and Miss Montrose his orphaned daughter whose future no one in the family had thought to secure.

He stared at the paintings of various family members lined up around the parlour walls. All sitters were handsomely garbed, and the paintings had been done by a master. So where did Miss Montrose fit in? Where had she lived before she came to live with her aunt? Had she always been the poor relative? If so, no wonder she was prepared to wed Bramley. Anything to have a roof over her head, he supposed.

He heard the talking cease and waited for Miss Montrose to return. He should have been more considerate, earlier, when he'd said she was free to do as she chose, for tonight she'd not sleep at all, wondering at the possibilities open to her upon the reading of her aunt's will.

Either she'd have inherited a fortune, or she was a pauper. He stepped up close to better examine a couple of two small, obviously more recently painted, portraits upon the wall. They depicted a man and a woman of middle age, both light-haired, with fine but stern features. Family members? He could see nothing to suggest who they were to either of the Misses Montrose. So much about Miss Eliza was a mystery.

Now he wished to know more.

He also wished for the courage to bring up the subject of that surprising kiss that hadn't been mentioned. Some ladies would have been mortified. She appeared to have brushed it aside as if it had never happened.

But he had caught her studying him. When he'd been putting wood on the fire, he'd caught her eyes on him, and the look she'd sent him when she'd thought he couldn't see had been gratifying.

But there was little beyond that other than a mild encouragement that he stayed for dinner to keep her company. She'd said little to indicate how preoccupied she must be by her future, and there'd been no hint of self-pity in her demeanour.

If she inherited wealth, she could do as she pleased. If not, she'd be hoping George Bramley did the honourable thing and did not renege on the marriage.

Bramley! The idea of marriage between Miss Montrose and that thuggish ruffian was intolerable. And yet, what alternative did she have should the cards not turn in her favour?

Lord! Of course, Rufus shouldn't have kissed her! And now he thought her even more impressive for being such a woman of principle, for didn't she have every justification for subtly—or not so subtly—pursuing him as an alternative suitor? It was clear she found him a good deal more attractive a proposition than she did Bramley. But unless Rufus gave her some encouragement further to their kiss, she wasn't going to carry this further.

This, he now realised as he ran his hands over a Sevres vase—yet another indication that while the cottage was humble, its accoutrements were not— was an increasing fascination and admiration for Miss Montrose. He'd not been on the lookout for a wife, and he certainly wouldn't have looked for a prospective bride with Miss Montrose's reserve. He gravitated naturally to the vivacious; the flirtatious.

Perhaps that was why he'd never got himself hitched. He

enjoyed these types of women, but subconsciously he wanted a wife with more depth.

Someone like Miss Montrose.

Someone whom he could rely upon to attend to necessary matters of business, and who would take an interest in estate affairs. He wasn't a large landholder, but his properties were extensive enough that increasingly they required his attendance, and he had the expectation of inheriting more. Miss Montrose, in addition to possessing the qualities that would make her an adept and conscientious landholder's wife, was extremely pleasing to the eye.

There was no denying that he was most assuredly attracted to her. Yes, she was affianced to Bramley, but it was quite clear that was for expediency only.

Well, Rufus was a betting man in his own way, and while he *could* afford a wife with nothing, if she answered his exacting criteria, as Miss Montrose did, perhaps she *would* inherit when the old woman's will was read the following day.

Perhaps he'd be on hand to offer her an alternative to George Bramley. Why not? He wasn't being any more dishonorable than Bramley himself, who should have come personally to see his betrothed if he wanted his horse back.

But even as he put it this way, he knew that, deep down, it didn't really matter which way it went. And that only a cad like Bramley would think this way.

He wanted Miss Montrose, regardless.

⚜

ONCE ELIZA HAD DESPATCHED MRS GOODINGS, WHOM SHE MADE sure was well out of sight at the bottom of the road before it forked, she sought out Mr Patmore from the parlour where he was staring thoughtfully at a Sevres vase, snatched her cloak from the hook on the wall, and bade him follow her.

She didn't feel the need for small talk or to explain who the visitor had been, simply nodded her head towards the glowering sky as she pushed open the door and said, "I'll wager we'll be rained upon. I trust you have dry clothes at the *White Swan*?"

He was clearly surprised. "You'd planned on coming out in the dark—alone—to take Devil's Run back to his stable? The horse is my responsibility now, Miss Montrose."

She stopped at the gate and put her hands on her hips. "Devil belongs to me, and you have been kind enough to take him to Mr Bramley; however, if I choose to take him to his stables right now, that is my affair. Are you going to accompany me?" She squared her shoulders, adding with brittle pride, "I understand if you prefer to return directly to your lodgings."

"And leave you to walk in the dark? Aren't you...afraid?"

"Of you? The dark? My reputation?" Eliza was feeling ridiculously independent now that the truth was dawning on her that she was—at least for a few days—mistress of her own destiny.

What did she care about reputation when that was long gone? Besides, Mr Patmore had been good company. Part of the reason for her clipped manner was to disguise the fact that she didn't want to relinquish him quite so soon, though she'd have to soon enough. It might be a long time before she'd again enjoy the company of a good and honourable man to walk out with. Perhaps not until Gideon was grown—and by God, she intended to be by his side during that journey from childhood.

"I hardly think you're going to take advantage, Mr Patmore," she said, latching the gate behind them while he still hesitated. "Not after today, when you've gone so far beyond the call of duty. Now, I suppose we shall have to lead Devil's Run." She let doubt colour her tone, and he asked quickly, "What would you do if I weren't here, Miss Montrose?"

She smiled and bit her lip. "I'd jump astride and enjoy the fact that in the dark no one would see."

"It sounds as if you'd like to be so wicked this evening."

The glint in his eyes caught her by surprise. So he wouldn't be scandalised if she'd done so? She'd pegged him as having a rather entrenched attitude towards behaviour that followed societal expectations.

Without warning, he leapt into the saddle—the one he'd transferred from his previous mount. "Come, Miss Montrose. I'll take you up in front. I promise I shan't tell and, as you say, in the dark no one will see."

A skittering of nerves ran through her as she stared at his extended hand. The idea was appealing. Too appealing. She knew she should resist, but she gripped his large, warm hand all the same, and he hoisted her up onto the saddle in front, his arms curving around her as he took the reins.

The sensation of enveloping, manly warmth was so unexpectedly and sinfully delicious, Eliza didn't know what to say or do. She shouldn't be in such a position, and yet it was quite the most exquisite feeling she'd enjoyed almost for as long as she could remember. Well, for seven years, that at least was true.

"Are you comfortable, Miss Montrose?" His voice warmed her ear while the rest of him did far more than that.

"Mmm-hmmm," she managed, resisting the urge to snuggle more deeply into his embrace for she must *not* give him the impression that she liked the closeness as much as she did. This was for expediency only. She had stubbornly insisted on going out on this final trip to stable Devil's Run for she'd not see him again for some time, while he had simply wanted to get them there faster so he could return to the *White Swan* to get some rest before riding the horse back to Quamby House.

They travelled at a gentle pace, and Eliza couldn't decide whether Mr Patmore's arms were more familiarly wrapped about her than was warranted, and wished she didn't hope that they were.

Any gentleman in his position would be acting just as he was, and the warmth churning in her body was simply a reaction to the fact that it had been so long since she'd actually felt a man's hands upon her.

Better get used to it, she thought with a stab of despair as she called to mind Mr Bramley, whose hands would be all over her soon. For even if her aunt didn't make Eliza her beneficiary, Eliza planned to use every bargaining tool at her fingertips to persuade him she was a good proposition. She had to, and she must not let any feelings for Mr Patmore divert her. Mr Bramley must be part of her future if Gideon was ever to be.

A smattering of rain took her by surprise, and she gasped. Or was it that his body suddenly seemed so much closer against hers as he spoke above the noise of galloping hooves and rising wind.

"We'll have to hurry!" His voice was right in her ear. Intimate. Unnervingly so. "Hold on!"

He hunched over her as they flew over the undulating ground, while the wind whipped their faces and the rain quickened.

It was the most thrilling sensation Eliza could remember.

He slowed to a stop outside the stables then dismounted, raising his arms to take her down, and she slithered off the back of Devil's Ride and into his embrace. Perhaps he'd have let her go had a gust of wind not whipped Eliza's hair across her eyes. With one hand still upon her waist, he lowered his head a little and gently untangled her unruly tresses.

Perhaps, in the glow of moonlight, he saw the spark in her eyes that reflected his own feelings, for something in his expression flared. There was a split second of arrested awareness before a subtle shifting in the mood between them, then the sharp excitement of melding bodies, arms entwined, and mouths unexpectedly fused in a kiss. She didn't withdraw. Instead, the jolt of something come to life within sent Eliza into the abyss; her mind a mass of coalescing thoughts; her body a jumble of nerve endings as she clung to him.

Another smattering of rain caused them to break apart, then her hand was in his, the reins of Devil's Run in his other, and she was stumbling after him. He hurried them both into the stables, Eliza in his arms again before he'd even sent home the bolt.

And as she stumbled backwards, her arms twined round his neck, she wasn't sure whether she'd put them there to steady herself, or through base desire, but that was a question for another time.

All that was important was the here and now; an array of sensory delights in which to indulge for a mindless eternity, or a quick and satisfying five minutes. Her body was on fire like it hadn't been for years, but the reminder of how she'd once responded to a man when her heart was engaged was like a drug.

His cheek was rough as she ran her mouth across its angular plane to kiss the smoothness beneath his eye; her nipples burned with excitement and want, perhaps more through the urge that he touch her there as she silently willed that he dispense with restraint.

With one arm around her waist, he swung her onto a hay bale, resting her on her back while he leant over her, cupping her cheek, kissing her lips and, oh joy, cupping her all-too-sensitive breast as he trailed kisses across her décolletage before hungrily kissing her mouth.

Eliza held him close, pushing her body against his, all but drowning in a long-forgotten abandonment that made her weak and loose-limbed with longing.

Her skirts had rucked up to her knees, and with her legs freed of the usual restraint, it felt only a natural progression to hook them about his waist, for he'd surely need no more prompting than to carry this to its natural conclusion. If Eliza had only this one opportunity to answer to a passion she may never again experience, she was mindless enough to do what was needed to spur him on.

It had entirely the opposite effect.

Raising himself, a chill draft swept between them as Mr Patmore withdrew his mouth from where she was sure he was heading once more to her breast. An aching chasm of disappointment filled the place where seconds before thrilling desire had pumped through her lonely heart just now come to life.

"I'm sorry!" He said the words a fraction of a moment before they'd have spilled from her own lips, and perhaps that was best so she'd not sound so ashamed, diminished and needy; all three of which threatened to choke her with mortification.

He helped her to her feet, brushing the hay from her skirts, gently withdrawing yellow stalks from her hair while she stared at the moonlight streaming through the window, and wondered if she'd ever feel the way she had just now.

Alive. Like she'd felt during the gallop to the stables, and here in the stables in Mr Patmore's arms, feeling the weight of his hard, masculine, dependable body upon hers, and the sensations that coursed through her when his mouth touched her skin.

CHAPTER 10

Rufus blinked at the young woman who'd just turned him from a man of restraint—a characteristic upon which he prided himself—into a lust-crazed young buck. How could he have forgotten himself to such a degree? Only just had he drawn back from the brink of dishonouring her, to put not too fine a point upon it. She was an unmarried young woman betrothed to another, and he had been set to seduce her until, fortunately, a rush of rational thought had saved them both.

She turned her face from her contemplation of the darkness beyond and shook her head. "You have nothing for which to apologise."

He swallowed. It was taking him some moments to recover from the exertion of this extraordinary encounter. Now that his mind seemed in reasonable working order once more though, he waited for her considered reaction. Would she show shame, embarrassment, and remorse? That's what ladies—of all stations in life—did after they had been enthusiastic participants of sexual congress, and though it hadn't reached that point, Miss Montrose had been surprisingly enthusiastic.

What might have happened if Rufus hadn't, by a hairsbreadth, retained his gentlemanly instincts? For he'd certainly awakened a fire of desire within this quiet, contained, young woman. Perhaps something had been unleashed when she'd shattered that stillness that was so much a part of her essence, her fascination, by plunging into the lake to save the children.

Perhaps Rufus had unleashed its twin. That other side. The sexual side about which young ladies mustn't speak. Yes, the ice maiden he'd thought her was a wildcat when it came to desires of the flesh.

He was struck by an even greater appreciation of her hidden depths. Before this latest encounter, he realised he'd intended offering for her. Regardless of whether she would inherit, he would make her his bride.

The thought filled him with such a great happiness, he moved to embrace her, cement what had just happened with a kiss.

But she drew back, shaking her head, though a faint smile played about her lips.

Her eyes sparkled, and her teeth were white. It wasn't just the moonlight imbuing both with perfection. She really was perfection, he thought with satisfaction. And she was going to be his wife.

"Miss Montrose," he began, staring like a mesmerised moon calf at the top of her beautiful shining hair.

Feeling another wave of tenderness, he gently removed an errant stalk from those magnificent tresses and waited for her to raise her head to him once more.

He cleared his throat and prepared to go down on bended knee. It might not be the most auspicious time or location, but a man who intended to do the honourable thing, ought to make his intentions clear at a moment like this. No point in having Miss Montrose toss all night in agonised fear that she'd almost given herself to a cad. "Miss Montrose, I would like to ask you—"

The pressure of her hand which prevented him from kneeling, and the tone in her voice, took him by surprise.

"Please, do not say anything right now, Mr Patmore."

A moment's uncertainty cut through his happy expectation, but her smile was reassuring. "I have a lot to think about." She pressed her lips together. "My aunt has just died, and there will be people coming from all parts tomorrow. Please don't complicate matters just at this juncture."

Rufus wasn't entirely certain he liked the way she phrased this. He hadn't complicated matters 'at this juncture' all on his own. But then, he quickly counselled himself, he was being churlish simply because Miss Montrose wasn't ready to hurl herself into his embrace and weep with relief over his timely marriage proposal that would rescue her from all uncertainty.

He nodded and offered her his arm. "If that is your wish."

"We can talk about Devil's Run if you like," she said, resting her hand on his coat sleeve. "That is, since we have a little walk before I'm home, and I really don't know what to think about this very strange day. Though I certainly am, as Aunt Montrose has said, the very wickedest and undeserving of young women." She gave a short laugh. "And now you've experienced that for yourself, haven't you?"

"If you think I condemn you for something in which I had as much a part too—"

"Please, Mr Patmore!" She held up her hand to silence him. "Let us entirely turn the topic. I am immensely grateful to you for all you've done for me these past two days. Please don't let a moment's...rashness...make you say or do anything you may regret for a lifetime."

He could feel himself gaping like a fish. She was giving him a reprieve. No, it didn't mean she didn't want to marry him, but that she wanted him to be sure he wanted to marry her. By sleeping on it and asking her in the morning.

"By God, you are an astonishing woman," he said, and he truly meant it. Miss Montrose was entirely the kind of wife he realised he both needed and wanted.

And the reading of old Miss Montrose's will would change nothing. Regardless of whether Eliza Montrose was left penniless or in possession of a fortune, she could accept Rufus's marriage offer in the happy knowledge that he'd been as willing to ask for her hand regardless of the outcome.

Together they trod the moonlit path, chatting companionably, their minds as attuned as their bodies had been, but with no sense of awkwardness or embarrassment.

And though it would have been nice to have kissed her once more in parting, he was happy that she clasped his hand warmly when saying good night. He read the desire in her eyes, but he understood she wanted a night to digest the momentousness of the day.

Happily, he returned to his lodgings, more than ever fired up by the thought that in the morning he could look forward to the rest of his life as the husband to that diamond of the first water, Miss Eliza Montrose.

ॐ

ELIZA KNEW SHE'D NOT SLEEP. BY THE TIME MR PATMORE HAD returned to her, and she had, by the utmost strength of will, resisted the impulse to call him back, her connection to reality felt reduced to the merest thread. She was physically and emotionally exhausted as she stood by her casement window and watched that lovely gentleman walk away.

What would it be like to wed a man who was thoughtful and kind and so marvellously passionate? She had no shame and certainly no regrets about what had happened this evening. In fact, it surely was the most fortuitous of encounters, for it reminded her that she had a heart that could beat with an excitement inspired by more than the need to save lives, such as when she'd plunged into the lake.

The last couple of days had reminded her what it was to feel romantic love when she'd thought her heart a dried-out husk.

And, therein, was the rub. What was the point of making this discovery on the eve of pledging herself to a man she knew she could *never* love?

Wearily, she changed into her nightrail and slipped beneath the covers of her narrow iron bed beneath the window. She could see the big round moon through a hole in the curtain that she'd intended to mend only last week when the ageing fabric had rent asunder.

Now there was no point. She'd not be living in this cottage much longer.

But did that mean she had to live with Mr Bramley as his wife? Mr Patmore had given her another option. A far more desirable option.

She shivered, not from cold, and ran her hands over her flat belly, up and over her breasts. Not long before, his hands made that same journey in a far more passionate exploration, and she had embraced every nuanced touch. She drew in a shuddering breath, and brought to mind once more the delicately featured face of the man who'd looked down at her with such feeling.

He'd asked her to marry him. Well, he would have if she'd let him, but she was so set on her course to wed Mr Bramley, and with her emotions so disordered, she'd been unable to countenance any other option.

Now she was filled with excitement as she wondered if indeed she really could hope for happiness. She drew in a shuddering breath, closing her eyes as she gently rubbed the flat of her hand over her sensitised nipples, and imagined it was Mr Patmore above her.

The idea was heavenly. Then she put Mr Bramley in his place, and her brain screamed in objection.

She sat up, gasping for air.

How could she marry Mr Bramley if she could marry Mr Patmore? Surely there must a way she could have Mr Patmore for her husband and keep Gideon close?

Thoughts chased themselves around her brain like wild chickens. She, that most self-contained of young women, could find no order, no discipline, as she pictured in wildly disturbing images first Mr Patmore tending to her desires in bed—and then her tending to Mr Bramley's desires.

Of course, she couldn't sleep. She pressed her hands against the sides of her head and tried to will away the pictures that haunted her. She tried not to scream, and when she feared she may do just that, she threw back the covers, put a shawl about her shoulders, and went down to the scullery to put a pan of milk over the embers of the fire.

While waiting for it to boil, she went to the parlour and looked down upon the face of her dead aunt who'd never looked so peaceful or contented in her life. She wondered if Aunt Montrose had ever sinned. Eliza knew nothing about Aunt Montrose's past, other than that her aunt had only lived in this village the past ten years having decamped from the other side of the county for reasons unknown.

Sometimes the cruellest and most sanctimonious of people were the greatest sinners. Eliza knew this. Success in life rested on getting away with one's crime.

She hoped there was no one left alive who knew her own sad and sorry past.

She shivered. Perhaps, with her aunt's death, she might now wash clear the stain of her sinning youth and forge a future as a happily married young woman with children. Hope prickled her skin. Yes, a brood of children by Mr Patmore, and somehow, with Gideon in the background, his interests assured, his future the one he should have had, had they not been abandoned by his father.

"Good night, Aunt Montrose," she whispered, feeling no grief but only expectation. "Regardless of what you have allotted me in your will tomorrow, I *will* have the happiness I deserve."

CHAPTER 11

Back at Quamby House, a distracted Fanny sighed and ran her hand across a porcelain milkmaid arranged on the mantelpiece. She'd thought about turning on her heel when she'd discovered the drawing room occupied by Mr Bramley, but then decided that as she was bored, it might be rather fun to needle him.

"Do you not think it strange that Mr Patmore hasn't returned with Devil's Run?" Fanny focused her interested eyes upon George Bramley, who was lounging upon the sofa doing absolutely nothing, but whose mottled complexion suddenly revealed the feelings he was clearly reluctant to divulge.

"If he's not back today, I'm going down there myself." He sat up straighter and sent Fanny something between a glare and a leer. "Lord, I hope nothing's happened to my horse."

"I'd be more worried that nothing has happened to Miss Montrose," Lord Fenton said, arriving at that moment and punctuating it with such gallantry Fanny was happy to reward him with a kiss. Antoinette had secreted herself away with her clandestine beau, and Fenton had been out riding when she'd much rather have been doing with him what her sister was doing with the very disreputable actor, Ambrose Montague, who'd forsaken a role at Covent Garden to do Antoinette's bidding. Quamby seemed much happier—Fanny agreed with Antoinette on this—as he was now at greater liberty to follow his own inclinations. Fanny rather suspected that involved several of Ambrose's fellow libertarians of the stage.

When Fanny had finished caressing Fenton, she sent George a darkling look. "I hardly suppose George is worried about Miss Montrose personally, since his awful proposal was entirely predicated on the outcome of her aunt's will. Goodness, George. You don't even have the grace to blush!"

"What awful proposal?" Fenton patted his wife's hand after he'd stayed her efforts to stand. "You make it sound like there's more to it than the usual proposal."

"As if you'd know what informed the usual proposal. What about the one you offered me?" She sent him an arch look then giggled. "That was hardly the kind of proposal a young lady with expectations like myself had hoped for. Much more in George's line, though I daresay his was in fact more respectable, eh, George?" She sent a narrow look at George, who was now nursing his second Madeira on his belly and looking slightly defensive.

He raised one shoulder slightly then took a sip of his drink. "Turned out Miss Montrose was a betting gel, so it suited us both."

"Ha! It only suited you, Cousin George, because you had a nice easy way out if she didn't get all her aunt's money should the old woman die before you and Miss Montrose wed." Fanny looked at Fenton. "Did I not tell you the whole story, dearest? No? Well, there it is. I can't believe Miss Montrose accepted you, Cousin George. Well, perhaps her aunt has died, and Miss Montrose has suddenly inherited all her money, and run off with the footman because he's a lot more of a gentleman than you. Why on earth would she even consider marrying you if you were so brutish as to wrap up your marriage offer in terms of a wager?"

Bramley drained his glass, placed it on a side table, and raised his hands as if defending himself. "Lord, Cousin Fanny, I don't know, but she did! We were discussing horses at the Assembly Ball the second time we met. I liked her well enough, and she's a beauty, there ain't no denying. I'd been told the odds were fifty-fifty she'd inherit a fortune from her cheeseparing aunt, only I pretended I didn't know this when I said vaguely that my love of chance was such that I'd stake a good marriage on a situation where the odds might favour my intended—or not—if I had an out. That's when she said she'd accept such a scenario as she'd be prepared to take any chance to escape the life she had with her own dreadful aunt, whom she said was likely to live another half century. So I suggested I'd marry her on those terms—a three-month betrothal, and if the aunt slipped off this mortal coil and didn't favour Miss Montrose within that time, then the betrothal was dissolved, but that if old Aunt Montrose were still hale and hearty, we'd go ahead with the marriage. I need a wife, and she'll do nicely enough, and she needed to escape." He shrugged. "I've heard of worse reasons to wed."

"So there is no feeling between either of you?"

"I already said that I like her well enough. She's very fetching in fact, and the more I see her, the more I like her." Bramley grinned rather lasciviously. "Perhaps you're right, though, and the aunt has died. That would be entertaining."

He raised his eyebrows as a great thundering of footsteps sounded in the corridor, and Antoinette burst into the room.

"Fanny! Fenton!" Panting with excitement, Antoinette held her side as she collapsed against the doorframe. "I've just received a note, and you'll never believe what it says! Old Miss Montrose, Eliza Montrose's aunt, is dead!"

Fanny exchanged an interested glance with her husband, before seeing how George Bramley was taking the news. His eyes were suddenly alight with expectation.

"And you'll never guess what else?" Antoinette, who was always one for blurting things out, put her hands to her mouth as she fixed Fanny with a panicked look before glancing at Bramley, who appeared not to be taking in anything more Antoinette had to say.

He was hunched over, his hands dangling between his knees, wearing a speculative expression as he gazed into the fireplace.

"I can't possibly guess," murmured Fenton wickedly into the silence.

"For goodness sake, darling, you know Antoinette has had second thoughts about revealing her latest indiscretion to all and sundry. Don't try and embarrass her."

"Oh, you could never do that!" Antoinette assured him. "And it is something I learned from my lovely indiscretion, who has been most assiduous in discharging my request for *you know what*." She sighed happily. "But, you're right; I think I'll wait for another time to tell you."

"Oh Lord," grumbled Fanny sending an annoyed look in her husband's direction before pleading, "Tell us, Antoinette. Has the will been read? Has Miss Montrose been favoured?"

"I haven't the slightest idea. I mean, nobody will know until tomorrow as that's when Miss Montrose's solicitor will play his part following the funeral. I take it you'll be there, Cousin George? To provide Miss Montrose the love and support she needs?" Dropping the ironic tone, she added, for Fanny's benefit, and to the accompaniment of dancing eyes, "The other thing which I'll tell you later is about the most interesting developments turned up by my darling Ambrose, who has been running all over London turning up old stones to shine a light on..." she slanted a meaningful look at George, who was clearly caught up in his own musings as he helped himself to more wine, "...the possible reasons for why a certain ice maiden in whom we are interested might deport herself in a certain fashion."

⚜

RUFUS WAS ANNOYED TO FIND THE COTTAGE OF THE LATE MISS Montrose again filled with well-meaning ladies preparing the refreshments that would follow the funeral later that afternoon.

Miss Montrose, he was told, was in the vegetable garden, which he was pleased to discover was a nicely secluded area behind a high brick wall, so when he strode in, and she rose with a look of what he thought was pleasure, he was confident they were far from prying eyes.

"I hadn't noticed it yesterday, but you're still limping, Mr Patmore!" she exclaimed, glancing at his ankle.

"There was a great deal of other more important matters to concentrate on yesterday than my ankle," he said, wishing he could take her hands in his; however, she was gripping, rather firmly, a bunch of carrots.

Dressed in black, he thought she looked curiously affecting. Not because black was a colour that suited her, for it accentuated the pallor of her skin and made her blue eyes look pale and washed out; but because she looked particularly vulnerable, and he wanted to be the man upon whom she would depend forevermore.

Light colours complemented her peaches and cream complexion, he decided. When she was his wife, he'd enjoy seeing her dressed according to the latest fashions, like his sisters took for granted. Whatever gave her pleasure would give him pleasure.

Poor Miss Montrose had never worn anything of the first stare since he'd known her, and he was a man who was aware of these things. It was one of the reasons he'd not considered a penniless wife, knowing that the expense of keeping up the appearances necessary to one's station was a costly business.

But where matters of the heart were concerned, he now realised one did what one had to, even if it meant he had to stint on his horses. It would be a small price to pay to have this sweet and lovely woman for his wife.

"Mr Patmore...I..."

He was surprised at her clear discomfort, and the fact she stumbled over her words for the first time ever gave him courage. A faint blush stained her cheeks, and she had difficulty meeting his eye.

He knew she'd enjoyed their encounter the previous night. Surely she wanted him as much as he wanted her.

And yet, she seemed strangely diffident.

Or perhaps she was simply exhausted. Her future hinged on what would be revealed in another couple of hours. Had her aunt favoured her or not? Except Rufus intended such an outcome to be irrelevant, and if he insisted on asking her now, before Bramley came charging in upon having perhaps heard the news, she'd know without a doubt that he was asking her because he loved her and not for any other reason.

She put up her hand to stop him from getting any closer. "You do not owe me anything, Mr Patmore," she murmured. "I will not be cast as the designing female who lured you."

"Of course not!" He could hear sounds near the back of the house and feared they would be interrupted soon. He had to say what was necessary without preliminaries. It was not a question that could wait until after the funeral.

"No?" Her smile was illuminating, and it filled his heart with overwhelming relief. She *did* love him. How could she look at him like this and not?

"Never!" He shook his head. "Miss Montrose, last night was a surprise to both of us, and of course, it's the reason I'm here. I admired you before for all those magnificent qualities you displayed at Quamby House and then after your aunt died— courage and self-control. But last night you showed me another side. A warm—"

"Mr Patmore! Miss Montrose!"

He forced himself to ignore the calls of the servant upon the back step as he took the carrots from her and put them aside, then gripped her hands and brought them up to his lips, forging ahead with his reasons. "I know on what basis you are to marry Mr Bramley. I believe he will renege if it is revealed your aunt has not favoured you. Regardless of the outcome this afternoon, I won't—"

"Miss Montrose! You have visitors! Fine and rich visitors and I need to give 'em tea, direct. Are ye there?"

Disconcertingly, she pulled away, sending him a worried look as she progressed towards Dora's insistent calling.

"We can talk about this later, Mr Patmore," she said. "After my aunt's will has been read." She turned back with a smile. "I would prefer it that way."

Another voice intruded. Older and more cultured.

"Eliza! There you are, girl. Come along now; there are people wishing to see you." An imperious middle-aged woman appeared on the back step beside Dora, glancing suspiciously in Rufus's direction before beckoning once more with more forcefulness. "Where are those carrots you were to fetch?"

"I have them, Aunt Catherine." She sent an apologetic look in Rufus's direction, explaining in an undertone, "She's Aunt Montrose's younger sister."

Voices sounded from within the house. More visitors, and a cloud crossed her face. "It sounds as if Mr Bramley might be here."

Rufus nodded briefly, staring at her retreating back. Yet again she'd given him a reprieve. She really didn't want to commit either herself or him to anything before the will was read.

He was frustrated, on tenterhooks, but it gave him time to muse over the insane desire that had taken hold of him. What did he really know of her? She was lovely to look at, but there'd been lovelier girls he'd known and not wished to marry. If it turned out she was penniless, his mother would be horrified.

But, like a lovelorn schoolboy, he stared at the birds lined up on the brick wall surrounding the vegetable garden and conjured up Miss Montrose's lovely face.

As much as anything was certain, he decided, she was the only woman for him.

* * *

ELIZA HANDED THE BASKET OF VEGETABLES TO DORA IN THE scullery, for her arms were trembling.

"Are you all right, miss?" Dora, usually lacking in sentiment, sent her a kind smile.

"Get along, Dora, there's much work to be done," Aunt Catherine, sweeping through in black velvet, dismissed her before turning to Eliza. "I got here half an hour ago and what welcome was there for me? I haven't seen you in four years, not since your mother's funeral, but you're as self-obsessed as you ever were. Who was that young man you were alone with outside?" She lowered her voice and put her face close to Eliza's. "Another of your fancy pieces? He certainly isn't Mr Bramley to whom I was introduced to in the parlour as your intended? Up to your old tricks again, Eliza? Lord, but I hope justice is waiting for you. You caused your brother's death, and then proceeded to break the hearts of both your parents. And now I see you consorting with a strange young man outside."

Eliza had never liked Aunt Catherine, who had competently raised five children after her husband had died suddenly. Eliza had thought that when a person was well provided for, they could probably manage to do most things quite competently. It just left more time to find faults in others.

Dutifully, she bowed her head and accepted the criticism. Lord, if Aunt Montrose favoured Eliza, she'd be in possession of a fortune and able to decide her future. Wouldn't that be the most deliciously happy state of affairs? Two days ago, all seemed gloom and despair. But now Mr Patmore had come into her life and set her aglow. She wished he'd not tried to ask her to marry him in the vegetable garden at such an inopportune time, but it did mean so much to her that he'd insisted on making clear that he was in love with her and not her money.

It was enough to decide her upon the fact that even if she were rich and able to decide her future, she would marry a man she loved.

And she loved Mr Patmore.

"Now, pinch some colour into your cheeks, Eliza. I'm sure Mr Bramley doesn't want to see you looking like a ghost. A husband expects his wife to be glowing at the sight of him, regardless of the circumstances."

The last person Eliza felt like greeting was Mr Bramley. In fact, the sight of his bullet-shaped head with its thick nose and bullish neck made her feel ill. She'd thought this was the man she'd have to marry if she were to achieve her heart's desire; that it was the price she must pay if she were to atone to Gideon for casting him into a cruel world where he would be a slave, a lackey, when his destiny should have been gilded.

Well, now she had been offered a different future, and she would embrace it when the time was right; though, as she was still betrothed to Mr Bramley, she'd have to follow through with at least the social niceties.

Mr Bramley rose from his seat in the parlour and all but swooped upon her, clasping her hands and kissing her fingertips, no doubt for the benefit of Lady Fenton who was smiling beside him.

"My poor bereaved Miss Montrose." Eliza noticed that Mr Bramley had staked out ownership of the most comfortable seat. "I have come to ease your pain," he told her, making no effort to illustrate his words with action. "I am only sorry I couldn't have been here yesterday. Nevertheless, within an hour of receiving the very sad news of your aunt, I was in my carriage."

"Poor Miss Montrose, you have had much to contend with lately," murmured Lady Fenton, elegant as always on a spindly chair. "But now, the future beckons."

"Indeed," Mr Bramley corroborated with a searching look. "I believe the reading of the will takes place this afternoon following the funeral tea. Ah, there's Mr Patmore! I was devilish put out when he never came back with Devil's Run."

Eliza was thoroughly relieved when Mr Bramley clapped Mr Patmore upon the shoulder and drew him out of the room so that she was alone for the moment with Lady Fenton.

She sank into a chair opposite.

When she'd first arrived at Quamby House, she'd not thought much of either Lady Fenton or her sister, to tell the truth. Their sophisticated gloss wasn't something she either admired or to which she aspired. In fact, she'd thought them vain, venal, and without substance. But after Eliza had jumped into the lake, they'd suddenly been so kind and interested, and so grateful, as evidenced by the fact they were here, although that was quite unnecessary.

Lady Fenton smoothed out her black silk skirts and fixed Eliza with an interested stare. "It was very gallant of Mr Patmore to remain with you in your hour of need, wasn't it?"

"Yes, it was," Eliza agreed.

"And did he have anything interesting to say?"

Eliza was shocked. So they knew? The speculative, almost self-satisfied look in Lady Fenton's eyes suggested she was entirely au fait with the state of both their hearts. She wasn't sure if she were horrified that her business was so open to scrutiny, or glad she needn't be so guarded.

Keeping her voice neutral, she answered, "It was good to see him when he came for Devil's Run. And then, of course, my aunt died, and he has been very...kind." She hoped the fire in her cheeks wasn't obvious to Lady Fenton. She looked up, blinking. "He needn't have felt he owed me anything. No one does, though I do appreciate you being here."

A short silence greeted her words, and it wasn't just that Lady Fenton was too busy nibbling on a sugar biscuit to answer. "So he's said nothing interesting, *yet*," Lady Fenton clarified. Goodness, she was a persistent one, but Eliza wasn't about to give anything away.

She shook her head briefly, for she'd already answered that question, then rose. "Please be comfortable here and excuse me while I attend to my Aunt Catherine, who seems to have taken the organisation of matters very much to heart. It's much more peaceful in here; I assure you."

WITH MUCH TO BE DONE, ELIZA DELAYED UNTIL THE VERY LAST minute returning to the room that now occupied her intended and the man she loved. They and Lady Fenton appeared to be engaged in some rather desultory conversation but turned as she appeared on the threshold.

She caught Mr Patmore's slight frown and blushed, unable to meet his eye as her insides began to crawl. She hated having to put on an act for everyone's benefit, but when she was married to Mr Patmore, she could be as transparent with her affections as Lady Fenton was. No one seemed to think any the worse of *her* for showing her feelings.

Married to Mr Patmore? Could she really hope for such happiness with such an honourable man?

Honourable man? The thought struck sudden fear into her heart.

"Gentlemen, the mourners are about to follow my aunt's coffin," she announced. "Lady Fenton and I will, of course, remain here to welcome you when you return. That's if you wish to join the mourners." She hoped they did. Simply looking at Mr Patmore's delicate mouth did dangerous things to her insides, while even a glance at Mr Bramley's stubbled jaw made her feel ill. She'd thought that her prosaic words would help dispel the kernel of guilt she felt growing by the minute inside her. She'd thought it was grief or fear, both of them natural emotions for farewelling the life of security she'd known these past seven years. Now she realised her feelings stemmed from another source as she caught Mr Patmore looking at her with blatant...was that really longing?

She hitched in a breath. If it were, how much would he condone her past? Could she hide *that* and live a lie? Should she be transparent with him before she allowed him to make his offer? She felt utterly helpless in the face of such conflict.

Last night, she'd allowed him the liberties only an abandoned woman would offer because she feared she was dying inside, and she wanted the reaffirmation of bodily responses to put the lie to that and damn the consequences. She'd never expected either her heart, or his, to become so engaged.

They all turned at the tragic bleat from the front step, as her cousin Susana sailed up the garden path and threw herself upon Eliza.

"Poor Aunt Montrose! What a tragedy." She dabbed at her eyes with her embroidered handkerchief, but Eliza could see no sign of blotchiness. Her blonde ringlets were pinned perfectly in place, as usual, her mourning dress was cut to advantage, and her blue eyes sparkled, not with unshed tears, but interest as she looked between Mr Patmore and Mr Bramley.

Dutifully, Eliza performed the necessary introductions, knowing Susana would be sizing up their respective prospects. An earl's nephew and a country gentleman of sizeable landholdings; both of them a cut above the kind of gentleman she was in the habit of dancing with at the local Assembly Ball, and definitely worth cultivating their acquaintance, for she showed no signs of wanting to go indoors as she boldly quizzed them.

"How very kind of you to come all this way and what a comfort and a support to Eliza." She affected a look that was part tragic, part heroic gratitude. "I shall miss my aunt more than words can say. She was a dear, kind woman who was always so good to me."

And now you're here to see how good she really was after death, Eliza thought as she led Susana inside. To her relief, the gentlemen left them to join those who would follow the coffin.

She was amused by the spark of excitement in Susana's eyes when she was introduced to Lady Fenton. Eliza could see Susana sizing her up, no doubt thinking that if the cool dark beauty could snare such a fine catch as she had—for the Brightwell sisters had in their day been notorious—so could Susana with her baby-blue eyes and girlish ringlets. Oh, Susana was undoubtedly pretty, prettier than Eliza with her childish looks and manner, but she was calculating.

As Eliza glimpsed the funeral procession wind down the street from the parlour window, she could keep her fear at bay no longer and went to sit down in a chair a little removed from the grouping, hoping to be left in peace. Soon her fate would be revealed.

Oh, Lord, make me the favoured one, she prayed silently as the village ladies and a few of Aunt Montrose's friends from farther afield partook of the food and drink Eliza and Dora had laid on. Anything else would see her effectively parting with her child. She wondered where Gideon was now. At Quamby House, playing with young George and Katherine? She couldn't wait to return there although there was no telling where she'd be living tonight and for the years hereafter. As Mr Bramley's wife at Quamby House, or as a penniless spinster in her aunt's cottage? That is, unless her Aunt Catherine insisted she was too young and that her lot must be to serve *her* with the same devotion she'd served her Aunt Montrose. Well, Eliza would not serve anyone. Somehow she'd find a way to be with Gideon.

It was in this frame of mind that she tried to appear at her ease with a fidgeting Susana, who clearly was harbouring the same hopes she was. And when the gentlemen returned from their doleful mission looking, nonetheless, in good spirits as they proceeded through the door and greeted the ladies, Eliza wasn't surprised by the coquettish manner her younger cousin adopted.

The more time passed, the more Eliza's spirits sagged. She relinquished her chair to an elderly village spinster, and introduced herself to a group of women she didn't know.

Aunt Montrose's lawyer was due to conduct the reading of the will in half an hour, which meant that the intervening time would be spent in an agony of having to entertain the fine people from Quamby House who had traversed half a county to be with her. She glimpsed Mr Patmore's eyes on her, no doubt waiting in antici- pation of a sign from her that she returned his feelings. And she did, but oh Lord, it wasn't that simple. Mr Bramley's furrowed brow indicated he was clearly in a fever of anticipation as to whether or not the money would go to her, and whether he was looking at his future wife or not each time his eyes landed upon her.

"Miss Montrose, how are you bearing up?"

Mr Patmore was at her elbow, offering her some Madeira and looking as if he really did care what she was feeling. She'd have loved to have been alone with him, but knew it would be easier to draw him into the circle of more general conversation.

"I'm sure I'm just as distraught as Cousin Susana at the loss of dear Aunt Montrose," she said, excusing herself from Aunt

Montrose's friends and taking a step towards Susana, who was conversing with Lady Fenton and Mr Bramley. "Aunt Montrose used to call Susana her faithful blessing and the epitome of womanly virtue," she added, inclining her head at Susana's sugary smile. "Especially when I'd displeased her with the pressure of the massages I gave her to ease her painful limbs."

"I always had such a light touch, cousin," Susana said with a simper.

"And such a pleasing manner to Aunt Montrose. You were indeed the favoured one."

"Oh, but it's so dreadful that Aunt Montrose's money may come between us," Susana said in plaintive tones. "Eliza has nothing. Not since the death of her poor parents, but at least I've not grown up in poverty after bringing shame upon my family." She put her hand to her mouth, adding quickly, "Though if Eliza has done wrong, she has paid for her sins with her tireless devotion to her dear departed late Aunt Montrose."

"And how have *you* paid for your sins, Miss Hilcrest?"

Eliza sent a surprised and grateful look in Lady Fenton's direction.

"I've never sinned." Susana didn't miss a beat until Lady Fenton rebuked her gently.

"My dear, who hasn't sinned whether in thought or deed? Why, to suggest that another is guilty of such a thing, *and* in company, is a sin in itself, and surely renders the one who makes such a charge a person of contempt." She smiled graciously. "Are you so blameless and yet make such odious comparisons with your cousin Eliza?"

Susana blushed hotly. "I didn't think it a crime to speak the truth. Besides, Eliza has no more devoted a cousin than myself, which I have already made entirely clear. Brave Eliza, yet I don't know how she'd have managed without me and her Aunt Montrose when her parents cast her out."

It was rare that Eliza was at a complete loss for words or that her insides churned so much. Indeed, not since she'd been forced to place Gideon into the foundling basket had she felt such emotion. Well, except for last night.

"I am sure a creature of such angelic demeanour as Miss Hilcrest could not possibly be guilty of any crime, however trifling. How can one look so like an angel and not have a clear conscience?"

Eliza stared at Mr Bramley, who was gazing at her cousin as if she were a gift from heaven. She couldn't believe it. He looked, for want of a better word, smitten. But then that's how he was— oleaginous. Oily. Slippery as an eel. He'd slip right out of this arrangement the moment he learned Eliza wasn't worth a penny.

Beside him, Mr Patmore's lips were pursed. He turned and offered Eliza a smile of support. What a noble, decent man he was.

She closed her eyes briefly. A good woman, a true and dutiful one, would reveal her wickedness to her intended before she accepted him. If Eliza could have done so, she would have, but it was only since last night that Mr Patmore had been a viable contender for her affections.

"Why, thank you for your support, Mr Bramley." Susana said with a coy look at Mr Bramley just as Eliza had seen her do at the few Assembly Balls they'd attended. "I'm not accustomed to having slurs cast upon my good character." She darted Lady Fenton a poisonous look while Eliza tried to meet Mr Patmore's smile without revealing her fear. If Susana were in possession of Eliza's sordid past actions, she realised how important it was to reveal everything to him before her cousin did. Or anyone else. *Was* it possible Susana knew about her past? Could anyone else? Eliza had only come to live with her aunt after Gideon had been taken from her, but despite Aunt Montrose's disapproval, the older woman had sworn that Eliza's secret would be safe, if only to protect the *family* name from being tarnished.

Susana raised her head and said proudly, with another look at Eliza, "I am proud of my blameless character and clear conscience."

While Lady Fenton returned her scarcely veiled assurances that she'd had no intention of casting slurs upon Susana or anyone else, Eliza's mind raced over the last few days that Aunt Montrose had been so ill. She remembered the crafty look on Susana's face when Eliza had come back from stabling Devil's Run with Mr Patmore and found Susana patting her aunt's hand. But her aunt had been unable to speak. She couldn't have revealed to Susana Eliza's past.

Eliza clenched her hands into fists as she tried to hide her devastation. Why would Susana have so blithely spoken of Eliza's sins when she never had before?

Mr Patmore, if he *alone* were in possession of the truth, might accept that Eliza had borne a child out of wedlock, but if this were ever to be made public, Eliza would be shunned by polite society. No husband could tolerate that. And as an unmarried woman, she could never hope to marry if her past were known. How could Susana have hinted at such a thing? How could she have been so cruel?

Very easily, of course, and it wouldn't have been the first time, she thought bitterly. Susana had always wanted to take whatever Eliza had, whether it were ribbons or pretty earrings.

Forcing her gaze away from Mr Bramley's face while avoiding Susana's sneer, she was disconcerted to find Mr Patmore observing her covertly. Oh Lord, she didn't need his sympathy. She didn't need anyone's sympathy. He must have attributed her painful preoccupation with her fears over what would transpire within the next hour.

Yet, whatever happened, Eliza owed it to Gideon to ensure he had a life worth living; that he not be reduced to mere servant status.

Mr Patmore turned to Mr Bramley and said in a voice light with amusement, "I'd be most interested whether *you* rest easy in your conscience, Mr Bramley. We gentlemen do seem to take for granted the licence to gamble and carouse to our heart's content, but I wonder at what point each of us stops to think it's time to adopt a more sober attitude, settle down...and marry." He slanted a look at Eliza before returning a gimlet eye upon his erstwhile friend.

"Conscience!" exclaimed Mr Bramley, with unexpected heat, turning a surprisingly fulminating glare upon Lady Fenton. "A subject that is indeed close to my heart. I wonder how some people can sleep at night, knowing that their sins have impinged upon the God-given rights of those whose very roofs they share." He made a show of collecting himself. "I am most amused that my cousin, Lady Fenton, should cast aspersions upon the supposed sins of others," here he directed a sympathetic look at Susana "when, as she so rightly points out, it is a very sin to suggest sin in another."

There was an awkward pause before Mr Patmore said in an ameliorating tone, "I think a discussion on sin is hardly appropriate at such a time."

To Eliza's astonishment, Mr Bramley said rather fiercely, "I would say a funeral is the most fitting time to address it. Death is where we're all destined, and one would wish to go there having enjoyed what one was due. It is a bitter pill to be cheated. I wonder how those who have come by ill-gotten gains can rest easy with *their* conscience."

Lady Fenton gave a theatrical sigh before explaining to the rest of the company, "Poor Cousin George has never got over the fact that he was the Earl of Quamby's heir until Young George was born. But would you not all spare a thought for poor Miss Montrose who doesn't know if she'll have a roof over her head by morning. Like you, Cousin George, she is at the mercy of matters beyond her control. It has nothing to do with the sins she has or hasn't committed. It's pure luck." She gave a soft laugh, adding, "Nevertheless, a little cunning can go a long way. How could women survive without wit and cunning when we are given no legal rights, eh Cousin George?"

An excruciating silence followed her words, until Mr Bramley's mouth turned into what Eliza supposed must be a smile but which looked more like a snarl. "Miss Hilcrest, my apologies for subjecting you to all this radical talk of women and rights and sin."

Lady Fenton nodded in apparent approval. "Quite right, Cousin George; it's not right to talk of sins and crime when we have two innocents among us."

"Innocents? Pray, do not hold back on our account," Susana said with a giggle. "A crime is a crime, and sometimes being forewarned of the dangers of the great world is being forearmed. I'd hate to think of committing a crime, simply because I didn't know it was a crime."

Mr Bramley shrugged and appeared to retreat into sullen indifference, and Eliza was about to interject to change the blessed subject when Lady Fenton said unwisely, though in a low tone apparently only intended for Eliza and Mr Fenton, "I apologise on Mr Bramley's behalf, but he feels very strongly about the rights of the children of parents who have sinned, would you believe?"

"Whose *mothers* have sinned," Mr Bramley muttered to Eliza's horror and with a pointed look at Lady Fenton.

Lady Fenton raised her eyebrows. "Pray, what is the difference? I am more than in agreement that it's an outrage that a child should bear the stigma of the actions of its parents, and it is one of society's many unfairnesses that it's the mother who bears full responsibility."

Mr Patmore concurred with a resigned shrug of his shoulders. "Yes, there it is. We may call society harsh or unjust but one's good name is everything, and once it is lost there is, sadly, no redemption."

"Redemption for whom?" Susana's apparently innocent question was followed by Mr Bramley's, asked with mild aggression, "For child or mother?"

"Both, in society's view."

"Goodness, Mr Patmore, that is a harsh line to take." Lady Fenton looked distressed.

"That's not to say I agree with society's narrow views, I assure you, Lady Fenton, for I do know you like to do your good works with the orphans from the foundling home. However, if we wish to participate fully in society, to be accepted and have our ambitions furthered, it isn't wise to display too liberal an attitude." He sent a warning look at Bramley. "We gentlemen do have, as I said before, greater licence than the ladies for misconduct, but there is a line beyond which we must not allow our vices to take us." He paused and said in a tone of measured significance. "Take gambling, for instance. A man who cheats loses his right to be called a gentleman. Surely you agree?"

He was referring to Mr Bramley's potential plans for Devil's Run, Eliza knew, but she was more concerned over the previous references to fallen women and their bastard children. She felt sick.

Mr Bramley inclined his head. "A man *caught* cheating is not a gentleman, I do agree. And a lady who is so eaten up with vice that she succumbs to the charms of a gentleman before she is wed, and then tries to foist that brat upon another, should burn in hell, do you not agree?" Though his words were less tinged with aggression than before, he continued to look pointedly at Lady Fenton.

Susana gave a little gasp, and Mr Patmore took this opportunity to intervene, saying in quite a different tone, "We forget where we are, I think. Miss Montrose has just lost her aunt and is looking decidedly distressed." He offered her his arm. "I think you need some fresh air. You have worked so hard to ensure all is in order during this time of grieving, and no one has given a thought to your need for a moment to gather yourself before the momentous next stage, which will determine your future. Allow me." Without brooking a refusal, he caged her hand and all but marched her away from the gathering.

She didn't know why she should suddenly come over all prickly, but she felt as dangerously put together as she ever had; that she might break into a million pieces if he said the wrong word. "Mr Patmore, I do not need your assistance. Or your sympathy," she added. "I can hold my own with my sharp-tongued cousin. She has spent her life scoring points over me, and I am very used to it. Nor must you concern yourself over Mr Bramley and myself. There is no need to treat me like a piece of Dresden china."

Oh Lord, why did she not take his concern in the way it was intended? His face was a picture of bafflement, as well it might be. Last night, there'd been passion and camaraderie. This morning, she'd held him at arm's distance. Now she was hurling figurative bricks at him.

His expression cleared, and he gripped her arms. "After your enthusiasm last night, I don't think you resemble anything remotely like a piece of Dresden china. There, I've said it. Made mention of what some might consider your terrible sin when it is I who have sinned if I do nothing to atone." His smile grew sweeter, his eyes crinkling at the corners "I will never forsake you, Eliza. Please give me hope that I might call you that. You have endured so much, so bravely, and I understand what this has all cost you." He indicated the house behind them with a nod of his head.

Eliza's mouth trembled, and she might have responded, only he placed a finger upon her lips and lowered his head a little.

"I believe there is a great deal of feeling there," he touched his hand ever so briefly to her heart, her chest, "that you don't know what to do with."

His touch sent the blood rushing to her cheeks and stoked the smouldering embers of her lower belly into a conflagration that threatened to consume her. If she didn't go now, she'd succumb to his curiously affecting blend of strength and masculinity mixed with genuine kindness. She used hauteur as her defence. "My actions last night were out of character. I'm not the woman you think me—"

"Oh, you are so much more, and I love you for it—"

"Eliza! Come indoors this moment. Have you no sense of occasion? Mr Wilkins is here to read my dear sister's will. Oh sir, I didn't see you, sir. Pray escort my niece indoors this moment."

Mr Patmore sent Eliza a wry look as he offered her his arm once again, and the door closed behind the clearly harried and exacting Aunt Catherine. For a moment, she thought he was going to brush a strand of hair from her forehead, but to her disappointment, he withdrew his hand at the last moment. "So everything for you hinges upon the next few minutes. Mr Bramley said you were a betting girl after his own heart, but if the wager you apparently agreed to doesn't go your way, then this is what you have to look forward to for the rest of your days?" He squeezed her arm. "That is, if you don't receive another offer."

Half an hour earlier, Eliza's heart would have been beating in expectation. Her smile of encouragement would have been in place, and she'd have been ready to accept this lovely man's imminent marriage proposal, throw herself into his arms and, in relief, allow him to direct her future.

Instead, she nodded slowly. "Indeed, Mr Patmore, but now is not the time to consider anything but the matter at hand. I think we should go inside. My aunt's will is about to be read."

CHAPTER 12

The servants had rustled up as much seating as could be managed in the tiny parlour, with its green sprigged curtains and borrowed furniture. It was a pretty outlook from a simple country cottage which made it all the more astonishing when the sum of Aunt Montrose's assets was finally revealed. Three times as much in the four per cents as anyone had ever speculated. It seemed Aunt Montrose had been in receipt of a bequest far in excess of anything she'd hinted at and, not being one to flaunt her wealth for fear of fortune-hunters, she'd told Eliza, she'd even kept it secret from her sisters and two nieces.

It was as if the old woman were in that very room, enjoying the anticipation with which her surviving relatives waited to hear how they'd been favoured. It positively crackled about them.

Eliza was glad of the fashion in bonnets which enabled her expression to be screened from the rest of the company, as she listened to Aunt Montrose's cousin receive a cow and a pig, Dr Rutledge a rather fine silver-topped cane that had belonged to her father, and Dora, the porcelain tea service. Aunt Montrose had been at pains to bequeath individual items to a great many, but after half an hour, there was still no mention of the bulk of her assets, and nothing for Eliza, or Susana, who fidgeted beside her cousin and darted increasingly anxious looks at her.

Susana had a comfortable home and a father ready to provide a reasonable dowry. She'd be disappointed to receive nothing, but she'd never be destitute as Eliza would, should her aunt exclude her.

As the sun dipped low on the horizon, the lawyer, at last, came to the division of Aunt Montrose's greatest holdings. He wasn't the dry, aged partner, Mr Cuthbert, who generally advised Aunt Montrose, but rather the junior, and he displayed the theatricality of David Garrick himself, pacing his words and holding his breath for the final pronouncement.

Now, here was what they'd all been waiting for.

Eliza's skin prickled; her mouth felt dry, and she heard Susana's quick breathing beside her.

The lawyer cast his gaze about the room, looked pointedly at Aunt Montrose's two nieces, and declared that the cottage was to go to Eliza, while Miss Anabelle Montrose's fortune in the three and four per cents was for Susana, to be held in trust until her twenty-fifth birthday, three years hence.

There was a collective gasp though the greatest came from Susana herself who held her hands to her cheeks and, thought Eliza, was about to cry out in pleasure until she heard her cousin's plaintive: "Must I wait *so* long?"

Eliza darted a look at Mr Bramley, but he turned his head away. No sympathetic, even understanding glance of the torment she must be enduring. His interest was purely pecuniary. She'd thought at one stage he found her moderately attractive; that he was anticipating the fact she'd be his wife for more than just her money. The idea had repulsed her at the time, but now that it was so clear it *had* all been about the money, the pain that clawed at her insides was almost too difficult to contain. Well, it wasn't just that; it was the whole pain associated with Mr Patmore and the principled attitude he'd adopted just before the reading regarding fallen women and illegitimate children.

"Why, Eliza, you have a house to live in; you cannot be churlish about that," Susana said brightly beside her. "I always told Aunt Montrose she must not take your good offices for granted, and she hasn't. She has given you a *house*."

There were the usual condolences, exclamations of surprise, and commiserations after the lawyer folded up the parchment from which he'd read, unclipped his glasses from his beakish nose, and immediately sought out Susana—the main beneficiary.

While they were engaged in a quiet corner, together with Susana's mother, since Susana's father—Aunt Montrose's son—was ailing, Lady Fenton and her sister, who'd just arrived, clustered around Eliza's side as if providing her the shield she so desperately needed at that moment.

"What will you do now?"

"You certainly don't beat about the bush, do you, Antoinette?" her sister replied, snapping her fan at her. "Can't you approach the matter with a modicum of delicacy?"

Lady Quamby looked offended, and then determined and business-like. "When time is of the essence, I'd say that getting to the point was the most sensible course of action. Miss Montrose is all but destitute. She has no dowry, though, of course, being in possession of a small landholding will make her desirable to any of the local farmers in the district. Is that what you want, Miss Montrose? To be a farmer's wife?"

Eliza ran a weary hand across her face. What did she want? She wanted to marry Mr Patmore, but she wasn't sure she had the courage to confront him with the truth.

He'd certainly been no champion of the innocent offspring of fallen women. He'd made it clear that while he didn't agree with society's opprobrium, he accepted that respectability was essential for getting on in the world. It had been a desperately painful illumination of his attitudes which, even though he was charming and in love with her, indicated he held to the societal line—a woman's reputation was everything and once lost, there was no redemption.

Even if she had the courage to tell him the truth, the consequences could be even worse than his disgust.

Her fear ratcheted up with each thought. What if somehow her crime were made public? If Mr Patmore didn't want to marry her, would he consider her so beneath the pale he'd warn Mr Bramley about Eliza's true nature?

Oh Lord, she didn't know what she should do.

And then she heard it. The happy shout of a young boy and, glancing out of the window, she saw Young George engaged in a playful bout of fisticuffs with her very own Gideon. Jack.

"You brought the boys!" she blurted out, and Lady Quamby swung her head around in surprise. "Nanny Brown had a megrim, and in the end, it seemed easier to take young Jack along too. He's the only one able to make Young George toe the line, it seems. I thought if I observed them for a few hours, I could learn a trick or two."

"Oh...what a charming idea," Eliza said faintly.

"Quamby thought we could employ Jack as the bootboy in a few years when he's big enough to work, but I think I'll need him to convince George or what my son *ought* to be doing rather than what he *wants* to be doing."

Eliza found it hard to breathe.

If she married Mr Bramley, she'd live in the same household as her child, enabling her to ensure with her dying breath that Jack became more than the bootboy.

But even though the idea of such a marriage was anathema, it would never come to pass, she thought in terror.

No, she was penniless, except for a cottage and prospects for marrying a farmer, in which case she could try to engage Gideon as a bootboy within the household. The foundling home would gladly give him up for that purpose. But how would that help him? No, she needed to be well connected, married to a man of influence.

The weight upon her shoulders was almost unbearable. Mr Bramley wasn't going to marry her. The wager had not gone her way, now that she offered him nothing more than a pretty face, if that, she thought wryly.

"Miss Montrose must come home with us tonight."

Eliza glanced at Lady Fenton, who was looking quite decisive as she fanned herself, for the parlour was growing close on this warm September afternoon.

"Yes, you can't possibly remain here alone," corroborated Lady Quamby. "Please, Miss Montrose? You must be our guest for at least a week while we decide what can be done for you?"

"I'm not a charity case. But I thank you, of course." She pulled herself together. Her self-absorption in her dilemma mustn't make her cold and bristly. The offer she'd just received was the best she could possibly have hoped for under the circumstances, giving her the opportunity to work on Mr Bramley while, of course, enabling her to see Jack. Helping Jack was her first priority, and if that failed, she'd see if her future could be salvaged in some other way. For without money, family or prospects, she had nothing to offer anyone, least of all her son.

Susana sidled up to her when she was for a moment alone. "My dear cousin, this is simply too terrible a situation for you to be in, but do not fear being left all alone. I wish to help you."

Before Eliza could manage the suspicious response that came naturally to her lips, Susana rushed on, "Poor Papa, bedridden as he is, would be only too glad of a nurse to aid him in his ailing dotage. In fact, we've already spoken of it, suspecting Aunt Montrose's greater fondness for me."

Fierce, boiling heat rose to the surface of Eliza's skin. She put her head close to her cousin's and hissed, "I will never play nurse-maid to anyone, ever again, do you hear? How dare you gloat in this manner?"

"Gloat?" Offended, Susana drew her shoulders back, saying crisply over her shoulder, "You'll be sorry you were rude to me, Eliza Montrose, when I'm in a position to grant you what you want, and when I shall soon be elevated so far above you. You've always thought yourself superior—I don't know why—but I shan't forget the way you spoke to me just now. Oh, Mr Bramley, I beg your pardon."

For she'd swung right into the barrel chest of Eliza's erstwhile betrothed, who perhaps even now was on his way to break off his unconventional arrangement with Eliza.

Eliza couldn't bear to see any more. Glaring at both Susana and Mr Bramley, she pushed through the throng in the parlour, only keeping her tears at bay in time to breathe in the less poisoned air of the great outdoors.

It didn't matter that she'd be considered rude, that everyone would assume she was upset because she'd been overlooked by her aunt. Well, it was true, wasn't it? And why should it be any surprise or indeed make her any less the person she was when she was suddenly destitute? She owned a house, yes, but unless she sold it and moved into something far more humble, she had not a feather to fly with. And she could just imagine her meddling Aunt Catherine invoking the Rules of the Montroses to ensure that a 'flighty' twenty-five-year-old miss did not run her own life.

Her black satin shoes were hardly made for walking, but she took the muddy track through the fields; climbing the stiles and splashing into puddles on the other side so that her newly dyed mourning gown was damp and filthy by the time she reached the paddock where Devil's Run cantered over to greet her.

She twined her hands about his neck and pressed her cheek to his muzzle when he drew close. His warmth and companionship were balm to her lonely soul as she wept into his shaggy coat.

"You're so far from a fiend *or* a champion I don't know what to make of you, but then what does anyone make of me?" she wondered aloud. "And what does it matter? I am destitute. A charity case. Who'll want me now?"

"I still want you, Miss Montrose."

She turned into Mr Patmore's strong, firm chest, pressing her hands against his shoulders only for a second before she yielded to his embrace. It was gentle and unpressured. A simple exchange of comfort, and she rested her cheek upon his breastbone for a moment and breathed in the wonderful, familiar scent of him as if it might sustain her forever.

"I suppose everyone thinks I'm most ungrateful. I didn't mean to be rude, running away like that."

"Lady Fenton has put all to rights, diplomat that she is. There was no mention of your exchange with Miss Susana."

"So you know of that, then?"

"Miss Susana was gloating. You had every reason to turn down her offer of so-called charity. She's a little fiend, I think, dressed up as a china doll."

Eliza was enjoying the feel of rough wool beneath her cheek and the familiar lines and angles of his body. It brought back last night together.

Though everything in her life was so uncertain, the way he was looking at her almost gave her the courage to blurt out the truth, right there and then. She took a deep breath, but he spoke first, "Your cousin seems to know how to turn a situation to her advantage."

She gripped his lapels and squeezed shut her eyes. She didn't want to look at him or anything else. It was as much as she could wish for, feeling for a moment a sympathetic embrace. "I should have known Aunt Montrose would favour her above me. I just didn't expect she'd be so discriminating in apportioning her largesse. She must truly have disliked me to have ensured I didn't rise above being a pauper, yet elevating Susana so greatly."

"Elevating her into the sights of a toady like Mr Bramley. I hope my words won't occasion you too much pain. I don't think so, for I know you don't love the gentleman."

Eliza sighed as she stepped out of his embrace. "He offered me what I wanted," she said softly.

"And I do not?"

She jerked her head back to look at him. "What are you saying, Mr Patmore?"

He put his head on one side and smiled as she stepped back. "I think you know very well. I've tried to ask you a question which you don't seem to want me to ask."

Dusk was gathering, and the path home was growing dim. She shouldn't be seen alone with a gentleman she wasn't going to marry.

But if she *were* going to marry him? She nibbled at her lower lip. Ultimately, she'd been nothing in Aunt Montrose's eyes. Perhaps that's what the general opinion was. She was less than nothing. She'd been made to feel it for seven long years. Jack would be conscious of such a feeling yet Eliza had the power to change that.

He leaned back against the fence, watching her closely, Devil's Run beside him. Two fine creatures, she thought unexpectedly, remembering with stirring consciousness the feel of his body against hers.

Cheeks flaming, she turned her head away. How grand if she could say yes, and then she'd have two male creatures in her life she admired on their merits. But not the one she wanted most. Not her son, for how could she now acknowledge the truth about Jack after all that had been said this afternoon?

"I...I *will* let you ask it," she floundered. She put her hands to her face. "Forgive me, Mr Patmore; my wits are disordered. I feel unhappy and, yes, cheated and...unloved. By my aunt, I mean. I do wish to let you speak, but not now. I need to be in a better position to receive you. It is very hard to accept that I've been passed over. I know I should be grateful I've been given the cottage, but with no maintenance, I have nothing. Please, don't say what you came here to say. Not when I feel such a charity case and will always associate your offer with when I was at my lowest ebb."

❧

"I BELIEVE IT'S PRIDE." RUFUS DIDN'T CARE IF GEORGE BRAMLEY would no doubt have liked to see the back of him earlier rather than later. Certainly, there was little charm forthcoming from that quarter and, in fact, Bramley had sloped off to pay some attention for the first time to his horse. It had been Ladies Quamby and Fenton who had urged him to stay the night after he'd delivered Devil's Run back to Lord Quamby's stables, and now they were seeing to his comfort in the drawing room of Quamby House, offering him Madeira and biscuits in the blue drawing room while Miss Patmore rested upstairs after her journey.

He clenched his fists and considered whether to say more of his suspicions. As they were looking expectantly at him, he went on, "This is an outrageous charge, and I'm sure I don't mean to slight Miss Hilcrest, but I'd swear that when I returned to the cottage with Miss Montrose just hours before her aunt died, I saw Miss Hilcrest, who was sitting at her aunt's bedside, slip a paper into her reticule. A most...crafty look crossed her face as she said goodbye."

"Heavens, Mr Patmore!" exclaimed Lady Fenton, looking more excited than horrified as she rearranged her crimson velvet skirts on the Chippendale sofa. "This is quite an allegation."

He nodded, pleased his audience was sympathetic and relieved that Bramley wasn't in attendance. "During the funeral tea, I gathered that the late Miss Montrose's regular solicitor happened to be taking the waters in Bath and that the matter of her will had passed to the junior solicitor, so not the man she usually deals with. Now, despite fearing it is way out of jurisdiction, I've made enquiries—"

"Enquiries, Mr Patmore?" Lady Quamby began fanning herself vigorously. "Surely you can't mean to accuse Miss Hilcrest of forging her aunt's will?"

"Good Lord, no!" Rufus expostulated. "What I wish to ascertain is if she induced her aunt to make an amendment just hours before she died, and to ensure that the will which was read out to all and sundry yesterday is in fact her *legal* will."

"Oh, my dear Mr Patmore; you are Miss Montrose's champion!" Lady Quamby gushed to his embarrassment.

He cleared his throat. He was pleased with his efforts, but they hadn't been *so* exacting for someone as self-interested as he. "It wasn't too much trouble to ask that a few enquiries be satisfied. You see, I'm certain Miss Montrose is avoiding any possibility that I mention the subject of marriage because she's ashamed she's penniless, and she thinks her earlier encouragement will come across as venal and grasping."

"Earlier encouragement?" Lady Quamby repeated with prurient glee as she pushed back her golden curls. "Oh my, Mr Patmore, that does sound romantic as does your desire to see that the law has been applied in order to champion dear Miss Montrose, only..." Her mouth turned down at the corners, and she fanned herself as she reclined upon the chaise longue and directed an uncertain look at her sister. "Fanny, do you think we should mention...*this other complication?*" she asked in a loud stage whisper.

Lady Fenton sighed as she looked between them both over the top of the newssheet she'd been reading before saying archly, "Of course we shouldn't, Antoinette. We must handle the matter with great delicacy. Aren't those the words you used just yesterday when you were afraid of wounding anyone's sensibilities?" She sighed again, louder this time. "My apologies, Mr Patmore. My sister has no sense of occasion, and now there is nothing for it but to be quite transparent and to tell you that—"

"There is another!" Lady Quamby interjected, swinging her legs over the side of the chaise longue, and looking quite tragic as she straightened, her hands framing her face. "Oh Mr Patmore, I didn't want there to be. You are quite the handsomest and most worthwhile of suitors and indeed, Miss Montrose's perfect match but..."

"But what?" he interjected more sharply than he'd intended.

Lady Quamby appeared to wilt. "Mr Patmore, I fear the reason Miss Montrose doesn't want you to ask her this momentous question is because..." She sucked a deep breath through her teeth as she bit her lip, then unexpectedly leapt to her feet, rushing across the room to clasp Rufus's arm as if she truly couldn't bear to impart the wounding news.

Rufus didn't know what to say or do, so he clenched his jaw and remained as statue-like as he could for indeed his heart was starting to crumble, just a little, in anticipation of what he feared he was about to hear.

"Go on, Lady Quamby," he muttered.

She rested her glorious tumble of golden curls against his shoulder and wailed, "Her old beau, the gentleman who broke her heart seven years ago by leaving the country suddenly following a tragic misunderstanding, has only this week returned and is in fact on his way here."

"Here?" He didn't know he could sound so calm. "Is this true, Lady Quamby?"

She nodded and wiped her eyes as she stepped back. "I received this news from a dear and faithful...friend...who happened to have made enquiries when he was in London last."

"Made enquiries?" Suddenly, everything was sounding very havey-cavey.

Lady Fenton rose and swept over, looking grave as she took his other arm. "Please know that we weren't meddling, Mr Patmore. It's just that we couldn't understand why Miss Montrose seemed so intent on marrying Cousin George and when, at the time, we feared the spark of fire between the two of you might...fizzle," she looked apologetic, "Antoinette thought a few enquiries regarding Miss Montrose's past might throw up some answers. That's when we learned of a gentleman by the name of Orlando Perceval, who had spent a summer seven years ago staying with Eliza Montrose, her brother, and parents."

Rufus raised his eyebrows, signalling her to go on. Could it really be true that Eliza continued to hold a flame to a gentleman who had abandoned her more than six years ago? A gentleman who'd not sent her a word in the meantime—until now?

Or perhaps he had. What did Rufus know? He certainly knew nothing of the state of Miss Montrose's heart, though her body had been willing enough two nights ago. Was that because she'd just heard that Orlando Perceval was riding post haste from the docks at Southampton, or wherever he was holed up, on a mission to rescue her?

He stared stiffly out of the window. "Thank you for that information, ladies. It does indeed throw some light on what had started to become a matter of some vexation." Then, more decisively, "I shall leave in the morning." He drew away, causing Lady Quamby, who was still attached to his coat sleeve, to stumble slightly.

"Nonsense!" Lady Fenton returned calmly, drawing her sister down onto the sofa beside her. "You need another drink, Mr Patmore. If Mr Perceval did indeed abandon Miss Montrose all those years ago, then what kind of man does that make him compared with a man of nobility and honour like you?"

"I'd say it makes him a man of enduring fascination, don't you think?" Lady Quamby suggested, not very helpfully. "No!" she added, "the comparison will be odious, and that's why you must stay here, Mr Patmore, so that she can compare the two of you and have absolutely no doubt as to who is the better man."

The last thing Rufus felt like was puffing out his chest like some prize bull in a contest over Miss Montrose's heart. She only had to indicate with a smile or crook of her little finger, and he'd ask her to marry him in a heartbeat. But if the two ladies before him were correct, Miss Montrose was consumed by doubt, and by thoughts of this other gentleman.

So, *did* he still wish to wed her under these altered circumstances?

He'd just have to hear the truth from her own lips and make that decision; though as he sat down and accepted a second glass of Madeira, he knew that he did.

⊰❦⊱

"I DO HOPE MR PERCEVAL COMES SOON. JUST LOOK AT MISS Montrose." With a nod of her chin, Fanny indicated the lonely figure of Miss Montrose taking the path by the riverbank near where the children were playing with Nanny Brown.

Antoinette's rejoinder was energetic. "I'm sure she can't be grieving over the old termagant to look so gloomy. But is she dwelling on Mr Patmore or her lost love, Mr Perceval? Perhaps she can't decide what to do. Except that, of course, she doesn't know that Mr Perceval will be arriving this evening, so she can't really be dwelling on that."

"She doesn't *know* that he's coming?" Fanny jerked forward, her tea spilling from her teacup. "Lord, Antoinette, do you realise that Mr Patmore thinks that's why she wouldn't let him ask her to marry him? Did no one tell her?"

"I wanted it to be a surprise for her." Antoinette sounded dubious.

"Don't you see, this changes everything?" Fanny cried. "*I* thought the reason she'd rejected Mr Patmore was because she knew Mr Perceval was coming!"

Antoinette looked pained. "It's possible she found out, though *I* didn't tell her."

Fanny nibbled the tip of her finger as she rose and began to pace. "Oh Antoinette, did you see how long-faced Mr Patmore looked this afternoon when he made that excuse about going to the stables to consult Cousin George over a horse. That's supposedly why he's staying another night. At least, that's why George thinks he is. He's got himself involved in that ridiculous horse race Cousin George has no chance of winning using Devil's Run."

"I'm so glad Mr Patmore changed his mind and decided to stay so that he really could show Miss Montrose who was the better man." Antoinette clasped her hands. "Ambrose tells me that Mr Perceval is quite an Adonis, but I can't believe he's more worthy than Mr Patmore. He's certainly not as loyal if he abandoned her seven years ago. And, your suspicions are quite correct, if I wasn't so very engaged by darling Ambrose, I could quite fancy a little dalliance with Mr Patmore."

Fanny made a noise of irritation. "Really, Antoinette, I don't believe Mr Patmore would succumb to your lures, even if you jumped on him. Oh, my! Look! Miss Montrose has suddenly come over all purposeful. Where's she going?"

"Good lord! Straight to Mr Bramley!" squeaked Antoinette, rushing to the window to push aside the curtain to stand beside Fanny. "I do hope she gives him a piece of her mind. Imagine the gall! That he should call off the betrothal not even a day after it was revealed she was penniless. He didn't even care what people thought of him."

⚜

Indeed, Eliza would have liked to have given Mr Bramley a piece of her mind except that she'd readily agreed to the terms of the wager which he'd proposed.

All morning she'd pondered her alternatives. It would take only a little encouragement for Mr Patmore to repeat his proposal, if his longing looks in her direction were a true indication of his feelings.

But therein lay the problem that would not go away. Marriage to Mr Patmore, wonderful though that would be, meant Eliza would live in perpetual fear he'd discover her sordid past. It was too dangerous to risk confessing. Undoubtedly, he was a kind and good man, but *what* man, in this day and age, would happily welcome his new wife's bastard son into his household? Possibly he'd forgive her past transgressions. He might well forgive the fact she'd borne a child out of wedlock. But would he agree to have that child living under his roof? Of course not.

Whereas if Eliza married Mr Bramley, and moved into the apartment that had been redecorated for that purpose, she would see Jack almost every day.

She slowed her pace towards Mr Patmore to watch her son playing a game of blind man's bluff with Young George, Katherine, and Nanny Brown. His clothes were torn, and his hair needed cutting, and to the casual observer, there was no doubt that he came from humble stock. Yet he was the quickest and cleverest of the three children—certainly to Eliza—as even with his eyes bandaged he seemed to sense where his adversaries were.

Katherine, dressed in white with a blue sash skipped around him, just a hair's breadth away, giggling, while Jack slowly circled on the spot, hands outstretched, a broad grin on his face. What a difference it must be to the lad to spend time and play as a child. Eliza daren't think too much about the cold and unloving environment he must return to each night.

"Oi! That ain't part o' the game!"

Eliza felt a mother's quick rage as Young George delivered the blindfolded Jack a second hefty kick on the back of the legs, this one felling him.

Before she'd reached the pair, Jack's blindfold was off, and he was now engaged in a serious bout of fisticuffs.

"Stop that this moment, children!" Her imperious demand as she grabbed them by their collars and hauled them to their feet, had Jack hanging his head and Young George raising a disdainful nose in the air as she jostled them to attention to deliver a warning.

"That was not fair play, George. I saw you kick Jack, and that's not part of the game."

"It's the way George plays," said Katherine. "Jack knows it too, only he didn't get out of the way in time. You'll have to be quicker next time, won't you, Jack?"

Eliza was about to castigate Lady Fenton's daughter but thought better of it when she saw the cheeky grin Katherine and Jack shared. Her heart rate eased a little. So Jack had an ally in Katherine. Good. She and Jack knew what playing with Young George entailed.

Jack grinned up at her. "No need to worry about me, m'lady. I know how to look after meself."

Her boy looked so supremely confident about this, his perky smile never wavering. Indeed, he had the character of the undaunted. He'd survive, but his voice and his lack of education or social backing would damn his chances to rise in the world.

She squared her shoulders. Quick, nimble, and clever Jack could achieve great things if he had the support he needed.

Surely no sacrifice was too great to ensure that happened?

Reluctantly she left the children to their game and when Jack sped out of view, she intercepted her former betrothed en route to the stables. "Good afternoon, Mr Bramley."

He had the good grace to look embarrassed after his initial surprise. "Good afternoon, Miss Montrose. I didn't expect to see you."

"I daresay most young ladies in my unfortunate situation would have been gone by dawn so as not to have to face the man who has just dissolved their betrothal. Yes, I understood the conditions of our arrangement, but surely it was most discourteous that you should reappraise me of it *by letter*."

He grunted and looked away. "Thought you'd prefer it that way, to tell the truth. Besides, like you said, you were happy to gamble on the outcome, and had your aunt died a week *after* we were shackled, you'd have won the wager."

She nodded. Was this a man she could possibly consider taking as her husband when Mr Patmore had offered for her? Another happy cry from the children playing on the lawns not far away made them both turn, and her resolve hardened. She took a deep breath. "I own a horse you want. Is it enough to make you reconsider your offer of marriage?"

"Good Lord, Miss Montrose; what a question?"

My, she *had* discomposed him. She was surprised and delighted and pressed her point. "I think Devil's Run is worth more to you for reasons I cannot fathom. I know you are a betting man, but as fond of the animal as I am, I can't imagine he'll win you any races. However, your motivations aren't something I'm interested in right now. I just have one counter proposal for you. A wager if you will."

"Heavens, Miss Montrose; you and your wagers! They've not been in your favour to date." He looked as if he might dismiss her altogether since she clearly would bring him no material gain. However, he went on, "No, my motivations have nothing to do with you, though it's true, I do want to race Devil's Run. My uncle, however, will ensure I have access to the horse when I need him."

"I've already ensured that will not happen."

She was caught out by the active delight she felt in his anger, so inexpertly hidden, though quietly expressed in the flare of his thick nose and flash of his dark eyes.

"Have you indeed?"

"I have. I spoke to him last night after he graciously corroborated his wife's invitation that I spend a fortnight here. I told him that I believed you coveted the horse he'd given me and would endeavour to take or borrow it, but that I desired this not to happen under any circumstances for my own reasons. Perhaps he mistook my motivations for pique that you'd thrown me over so easily."

For a moment, they glared at one another. "Well, that's true enough, isn't it?" he muttered. Then, he couldn't help asking, of course, "And what is your proposal?"

"That you agree you will marry me if Devil's Run wins the race you need him to win next Saturday. Then, of course, you will own him, since what is mine will be yours, legally, once we're married, and as your wife, I can make no further stipulations regarding your property."

He opened his mouth to let forth a no doubt angry rejoinder, but then closed it again, staring at her in some perplexity. "You wish to hold me to a marriage that I believe neither of us greatly desires. Certainly, not without the underpinnings of the wealth that might have made it tolerable. It is true; you are not without your attractions, Miss Montrose, but you would not be my first choice, with or without a fortune. I'm not sure such a straight talking and determined woman as yourself would suit me."

"You'd prefer a shrinking violet you could bully and make cower?"

He stared at her. "*That* is what you think of me yet you wish to marry me? Your logic is beyond me, Miss Montrose."

"You have access to Quamby House; your sisters-in-law move in the circles I would enjoy being part of, and I need a husband. I am twenty-five years old and time is running out for me. I know you must be in the market for a wife, otherwise you'd not have proposed." She pushed her point when she saw him hesitate. "And there must be advantages to a marriage in which you were given licence to follow your other...interests?"

He shrugged as he continued to walk towards the stables. "As I said, Miss Montrose, you are far too direct for me."

"Then I shall take Devil's Run with me tonight and hide him." Lord, where had that piece of bravado come from?

He halted and turned, and a slow smile curled one side of his mouth. "Don't think you could get away with making such threats after we were married, Miss Montrose." He chewed his lip. "But your talk has hit a nerve. Perhaps I would enjoy putting you in your place if I were to marry you. How would you like that?"

He said it as a dare, but Eliza merely shrugged. "I'm not sure how I would enjoy being subjugated by any man; that's true. I only know that I want the trappings of comfort so greatly after living as a slave to my aunt that I'm prepared to swallow my pride to get what I want."

"All right, you gift me Devil's Run now, and if he wins next Saturday's race, I'll marry you."

His response was so unexpected the blood rushed from her head, and his thuggish face swam before her eyes. "You'd really do that?"

"I want him enough to back up what I just implied—that I believe he can win me an inordinate amount of money. As for you, Miss Montrose, you're not displeasing to the eye. I've warned you what's in store for you, so not even the devilishly exasperating Lady Quamby can blame me for the hell I'll no doubt put you through, but since you're so insistent—desperate, of course, now you have nothing—I daresay having a diplomatic wife to smooth my path while letting me do as I wish will make life easier."

It wasn't often Eliza was struck dumb. He was actually acceding to her grand plans, and a great deal more simply than she'd expected. But was she making a mistake? Suddenly, she doubted herself. The only reason her heart was involved was because of the access he gave her to Jack. Mr Bramley had a cruel streak; it was true. If he ever discovered her connection to the boy he would punish them both.

Yet why should he? Eliza was discreet. She didn't wear her heart on her sleeve. She was cautious. She could manage the situation.

Her mind strayed to the one great complication—Mr Patmore.

She wanted to marry him, and he wanted to marry her. In fact, she could imagine he might go to great lengths to dissuade her from marrying Mr Bramley. He'd never understand her real motivations and might imagine false ones.

Nervously, she twisted the ends of her shawl between her fingers. "A...private wedding, perhaps, Mr Bramley? After you've finished celebrating Devil's Run's success on the course?

He shrugged. "The legalities have already been attended to. The banns have been called, and I daresay the sooner I can enjoy my husbandly privileges the better." He sent her a lascivious leer over his shoulder as he turned. "Devil's Run will be mine, and you will have my name and my protection." He laughed at this, as if he found it amusing while he kept walking, then stopped and turned to salute her. "Thank you, Miss Montrose. I daresay we'll deal well enough together. We both want something from each other. It's how the best bargains are struck. I've given you fair warning of what to expect, and in return, I'll provide you with the comforts a man in my position is able to grant.

"I'll arrange a private wedding in St Mary's in the village at midnight next Saturday after the race is fairly won. The vicar will be feeling particularly amenable, and in truth, such a ceremony would be preferable to me also, than one that has my blasted cousins-in-law weeping and wailing and trying to persuade you to cry off." He shook his head. "They didn't take to you; you know that. Not when you first came here, but since you rescued their snotty brats, they and old Quamby can't do enough for you. Reckon it could be useful having you around, m'dear."

Eliza watched him leave, her heart heavy in her chest. What had she done? Why had she persisted? But the arrangement had been mutually agreed. She'd be living in residence in Quamby House within a week, and Jack would be in close proximity.

Wasn't that all that mattered?

CHAPTER 13

It was excruciating having to face Mr Patmore in the drawing room that evening as the company—surprisingly subdued, Eliza thought—sipped sherry prior to going into dinner.

He was the first to arrive at her elbow to engage her in conversation, and she was aware of the interested glances from her hostesses. She was also aware of a heady acceleration of her heart rate, but that couldn't be helped or pandered to. Until the race in a few days' time, she had to keep her silence.

"You look very lovely this evening," he remarked, his eyes taking in her newest and most flattering ensemble, a gold net gown with ruffles around the hem and upon the sleeves, complemented by feathers in her hair. Eliza had worked hard on this creation when she'd learned she'd be a guest of the Earl and Countess of Quamby. Little did she know how greatly the visit would change her life. "Lovelier than I've seen you," he added. "And that's saying something. Could there be some special reason your eyes look so bright and your cheeks so full of roses?"

Goodness! What was he suggesting? There was definitely speculation in his gaze, and she wondered if he were fishing for a response from her that might indicate she was ready to hear him speak his heart tonight.

Fingers of pain clutched at her. It would undo her to have such a beautiful man remind her that he couldn't be hers. Oh, why had he made his thoughts on bastard children so abundantly clear to all and sundry the other night? Under different circumstances, she might have had the courage to marry him and take the risk he'd never find out about Jack. She might even have had the courage to confess all, making her a better woman than she knew herself to be.

But hadn't he shown his moral fibre in gently restraining her passions that would have had her cast all caution before the wind, while at the same time making very clear his feelings were equally aroused?

Clearly, he was a man of principle and moral righteousness. Of course, he'd not sanction a bastard in the family—or forgive the mother of one.

"Mr Patmore...you are too kind," she said, dipping her eyes as a ripple of interest in several new arrivals swept the room.

"I heard we were expecting visitors." Mr Patmore stepped a little closer, his attitude protective though some might consider it proprietorial. Eliza liked it. She raised her gaze and caught his eyes boring into hers, as if he were attuned to her every nuanced response, and her breath caught in her throat. She didn't care if her look was transparent with longing; there was only so much she could do to dampen her true feelings.

If Mr Patmore were her husband, or even her betrothed, she'd surreptitiously insinuate her hand into his and offer him all she had with just a look.

But he wasn't and could never be, and besides, her hosts were stepping apart to welcome the new additions to their gathering, and soon it would be incumbent upon Eliza to show her good manners and greet them when all she wanted was to bare her heart and soul to Mr Patmore.

"I believe Miss Montrose and one of our guests are already

acquainted." Lady Quamby smiled brightly as she prepared to do the introductions. "Though I don't believe she has met Mr Ambrose Canning."

Reluctantly, Eliza transferred her gaze from Mr Patmore to the two tall strangers who'd just arrived.

Except—one of them wasn't a stranger.

No, she and he were certainly more than just acquainted.

"Mr Perceval." It came out as a faint breath.

Mr Patmore put out a steadying hand as she stumbled backwards.

"It's been a long time, Eliza."

Orlando. It really was him. Seven years older and just as handsome with his fine features dominated by a patrician nose, his fair hair slightly curling, characterised by the cowlick Eliza had loved to study when he wasn't looking, just as he was now studying her. "Eliza?" There was a diffidence in his manner that was at odds with the Orlando she knew. But then, of course, he'd wonder how she'd receive him after all this time. After what had happened.

Nor did she know how to respond, except that she was relieved to have to follow through on the social niceties to greet the dark, theatrical looking Mr Canning, since it gave her time to gather her wits before turning back to her erstwhile...lover.

"A very long time." What else could she say? She cleared her throat, aware of Mr Patmore's very interested gaze. "What have you been doing all this time?"

"After a tour of the Continent, I returned to the West Indies."

Inanities. Her brain was churning with all the questions she had for him. Of all the things she had to tell him. Yet, would she? Seven years had passed since they'd parted, and Eliza was a very different person from the schoolgirl he'd promised to marry. Did he even know about Jack?

"Miss Montrose?" Lady Fenton's concerned voice broke her reverie. "Are you well?"

Eliza put her hand to her forehead; her brain whirling with the enormity of what Orlando's visit might mean. "Are you married?"

There was a moment of surprised silence. Perhaps *shocked* was more apt, and Eliza felt her cheeks burning as she took in each face trained upon hers: Ladies Fenton and Quamby, Mr Canning's, and Mr Perceval's. And, dear Mr Patmore who'd remained loyally by her side and was looking a little pale, she noted, though not nearly as pale as she must be looking since she truly feared she was about to faint.

But not because she was hanging on Orlando's answer. His expression was concerned, but not filled with frustrated longing; not like a man who's been torn from his one true love.

Once, she'd been crazed with passion and sick with loss over Orlando. Since she'd come to Quamby House, her reason for living had been restored to her. She'd found the conduit to all the love she needed—Jack. She'd felt desired by Mr Patmore, a kind and honourable man whose love she returned.

Rufus Patmore. *He* was the man she loved, she realised with painful clarity. She *had* to find the courage to confide in him.

"I married three months ago, Eliza." He cleared his throat, hesitating as he weighed up his next words. "My wife is on the plantation, expecting our first child in September, so my visit to England is only for a few weeks." He paused, awkwardly. "It's a great surprise to see you here, Eliza." He sent an uncertain glance around the rest of the company who were looking on with rapt interest. "Naturally, I'd have paid my respects if I knew where to find you."

Paid his respects... She nodded. Words wouldn't come. Silence had descended until Lady Quamby said with forced cheerfulness and a flick of her golden curls modishly secured by a pearl-encrusted comb, "Let me introduce you to my cousin, Mr George Bramley, who has just arrived. He'll be most intrigued to learn where you got that dashing scar across your cheek, Mr Perceval. Cousin George has always had a desire to be a skilled swordsman, haven't you?"

This naturally deflected attention onto Mr Bramley and should have given Eliza a reprieve, except that Lady Quamby *had* to break into Mr Bramley's incoherent utterings to ask ingenuously, "Oh, *do* tell all, Mr Perceval! You sustained an injury, but you must have come off triumphant. Whom did you run through with a rapier?"

Whom did Orlando run through with a rapier?

"Miss Montrose! Eliza!" A dozen voices seemed to be speaking at once while the world closed in on her. And as her knees buckled and her head spun, she felt a pair of strong arms scoop her up before she hit the floor; at the same time as she wished she might disappear into a mote of dust and never have to face Orlando or Mr Patmore—and definitely not Mr Bramley—again.

❦

SHE MUST HAVE REGAINED CONSCIOUSNESS QUITE QUICKLY, FOR when she opened her eyes, it seemed that Mr Patmore had just laid her upon the chaise longue in the smaller drawing room along the passage while Orlando hovered at his side.

The room was dim and very quiet. She could hear herself breathing. In fact, she could hear the breathing of the other two men also, before Orlando gripped her hand murmuring, "Such a very great shock, Eliza. I don't know what you must be feeling."

Before Eliza could respond, he swung around to Mr Patmore, his expression tortured and intense. "Eliza and I knew one another, well, many years ago, perhaps you weren't aware. I left the country suddenly because..." He touched the scar on his cheek, and the words he'd not yet said caused Eliza to cover her eyes with her hands.

Orlando sank down onto his knees at her side, though he raised his face to Mr Patmore. In a low voice, he explained. "I left the country after a duel which left Eliza's brother dead."

Eliza struggled to sit up. "Edmund tried to kill you! It was not your fault he died because of his own stupidity!" His image was blurred through her tears as she looked at the beautiful mouth she'd kissed so many times in her youth. And though her heart ached, it was not through the pain of still loving him, but of what might have been had the lonely years not turned her longing into confusion tinged with resentment. "You didn't have to leave!"

All those withered hopes and dried-up dreams coupled with the seven years of punishment, made all the more excruciating by the knowledge she was again giving up the chance of love with the *other* gentleman staring down at her, that kind, honourable, *noble* Mr Patmore, broke the dam waters and for once Eliza's self containment deserted her.

She began to sob.

And she could not stop.

All she could do was wave one hand in dismissal and say through her tears, "Please leave me, gentlemen. At least until I am myself once more."

◌◈◌

SHAKEN, RUFUS RETURNED TO THE COMPANY THEY'D RECENTLY left. The Brightwell sisters, both looking far more subdued than usual, swept over to the two men.

"We had no wish to cause Miss Montrose such distress," said Lady Fenton, before her sister turned an accusing look upon Mr Perceval.

"I was assured you weren't married, Mr Perceval, else I'd not have considered opening up old wounds. That is the reason she fainted, is it not? Because she couldn't bear the idea that you had returned, yet remained as ever beyond her reach for tragic reasons beyond our understanding. My apologies, Mr Patmore."

Rufus blinked as Mr Perceval focused a level stare upon him. "You are...courting Miss Montrose?" He watched Lady Fenton slip away in order to usher her husband, Mr Bramley, and the theatrical fellow whose name escaped him, into the dining room.

Lady Quamby offered them a beseeching look as she answered for Rufus. "In a manner of speaking, but when she seemed so reluctant, I delved into the past a little and discovered...well, you, Mr Perceval."

"Me?" He sounded surprised. Rufus, meanwhile, was feeling like a deflated hot-air balloon. For seven years, Miss Montrose had carried a flame for a thwarted love affair that made her incapable of loving anyone else. It was, he supposed, the reason she was prepared to marry Mr Bramley, rather than himself, since it ensured loyalty of the heart was never going to be an issue. Clearly, thought Rufus, bitterly, Miss Montrose *liked* him. Just not enough to want to marry him.

"We learned that you spent a summer living in her father's house," said Lady Quamby, as her sister joined her side.

"My father was acquainted with Mr Montrose, and I traded on that friendship to lodge with the Montroses while I waited for my inheritance to come through. An uncle had left me a plantation in the East Indies."

Lady Quamby let out a plaintive sigh. "And you fell in love?"

Mr Perceval gave a slight inclination of his head.

"But then you duelled with the brother and killed him." Rufus realised he sounded more aggressive than he meant, but by God, this was the man standing between him and the woman he loved. And Perceval had wronged Eliza grievously. Yes, Rufus wanted to marry Eliza himself, but that was because he wanted to make her *happy*.

Lady Fenton said sharply to her sister, "You asked how Mr Perceval received his scar, Antoinette. What an inopportune moment to make such an enquiry when they had only just been reunited." Then, to Mr Perceval, "And you received the scar in a contest which killed Miss Montrose's brother?"

Mr Perceval raised a hand. "It was self-defence. He lunged at me with a rapier when I was unarmed. Somehow, in the fray, Edmund died. Shortly afterwards, I left the country. It was considered death by misadventure, though Eliza's family never forgave me."

"And that's why you couldn't marry her." Rufus nodded, as understanding dawned. Perhaps the brother had taken exception to Mr Perceval as a suitor for his sister, then after the young man's death, Eliza had borne the opprobrium of her family forever, and she'd been banished to live with her aunt.

Mr Perceval shifted uncomfortably. "I was already married."

Rufus looked at him with suspicion. "Miss Montrose didn't know?"

He shook his head. "She learned it after her brother's death. It was wrong of me, and I accept that she considered I was courting her." He shrugged. "But she was very young. Too young. It's the reason I never sought her out afterwards. After I'd left her home. I had nothing to offer her."

"But you said you married three months ago, Mr Perceval."

"That's right. My first wife was confined to an insane asylum for many years before she died. I became a widower a little over a year ago." His nostrils flared. "When Mr Canning befriended me at Whites and invited me to a weekend house party, I had no idea I would see Miss Montrose again. I learned she was one of the guests only as we were on the final stretch and passing through the village High Street and, after being talked out of turning tail and fleeing, I decided it would be my moment to atone. Only, I fear I've only made matters worse for her by stirring up the past. I'd hoped to find her happily married."

Lady Quamby appeared determined to make the best of matters. She pushed back her shoulders, raised her beautiful head so that her baby-blue eyes sparkled directly at Rufus and said, "That is what *we* hope shall come to pass before too long." Raising her glass, which had just been refilled by one of the footmen, she declared, "This tragic tale of lost love *shall* have a happy ending under this roof. You have found your heart's desire, Mr Perceval. Now, Miss Montrose can see that she is free at last to follow *her* heart without any guilt associated with such long-distant dramas."

Rufus only wished he shared her enthusiasm.

CHAPTER 14

Eliza felt little better in the morning. It was as if she were slowly convalescing from a great illness. How foolish she must appear.

Seven years ago, she'd not even been out. She'd not been presented. She'd been a schoolgirl who'd fallen desperately in love with a much older— married—man.

A man whose sudden reappearance into her life had stirred up the past and caused her to faint, which was something she'd never done. Not even when she was carrying Jack, for she'd been strong and robust throughout her pregnancy, which is how she'd managed to make her escape with him so shortly after his birth.

As she idly walked the gravel path that wound down the grassy hill and circumnavigated the lake, she felt weak. Weak and foolish. Certainly on a fool's errand if she persisted in this ridiculous idea of marrying Mr Bramley so she could do her best by Jack.

Now Jack's father was here. Oh yes, hadn't that kept her awake all night. Jack would be arriving in the donkey cart, and the children would be rushing about, no doubt tripping up the adults, and Orlando wouldn't even know his own son.

Was it her duty to both Jack and Orlando to reveal the truth?

Orlando seemed another world away. A different man from the one she'd hoped to marry. The man who'd whispered words of love and promises of marriage as he'd loved her in the secret tower room had been in no position to offer her anything.

He'd lied to her. Oh, she believed he loved her at the time; that he would have married her if he'd only been free to do so, but he'd behaved, ultimately, so dishonourably. Was this a man to whom she should entrust her son? *Their* son?

"Eliza!"

She swung round at his well-remembered voice. How often she'd heard that breathless note, the prelude to her throwing herself into his arms.

Their 'courtship' had been a long one of friendship, companionship, and only, at the very end, love and passion. Too brief to know if it would last, she supposed, but long enough to create a child, though Eliza had only truly lain with Orlando twice. So much frustrated passion and longing had led to the culmination of their overheated desire for each other before Edmund had stumbled upon them.

They'd been careless, and what else was Edmund to do when he knew what Eliza didn't—that Orlando had a wife.

"Orlando." She spoke his name carefully. She didn't want to imbue it with any of her true feelings, for fear it would make her vulnerable somehow.

He clasped her hands, squeezing them as he brought them to his lips.

"Don't do that!" she snapped, pulling them away and continuing to walk. "You're still a married man. Just like you were the first time."

He didn't answer immediately as he matched her stride across the lawn. "Eliza, you were so young when I met you. I should never have let myself fall for you that magical summer, but these things happen. And it had been so long since Millicent had been well that I didn't consider myself a married man."

"You still had a wife."

"Yes, who was dangerously ill and had tried numerous times to kill herself." He put his hand on her shoulder to make her stop. "I truly loved you, Eliza. I would have married you if I could have, and I truly believed it would be possible."

"A pity Edmund took honour to the limit." Her tone was ironic, but she stopped when she saw three children tearing across the grassy slope towards them, biting her lip as she anticipated the collision between Jack and his father, but of course, the children were involved in their own game of tag. They had no interest in two serious-looking grown-ups, though, laughing, they ran in circles several times around Eliza and Orlando before heading for a large oak tree Eliza knew they liked to climb.

"Those are the children of Ladies Fenton and Quamby," Eliza told him when he made no comment. She swallowed, and added carefully, "There's a boy who comes each day from the foundling home to play with them. He's a very clever lad." She hesitated. "You'd like him."

Orlando sent her a look as if he were trying to fathom whether she was teasing, but before he could answer, Lady Fenton arrived, a little out of breath.

"Miss Montrose, are you all right?" she asked, glancing between Eliza and Orlando, before adding quickly in answer to Eliza's rather scandalised look, "Good, I was sure you would be, but I'm trying to catch Katherine as Mrs Candlewick is here to fit her for a new dress. She doesn't want to come indoors, but she has to. Please try and restrain her if you can. The little hoyden already knows she's going to be punished."

"Then perhaps you'll never catch her, at least not this afternoon," Orlando said with a smile.

Lady Fenton made a noise of exasperation. "I fear you're right, but she has to learn. And she *does* want that dress, only she's utterly besotted with that foundling boy. I truly think the highlight of her day is getting into some scrape or another with him. Or finding some new way to vex Young George. Oh look, there's Jack now.

Jack!" She called him over, adding to Eliza and Orlando, "I can count on him to make my daughter toe the line."

Dutifully the boy trotted over, tugging his forelock as he executed a neat little bow. As it always did, Eliza's heart did strange things.

"Eliza?"

She realised she was still looking at him. *Smiling stupidly? Giving herself away?* Lord, she hoped not. She slanted a glance at Orlando, too afraid of seeing in his eyes the dawning realisation that before him stood his son. Instead, lines of faint puzzlement creased his brow.

"You invite orphans here to Quamby House, Lady Fenton?" he asked, taking no account of the fact the boy remained where he was as he'd not been dismissed. "Are you not worried something will go missing?"

"I understand your sentiments, Mr Perceval, and indeed it was difficult to persuade my husband and the earl of the merits." Lady Fenton patted Jack on the head. "However, my cousin was most insistent that we do what she called her 'God-given duty to succour the little children'; those who came into the world with nothing."

Orlando's gaze encompassed the great lands that surrounded him. "With all due respect, Lady Fenton, is it wise to put hopes into the minds of children who are quite frankly, on quite a different social footing?" He laughed, as if trying to lighten the tone, for Eliza noticed that her hostess was looking distinctly pink. What, really, were her thoughts, though more to the point, what were Orlando's? Eliza was finding it quite difficult to breathe.

"Believe me, Mr Perceval, I once shared your views, but only because I'd not given a thought to those less fortunate. I was too concerned with raising myself in the world." Her lips twisted in a wry smile. "However, a few years ago, my cousin nearly ran over a poor infant whose mother had had second thoughts about placing him into the basket for motherless babes. She was stricken with mortification at the thought she might have killed them both, and it seems to have excited her conscience. She takes in an orphan several days a week to play with her son, and we have done the same with young Jack."

She bent down to address the boy, but Eliza was too shocked to listen to what she was saying. Lady Fenton's *cousin* had been the young lady in the carriage who had nearly run down Eliza and Jack all those years ago? Mrs Thea Grayling, whom she'd met at the beginning of her visit here? It was a revelation. It changed nothing, but now she realised to whom she owed so much for changing Jack's circumstances for the better.

Orlando, who was standing behind his son, placed a hand on the boy's head and asked, "I hope you proceed with caution, Lady Fenton, though I wouldn't presume to tell you how to conduct your affairs. I just fear that we would be turning society on its head if we allowed all beggars and bastards to believe they were as entitled as we are."

"Entitled to what, Orlando?" Eliza burst out with far more heat than was warranted. "I believe it's pure luck as to where we're born in the great scheme of things. Why, *you* could have been as unfortunate as Jack here. Or rather, your *mother* could have been. What if she'd been abandoned and left with the care of you, through no fault of her own? Should the children be made to suffer? Are they not as entitled and intelligent? Jack is certainly intelligent, you said so yourself, Lady Fenton. You know your numbers, don't you, Jack?"

The lad looked surprised, as well he might, but Eliza was too distraught to know how to manage the quagmire into which she'd flung herself. "Forgive me! Good day, Lady Fenton! Orlando!"

She turned on her heel and walked rapidly down the hill towards the stables, while Fanny sent a surprised glance in Mr Perceval's direction before her gaze dropped to the clever charity child in front of him—a handsome, fine-featured boy with light, slightly curling hair.

Characterised by a cowlick and a patrician nose.

She frowned, glancing up again at Mr Perceval. "You can go

now, Jack. And if you can get Katherine to go back into the house before Mrs Candlewick is due to leave in half an hour, I'll make sure Cook sends you back to the home with cake to share with the other children."

⚜

R<small>UFUS</small> <small>SAW</small> M<small>ISS</small> M<small>ONTROSE</small> <small>LEAVE</small> L<small>ADY</small> Q<small>UAMBY</small> <small>AND</small> M<small>R</small> Perceval in some haste. Without thought, he began to follow. She appeared distressed, brushing at her eyes with the back of her hand as she hurried in the direction of the stables.

In a more considered frame of mind, Rufus might have questioned the wisdom in detaining her.

"Miss Montrose!" He found her inside the lofty building that housed the earl's half a dozen mounts.

"None of the grooms are anywhere to be found," she muttered. "I'd hoped to have one of them saddle up Devil for me."

"So you could clear your head with a bracing ride?" He ventured closer. Her lashes were damp and her nose pink. She looked utterly ravishing, and so desperately in need of comfort.

She nodded, avoiding his eyes and apparently trying to control her emotions for she began to pace, first to the stall where Devil was contentedly chewing straw, then to another doorway from which she gazed back to the place she'd just left.

"Miss Montrose, you have endured much these past few days." He went to her side and, bravely, gripped her hand, bringing it up to his chest and forcing her to look at him. The tragedy in her gaze nearly undid him. He wanted to kiss her without preamble, but wasn't sure how that would be received.

"Mr Bramley has thrown you over, and now you learn that the man you loved for so many years has only recently married. All this when your aunt is only just buried having neglected to recognise you for your services these many years." He squeezed her hand. "But don't think yourself alone. I am here for you." He swallowed. "If you'll have me."

With a cry of what he first believed was pain, she threw herself into his arms, a response that was as unexpected as it was pure heaven.

Kissing her fiercely, Rufus drew her into the shadows of the barn, backing them into an unoccupied stall. Her mouth was as sweet as he remembered, and her body as soft and desirable. He cupped her face and deepened the kiss as fiery heat threatened to consume him. God, he wanted this woman, and she would be his, as her passionate responses confirmed. An overwhelming relief swept over him as he drank in her scent, her goodness, her incomparable desirability.

"My darling, you are not alone," he whispered, as they finally stepped apart to draw breath and digest what they had done. "I love you. Yes, truly, madly, more than I could believe possible. You are an angel of goodness, a paragon of virtue beyond compare." When she looked as if she might cry once more, he drew her into his embrace again, stroking her hair as he went on. "I've never wanted anything as much as I want you to be my wife. You are perfect as you are. Your good heart has held true to a man whose memory you cherished for seven long years, and while I know today has been a shock, I hope it has helped sever the final ties that might bind you to him."

"Please, Mr Patmore, you paint me in too rosy a light." She struggled out of his embrace and stared at him, her expression stricken.

He shook his head. "Believe me, Eliza. If I may call you that. I am thirty-one years old, and I've not come even close to marrying because I have never fallen for a woman whose blameless character matches her charm and goodness. You are all these things." He knew he was gushing, but he was overcome with the need to highlight how deeply he felt about her. "You are a paragon, a brave and noble young woman shouldering your responsibilities to your aunt all these years without complaint merely because your lack of fortune put you in such a position. I don't care about your fortune. No, I care nothing for that; only that you are pure and kind and virtuous, and I would be so very proud to call my wife." He went down on one knee and stared up into her face. "Please, Miss Montrose. I'm begging you to make me the happiest man alive by agreeing to marry me."

She looked shocked rather than overjoyed, but then this was yet another tumultuous event, he supposed, in a very few tumultuous days. She opened her mouth to speak, closed it again, then turned her head away while two large tears coursed down her cheeks.

"Oh, Eliza!" he cried, mistaking her emotion for joy at his offer.

"No, Mr Patmore." She shook her head wildly as she retreated a step. "You don't understand. All these things you're saying. They—"

"All true!" He gripped her wrists. "I wouldn't say them if I didn't believe them. You are everything I've ever wanted in a wife. I have the utmost respect for everything you represent—uncomplaining virtue and acceptance as evidenced by the way you've served your aunt these long years. Please, Eliza, consider what I've just said. We could be so happy living between London and my estate, which is only three hours from here and five from London. I would not be an exacting husband. You'd be mistress of a household of servants and would have complete say over how matters were conducted. I have developed an interest in politics this past year, and you're exactly the kind of wife I'm looking for. A woman with an unblemished character who would be my hostess and represent me in the admirable, self-contained manner that so drew me to you. And that was before you showed me that you also were a woman of great love and passion. Please, Eliza."

He couldn't believe that she was shaking her head slowly, her expression sorrowful.

"You do me a great honour, Mr Patmore." She touched his cheek. "But as you rightly observed, I am a woman who needs to give careful consideration to matters of great import, so it would be wrong to give you an immediate answer."

He felt a great swell of relief lift his spirits. "Tomorrow?"

A shadow crossed her face. "The day after tomorrow, Mr Patmore. I have my reasons, but you will get your answer then."

It wasn't what he was expecting, but he had to accept it. He turned away, for one of the grooms had just returned, and Miss Montrose had hurried across to request him to fit Devil with a sidesaddle, almost as if she couldn't wait to be out of Rufus's company.

When she suddenly rushed back to his side, his heart swelled with hope, but all she had for him was: "One small but important request, Mr Patmore. Please don't tell anyone that you have asked me. Not Ladies Fenton or Quamby and not Mr Bramley. Can you *promise* me that?" She gripped his lapel, and her expression was so intense Rufus didn't know what to think.

He nodded, unconsciously touching his lip which still felt the exciting effects of their kiss. "If you wish, Miss Montrose. But you will give me your answer in a day?"

"The day after tomorrow, for you will be much occupied with the race tomorrow, I believe."

"As a spectator, merely, though I had hoped to travel north, back home, in the afternoon." He said it diffidently in the hopes she might say that then, of course, he would have his answer in the afternoon so that he might do just that, bolstered by the need to arrange matters regarding an impending wedding.

But she did not.

CHAPTER 15

The moment Fanny had farewelled their short-lived houseguest from the front portico, she swung round to her sister.

"Did you notice his cowlick?" she asked.

Antoinette was more occupied noticing the cut of her beloved Ambrose's coat—or rather, the lovely smooth swell just below the waistline as he bent to adjust his boot before climbing the stairs to join them—than Mr Perceval's cowlick. She therefore had to be asked a second time the question which had been hissed in hurried tones as Ambrose would soon be within earshot.

"Ambrose doesn't have a cowlick—do you, my love?—though he has many more interesting things which I've just been admiring." She contoured his rump with a quick skim of her hands before turning as the double doors were opened to admit them. Even the arrival of the dignified Bentink upon the threshold couldn't stop her whispering loudly in her lover's ear, "Why, you are just the cleverest spy in all England, Ambrose, you little cherub."

Fanny throttled her frustration as her sister, stepping inside as she clung to Ambrose's arm, added, "I know it was all very tragic for Miss Montrose to learn that the man she's been in love with all these years and who abandoned her—after murdering her *brother*, no less—is as ever out of reach, but don't you think it's a wonderful thing for her to know she can, guiltlessly, bestow her affections on a far worthier suitor—Mr Patmore? Why, it couldn't have worked out better, really. And it's only due to your astonishing sleuthing and acting capabilities, Ambrose. Why, you should be working for the Home Office or Foreign Office, not on the stage, though I suppose the qualities and attributes are interchangeable," she said airily. "But Mr Perceval, while handsome, certainly had none of Mr Patmore's *cachet*."

"A dull dog, if you ask me," Ambrose said with a decisive nod. "Had to goad him to put a wager on a sure bet, and do you think he thanked me when it came in?" He shook his head in answer to his own question. "Said he wasn't one for taking chances. Couldn't wait to get back to that God-forsaken bit of dirt across the sea, where there were no surprises waiting for him except a comfortable wife and soon a new heir, he hoped. Devilish uncomfortable this whole affair made him. Good he knew it was time to bow out gracefully."

"No, there really was no comparison to be made," Antoinette rattled on as they arrived at the drawing room, "and I think Miss Montrose realised that, so I daresay Miss Montrose and Mr Patmore will come back from the stables smelling of April and May with a wedding to announce."

Fanny nibbled her little finger. "I hope you're right, Antoinette. She certainly seemed upset when she left us. Do you know if Mr Perceval and Miss Montrose had any private conversation? I mean, it was a rather abrupt departure on his part. I was sure he was staying three days and there'd be plenty of time for them to settle their differences, digest the past, come to terms with what had happened." She felt unsettled and uncertain.

"It was, I agree—and I'd also adore a dish of tea. Ambrose, can you arrange that, dearest? No, don't just go to the bellpull. I want you to find one of the servants and ask them personally. They're so slow in coming when I pull on that thing. And make sure you're gone for at least five minutes. Now Fanny, why were you asking me about a cowlick?"

Even with Ambrose out of earshot, having obediently gone to do Antoinette's bidding, Fanny had nothing worth saying. With the passing of only half an hour since the faint stirring of consciousness when she'd glanced between Jack and Mr Perceval, Fanny was already counselling herself not to see dramatic coincidences when there were none.

"Never mind, it was nothing. And I'm sure you're right when you say the pair of them will come back and happily announce their betrothal. Ah, Katherine, you've deigned to do my bidding. Well, it's too late now. I asked Jack to send you here *immediately*— and certainly before Mrs Candlewick left—but the naughty boy obviously didn't heed my request, or chose to ignore it."

Katherine stared dolefully down at a grass stain on the hem of her white muslin. "He was coming for me, Mama, truly! Oh *please*, can't I have a new dress," the little girl begged. "We could go into the village and see that dressmaker lady at her cottage and have iced buns in the High Street." The thought made her eyes light up, but her mother shook her head. Fanny wasn't one to pander to anyone when her mood was disordered. "Clearly, Jack wasn't coming for you, despite what I asked of him, and you are far too fond of that child. What will you do when suddenly he's big enough to be sent away to become a bootboy and can no longer be your plaything at your beck and call?"

Katherine gasped and looked as if she were about to cry. "That won't happen, will it, Mama? Won't he stay here forever and ever? He's my *friend*. My absolutest *best* friend. He makes sure that awful George doesn't do all the horrid things George likes to do when he catches frogs or birds."

"Well, he's not much use to me if he doesn't carry out my instructions," muttered Fanny irritably. She was feeling unaccountably out of sorts, and wondered whether it was because the visit by Mr Perceval seemed so unsatisfactory, and he'd caused Miss

Montrose so much hurt when really, it was she and Antoinette who'd orchestrated the reunion.

"But Jack *was* coming to get me. I saw him running up the hill. I was in my favourite tree—you know, the oak near the lake—and he knew that's where he'd find me, but then Uncle George grabbed him by the arm a little way away, and I heard him telling George he had an important job to do tomorrow with Devil and the race."

Fanny's ears pricked up and Antoinette, who'd been gazing dreamily through the window, asked, "What important job was that, dear?"

Katherine shrugged. "Not very important. Only to hold Devil's reins and keep him quiet and from running away from the middle of the course until someone else came to fetch Devil to finish."

"To finish what, Katherine?" Fanny asked with studied calm.

"The race, of course. Uncle George said he had a shilling for Jack if he didn't tell anyone, and another shilling if he met him somewhere, and then he'd tell him exactly what he must do. Mama, can I have a shilling for telling you?" The little girl sent her mother a shrewd look. "It's valuable information if Uncle George is wanting to pay *Jack* not to tell anyone."

"Yes, but only if you don't tell anyone, either," said Fanny, reaching for her reticule. She rummaged for a coin, held it out, then withdrew it, saying, "On second thoughts, not yet, else there'll be all sorts of questions about where you got it and then people will wonder why you're being so close-lipped, which wouldn't be like you at all, would it, Katherine?"

"But Mama!" the girl cried, upset.

"Katherine, think of it as a valuable lesson. And if you learn it well, I shall give you two shillings tomorrow, instead of one today. Now, no need to say a word of any of this, for here comes Ambrose."

Indeed, here he was, beaming, in advance of one of the parlourmaids bearing a tray of tea as Fanny dismissed her daughter, saying, "So you may have your new dress, Katherine, and you may also tell Jack to come and see me, immediately. Tell him as a special treat I've asked Cook to give him the rest of yesterday's seed cake."

"But I was going to have some for nursery tea, Mama—" began Katherine.

Her mother cut her off. "Go and fetch Jack now, and you may have a small piece before Jack goes. In fact, tell Jack I'd like him to join you and me for an impromptu tea party in five minutes. Young George is in bed with the toothache, is he not? Ah, sadly he can't join us then."

ॐ

BUT WHEN THE EXCITED AND HUNGRY SEVEN-YEAR-OLDS DULY turned up, literally dancing with excitement, Fanny had to send them away with a hurried command that Sally organise for Cook to provide a children's tea in the orchard, as Cousin George had just burst into the drawing room not ten seconds after an unaccountably forlorn-looking Mr Patmore.

George was nearly apoplectic with rage. "That...woman...has just taken Devil for a ride, and Jennings has no idea when she'll be back. Lord knows, but she's likely to break the horse's leg and he'll be no good to anyone, just like Carnaby, eh, Rufus." His face was mottled and his hands were fists, as he stalked across the drawing room and noisily set to pouring himself a drink.

"Is Devil not hers to ride?" Fanny asked as she glanced at Mr Patmore, waiting for him to defend his future bride. He seemed to be looking rather longingly towards the cut-glass decanter which her Cousin George was handling with his usual lack of care. "Careful, Cousin George; you're going to chip the stopper," grumbled Fanny, reflecting that it was a relief he wasn't going to be entrusted with delicate Miss Montrose for a wife.

"Yes, Devil is hers to ride when she chooses," Mr Patmore corroborated with a weary sigh as if his mind were on other matters.

"That may be so, but she has given her consent for *me* to race the horse tomorrow." George began to pace as was his wont when he was agitated.

Mr Patmore tapped his fingers on the edge of his seat. "She was anxious to go for a canter when I saw her earlier. The groom fitted Devil with a sidesaddle." He forced a smile at the assembled company. "I'd say a bracing ride is just what the young lady needs after what has occurred, do you not? I hear Mr Perceval has just left. I'm glad. He discomposed her, and that is all. I believe..." He broke off.

My, my but Mr Patmore looked *very* sober, Fanny thought, her own thoughts whirling over Cousin George, his plans with Devil, his anger over Miss Montrose taking him riding. So, Cousin George really was up to no good over that horse race. And Mr Patmore was all in a lather. What could have transpired between himself and Miss Montrose? It sounded like marriage hadn't been discussed at all. Or if it had, there'd not been the outcome he'd desired.

Everyone had descended upon Fanny all at once, so that she'd barely had time to mull over what Jack had said earlier. Now, she asked on sudden impulse, "Mr Patmore, do you have a large wager on tomorrow's race? Antoinette and I are still deciding which way to bet with ten such highly contestable entries."

He remained distracted, staring at the decanter before attending to her with a sudden show of good manners as he rose to lean against the mantelpiece. "Forgive me, Lady Fenton, but yes, I do have a very large wager on the race. More than I usually bet on anything, but your cousin here is damned persuasive, especially when a fellow is in his cups."

"And on which horse did you place your money...how much?"

"A thousand on Devil's Run," muttered Mr Patmore, looking so uncomfortable Fanny wondered with a real pang whether he was as complicit as Cousin George in rigging this race. She'd not have thought it, but by the look of him, feared it was the case.

"And who is riding Devil, Cousin George?"

"Whittlesea, the chap who rides all my horses," replied George.

Antoinette sniggered. "And the chap who wins only half of them. You seem to have very great faith in the fact he'll win tomorrow's Cup for you."

Fanny looked innocently at George over her teacup. "Please don't be so rude as to help yourself to the brandy and not offer your guest."

With ill grace, George brandished the decanter roughly a second time, continually glancing out of the window for a sign of Miss Montrose's safe return, no doubt. Or rather, Devil's.

"So, Mr Patmore, you will remain with us at least until after the race. That's good," said Fanny, trying to conduct the conversation as if it were a normal afternoon tea which it was far from being. Her brain was in quite a muddle as to what she should do about the information she'd gathered from her daughter regarding the race. She'd have loved to have revealed George for the cheat he was, but Mr Patmore's possible complicity altered everything. What if he'd incautiously laid down his money in the hope of making a fortune to enable him to wed Miss Montrose? What if future happiness for Miss Montrose and Mr Patmore hinged on Devil's Run winning the Cup?

She felt sick, and was relieved when a knock on the door broke some of the unease as the parlourmaid entered bearing a silver salver on which rested a cream wafer for Mr Patmore.

Raising his eyebrows, he broke the seal and began to read before taking a few quick strides towards his hostess.

"My apologies, Lady Fenton, Lady Quamby; it appears that some rather urgent business has cropped up and I will have to leave earlier than I'd anticipated."

"Now?" squeaked Antoinette, looking from their guest then through the window as if she might conjure Miss Montrose upon the instant.

He looked conflicted. "I had hoped to remain until the day after tomorrow when I was waiting for... Well, it doesn't matter. This is something I must attend to, immediately."

"What about the race, old chap?" Cousin George looked dark as he downed his third brandy. "That's what it's all about, isn't it?"

"Not in this case," Mr Patmore said, adding more carefully, "Despite having a large sum riding on tomorrow's race, I really should try and get at least a couple of hours on the road before dusk."

"As you wish, Mr Patmore," said Fanny, feeling that this day was fast going down as the most unsatisfactory she had ever spent. All their careful plans, matchmaking, spiriting into their midst lost loves, who then proved not just worthless but destructive, had come to nothing. Was Miss Montrose refusing Mr Patmore because she continued to hold a flame for a man she could never have? Did she still feel unable to let go of her girlish infatuation, despite learning from his own lips that he was again married and forever out of reach? Or was it something else? Something deeper? Something regarding some old sin? "Do not tarry on our account. If you wish to organise...*certain matters* before you go, please feel free to leave now." She meant go and intercept Miss Montrose, but she wasn't at all sure that that was going to result in any great joy. Not judging by the look on Mr Patmore's miserable face, or by the fact that Miss Montrose seemed disinclined to see him again. No doubt Miss Montrose would be the next to march in and say she was off home to inspect the meagre furnishings of her cottage and see what she could sell in order to maintain herself. A cottage was a fine thing if one had an annuity to pay expenses. Which Miss Montrose did not.

"And I must find those children and send that boy on his way," Fanny said on a sigh when Mr Patmore had gone. What *was* she going to do with this new information gleaned about Devil's bogus role in a race in which her cousin and Mr Patmore stood to make a fortune? And Miss Montrose, too. She felt sick.

Jack and Katherine were sitting on a low bough of Katherine's favourite climbing oak, both eating large hunks of cake and laughing uproariously. They stopped when Fanny arrived beneath them.

"Hello, Mama; please don't tell me Jack has to go home. He will come back, won't he? He's not going to be a bootboy *yet*, is he? Why can't he be *my* bootboy? Sally never polishes my boots shiny enough. Not like Jack would. Jack always does what I say."

"Nah, not always, Miss Katherine, and 'sides, I ain't goin' to be a bootboy," Jack said cheerfully. "That nice Miss Montrose said I could be anythin' I wanted. Tomorrow I'm going to be a groom lookin' after the horses durin' the race, and in the evenin' I'm goin' to be a grooms*man* after', 'elping the nice lady to the church for her secret weddin'." He chuckled at the play on words.

Fanny, who was about to tell Jack that Roberts was waiting with the dogcart and that he must hurry off, wondered if her ears were deceiving her.

Wedding? Her heart lurched. So that was why Mr Patmore was behaving so oddly and why Miss Montrose was so distant. They planned to elope?

The lift to her spirits was short-lived. A secret wedding in the local church? Why, the banns hadn't been read. Cousin George had only just cried off, so *those* banns had been read, but the legalities weren't in place for Miss Montrose to wed an alternative bridegroom.

"Can I come to the wedding, too?" Katherine asked, her eyes shining. "There were raspberry ices at Miss Honey's wedding last month."

"Nah, reckon it's a waste of time if yer wantin' raspberry ices, cos there ain't goin' to be anyone there 'cept the nice lady and Mr Bramley and me and the vicar and his housekeeper."

"Mr *Bramley*?" Fanny raised her eyes and stared, open-mouthed at the boy who had added this after finishing the last bit of his cake and was now swinging his feet. "When did Mr Bramley mention this?"

Jack shrugged. "When he told me me duties 'bout Devil winnin'. 'E said if Devil won, then the lady'd won her wager fair and square, which weren't so bad a thing when all was said and done, but e'd 'ave to go to ground a bit, and I'd need to attend to some things to 'elp the lady get to the church by the midnight hour."

"You've got a good memory, Jack," said Katherine admiringly. "Can I have that piece of cake that's in your pocket?"

"No, you cannot!" Her mother spoke sharply. "That's going to the children at the foundling home, and Roberts is waiting with the cart to take Jack back." She continued to stare at the boy who looked so pleasant-natured and contented on his perch. "What time tomorrow did Mr Bramley say he'd fetch you?"

"Well, the race starts in the mornin' so 'e says I better be ready to be fetched from dawn."

"*Please,* can I have another piece of cake?" begged Katherine.

"You cannot!" Her mother repeated at the same time as Jack took a piece from his pocket and handed it over. He grinned at her daughter. "Reckon I were keepin' this for meself, but Kathy—I mean, Miss Katherine—wants it more 'n me and Cook's wrapped up more'n half a cake wot she's keepin' in the kitchen for me to fetch afore I go back." He swung himself down from the tree to stand before Fanny. "So, I'll be off then, m'lady?" He bobbed his head first to Fanny then Katherine.

"Yes, yes, you go," Fanny said faintly, watching him saunter down the hill and wondering what on earth she should do now. But when she saw Mr Patmore striding towards the stables, she realised that only one thing now would answer—the truth.

So, picking up her skirts and hurrying the short distance she intercepted him, coming up behind and surprising him with a hand on his shoulder.

"Mr Patmore, I think there's something you should know." She swallowed, wishing she had a complete picture of what was going on, so that she might hold back on certain facts that could prejudice Mr Patmore's regard for the young lady she saw as she looked over his shoulder was just riding in.

With a sigh, she added, "Several things, in fact."

CHAPTER 16

Eliza dismounted and, at the stable door, felt her heart sink as she watched Mr Patmore walk purposefully towards her.

"Miss Montrose, good afternoon. I hope you enjoyed your ride," he said with careful formality as he offered Eliza his arm. "Shall we walk? I have a few things to say in private as I must leave earlier than I'd intended."

"When?" She realised how much she didn't want him to go, at the same time she realised how much easier it would make her life if he weren't lurking in the background. The possible wedding to Mr Bramley tomorrow night made her feel ill. If Devil didn't win, it may not come to pass, in which case she would she throw herself at Mr Patmore because she'd exhausted all other opportunities?

"This afternoon, in fact. Pressing business demands my immediate attention." Career advancement? She wondered what kind of wife he'd choose when his position in politics or the diplomatic service would demand some unblemished hostess at his side.

Oh, if only Eliza knew if Susana really were in possession of the details of Eliza's reasons for being disowned, so that Eliza could take a chance with the wonderful man gazing at her with such serious consideration. Her cousin was spiteful; she'd be the first to reveal Eliza's shame if Aunt Montrose had told her on her deathbed. But if Susana *didn't* know, perhaps it might be possible to reveal the truth to Mr Patmore.

He may still be prepared to marry her if he could be assured that no one else was in possession of her secret. On the other hand, as a rising politician, he may not consider it worth the risk.

"Will you be sorry to see me go?"

Eliza looked into his eyes and tried to read what was in their depths. How far would he condone her sin? Ought she confess right now?

But, always came the niggling fear that for all that he might love her, he might consider her damned. And Jack damned. Their society wasn't kind to women like herself, she knew to her cost. If her own mother and father had cast her out, and the man who'd brought her so low held the same narrow attitudes, how could she risk revealing her darkest secret to the one man whose opinion mattered above all others?

If she had a fortune, she'd have time on her side, and be buffeted from the vagaries of ill fortune. But she was penniless. All she had was her name. And if it were revealed she was a woman of bad character, the society upon whom she relied for succour would cast her out, just like her parents had.

"Very sorry, Mr Patmore." She dropped her eyes, waiting for him to speak, unwilling to break the silence, for what more could she say?

"I thought you might consider giving me your answer now."

Now?

She stiffened. "I'm afraid I can't, Mr Patmore. I said, tomorrow."

"And is there a reason for that?" He sent her a very level look.

And she met it, thinking, *now I must tell him. Now is my chance.* Then suddenly her mother's face intruded in her mind, twisted with disgust and scorn, her words screaming themselves in her head. "Disgusting trollop!" "Forever damned!" "A smear upon society!"

If her own mother, whom she'd believed had loved her, could say such things, how would the man before her react? His opinion meant everything; he truly believed she was a woman of virtue, the ideal wife for a man looking forward to career advancement.

"I have my reasons, Mr Patmore. The day after tomorrow." She turned to leave, but he put his hand on her wrist, and the touch scorched a pathway to her heart. She closed her eyes, briefly, opening them upon a smile as she met his gaze.

"You shan't see me again, Miss Montrose, as I leave immediately, but I would like to know if I may have hope." His grip tightened, and he seemed to be willing more from her than she could give. When she said nothing, he hung his head, and she felt she would die of misery. "I hold you in the highest regard, Miss Montrose, and I would hope my feelings are returned."

She nodded. "They are, Mr Patmore." She took a deep breath to prepare herself for the inevitable breaking off of contact. "I admire you more than I can say."

His mouth quirked. "Admire me? That's not very hopeful."

"Admiration is more enduring than love, Mr Patmore. Safe travels. I shall write and, as promised, you shall have your answer the day after tomorrow."

⚜

"Ambrose has seen Whittlesea, and we know how it's going to happen, and *everything*!" Antoinette rushed into Fanny's bedchamber, squeaking when she saw Fenton in all his naked glory, reaching for his buckskins.

"Gad's teeth, Antoinette! What are you about?" Fanny thundered, pulling up the counterpane to cover her own nakedness. "Have you never heard of knocking?"

Antoinette stared at her brother-in-law a moment before tearing away her gaze, saying with a grin, "My, you are lucky,

Fanny." Then more urgently, "Ambrose was ever so clever. He pretended to be one of the riders who'll be competing in the Cup, and he ferreted out Whittlesea and said he was passing on a message from Mr Bramley that he'd changed tactics, and instead of Devil's Run waiting in hiding to finish the last of the race, he wanted Devil to *start*."

"But Antoinette, you had no right to tell Ambrose to pass on such a thing! I know we discussed it all, but I gave you no orders to act independently," Fanny cried.

However, Fenton went to sit on the bed and said consideringly, "There's more than just money riding on this race, my darling, and now that we know the truth, it'll get out. No, Ambrose and Antoinette were right. Devil must run an honourable race."

"Devil is a plodder. He'll never win!" Fanny wailed, flopping back onto the mattress. "And Miss Montrose and Mr Patmore both stand to win a fortune if he does. Or lose one if he doesn't. Why, their whole futures may be riding on it."

"Mr Patmore does not want to win *dis*honourably."

Antoinette picked up one of Fanny's stockings and her chemise in order to sit down upon the kist at the end of the bed. "Win what? Miss Montrose, or his wager on Devil?"

"Oh, he wants to win both, of course," replied Fenton, sitting on a chair by the bed to pull on his boots, "but not dishonourably. When a fellow's in love, fortune doesn't count for everything." He stood up, chucked his beloved wife beneath the chin, then swooped for a kiss.

"No," said Fanny, emerging from Fenton's show of love as she struggled up onto the pillows. "Reputation counts for more than fortune. And if I'm correct, Miss Montrose might have neither, which I suppose is why she considers herself lucky that Mr Bramley is going to marry her tonight. Except that I shan't let that happen."

Antoinette sighed. "If Mr Patmore won't marry her, then perhaps we *should* let Mr Bramley marry her. Oh, that's Mary at the door. I hope she has my morning hot chocolate on the same tray."

"Well, I didn't invite you into my boudoir to drink hot chocolate, Antoinette," said Fanny, who had been feeling greatly moved by Miss Montrose's plight, but now was feeling more moved by her husband's bare chest. "Thank you, Mary. And Antoinette, you go and congratulate Ambrose for doing what you told him to do when *I* was deciding on the best course of action." She couldn't help grumbling her displeasure again. "I don't know why you even considered you had the right, for you don't have all the facts. None of us do." Antoinette was the younger sister, and Fanny knew *she* was the clever one.

"You were too much of a lie-a-bed, Fanny, and Ambrose was up early, and he, in fact, only met Whittlesea by chance." Antoinette took her cup and saucer of hot chocolate and went to sit down at Fanny's dressing table, despite her sister's glare. "Anyway, I'd told Ambrose about Cousin George's dastardly tactics, and so Ambrose decided that since he knew Devil didn't have a chance of winning the race if he had to run the full course, he'd place a wager on him *not* winning, so that's why he told Whittlesea what he did. Which was really the only thing to be done since it's sure to get out. Except, of course, Cousin George doesn't know we know, or that Whittlesea has been met by Jack with Devil."

"And all this before I was even awake?" Fanny exclaimed.

"I'm sure you were *awake*, Fanny," said Antoinette with a sly look. "Just not inclined to get out of bed right then. The race is due to start in two hours, and everyone's going to be assembled in three hours at Bell's Bottom to meet the winning horse as it breaks through Jackson's Marsh and then crosses the flat. You'll be there, won't you? Ambrose and Quamby and I certainly will be."

"Pass me my shawl, Fenton," Fanny said imperiously as she swung her legs over the bed and pushed back her tumbled dark locks. "Of course I'm going to be there, but I have a few things to arrange first. I can't believe you let me stay in bed so long."

"I thought I was indulging you, dearest," said Fenton with a wink at Antoinette. "Damned if I do and damned if I don't. Now, I can see you're in commandress mode, so you'll find me in the breakfast parlour once you're ready to issue orders. Come, Antoinette; let's leave your sister to her toilette before a silver-backed hairbrush comes our way."

⚜

GEORGE BRAMLEY WATCHED THE LITHE FIGURE OF MISS Montrose, who was likely to be his bride before the night was out, and congratulated himself on winning a woman who was not only beautiful, not only beholden to him, but utterly desperate to wed him.

He'd never met one of those, and the more he thought about it, the more he liked the power this gave him. He would get a lot of pleasure out of reminding Miss Montrose that without him she was nothing, and that she'd have nothing. Well, she'd continue to have nothing unless she learned that George Bramley's way was the only way. He rubbed his hands and felt his breeches swell with the anticipation of showing her tonight who was master.

Devil's Run was going to make him a fortune, bring him a bride who, it had to be said, was everything a man could want when it came to lush womanhood. She might not be in her first flush of youth, but she had a good few years left in her yet. Besides which, she'd already given him carte blanche to carry on his affairs as he chose. If she thought that meant leaving her alone, she'd be in for a surprise, but it gave George licence to act with impunity and without suffering regular baleful reminders of what he owed her. Well, he owed her nothing since she'd been the one to beg him to marry her.

George was in an expansive mood by the time he settled himself under the canopy erected for the spectators and sipped champagne. It was at the top of a slope by the edge of a beech wood.

He'd dressed with care that morning in a wasp-waisted burgundy coat in the new style, with narrow trousers and a low-crowned beaver to top it off. The owner of the winning horse had a figure to cut. And at midnight when he wed Miss Montrose, *he'd* be owner of the winning horse, and Devil would win him many more races.

He tossed back his drink and marvelled at his good fortune. In markings and build the gelding was the twin to Maggot, the fleet-footed gelding George had happened upon in the stable yard of the *Dusty Crow* during one of his carousing sessions. At first, he'd thought his wits were addled or his eyes deceiving him, and that Devil had followed him all the way from Quamby House. But no, this horse was a dead ringer for Devil.

Parting with a good portion of the night's winnings, George had acquired the horse, which Whittlesea had been stabling for the last two weeks in anticipation of the great race today.

Now all George had to do was patiently enjoy his prime position at the top of the flat, and watch Devil struggle through Jackson's Marsh and across the winning line.

⚜

RELUCTANTLY, ELIZA TRAILED AFTER LADIES QUAMBY AND Fenton who were, as ever, in disagreement over the benefits of one cushioned chair beneath the canopy as the other.

"You know that even the moonlight is likely to turn me as brown as a gypsy and besides, that's far too close to Cousin George," complained Antoinette.

"Then you sit further into the shade, and I shall sit here with an interrupted view of Cousin George's ugly visage so that I might delight in his horror when Devil finishes so far back," said Fanny. "Oh, sorry Miss Montrose; that wasn't very polite of me since Devil, of course, belongs to you, and you must have a great deal riding on him."

Eliza nodded weakly. She did, although not in monetary terms. Devil couldn't possibly win the race, and it was this thought which had increasingly encouraged her as she'd tossed and turned throughout the night.

No, Devil could not, and would not win, and Eliza would therefore not be forced to marry Mr Bramley. Only hours before, she'd feverishly thought this her only option, but clarity had surprisingly surfaced through her sleeplessness.

Brushing back a strand of hair from her forehead, she caught the speculative glance of Mr Bramley, and her stomach heaved. No, she couldn't subject either herself or Jack to a life under the stewardship of Mr Bramley. Better to be a pauper and have Jack in her household as a bootboy, than to be wed to Mr Bramley with the dangerous hope that the Quamby household's fondness for Jack would shore up his future.

"Ah, Fenton, darling, come and sit beside me." Lady Fenton patted the cushion beside her and fleetingly squeezed her husband's hand, which earned her a brief kiss on the cheek before he settled himself with a coupe of champagne.

What Eliza wouldn't give to enjoy such domestic felicity. Lord and Lady Fenton had been married more than eight years, and yet they remained exquisitely in love, despite the occasional tiff that only seemed to bring them closer together.

Eliza might have had that too if she'd been thinking with less fraught emotion. All through the night, she'd been disturbed by images of Mr Patmore's kindness to her, his patent admiration, his desire to facilitate her every wish—and his patience. On so many occasions, she'd prevented him from making the marriage offer he was so obviously keen to make, and when finally he'd gone down on bended knee, she'd told him to wait some more.

And now he'd gone.

She was barely able to attend to the chatter about her as she took another sip of her drink. Mr Patmore was loyal and in love. And she'd only asked him to wait until tomorrow. She sighed. If she had pencil and paper, she'd scribble an answer to him right now and see it was despatched to him.

There was a minor ripple as Lord Quamby arrived, striking in a flamboyant waistcoat of claret and gold, a lace-encrusted flared coat in the old style, and the most extraordinary pair of striped trousers Eliza had ever seen.

He was leaning heavily on his sticks and accompanied by the most handsome young man Eliza had ever seen, but now Lady Quamby jumped up and with arms open wide, gushed, "Darling Quamby, you came after all! I'm so glad. It's going to be the most exciting finish. Only seven contenders still in the race, we've just been told, and Devil just bound to win. I hope you don't mind that you gave him to Eliza."

Eliza blushed hotly. She was unaccustomed to gifts of any kind, and now felt highly visible to the assembled audience of about two dozen from the lowliest serf to the villagers, and now Lord Quamby himself.

"I believe in rewarding great service," the earl said with a benign smile at Eliza. "Your aunt didn't serve you well, my girl, but I hope this horse will as you forge yourself the future you deserve." Grunting, he took a seat between Antoinette and Lord Fenton, saying over the top of the glass he was just handed, "Just sorry it wasn't with that nice young man who's been dangling after you since my good-for-nothing nephew threw you over." He sent a baleful look at Mr Bramley, who had raised his opera glasses to scan the horizon and appeared not to be listening.

Eliza's heart hitched. Studiously, she avoided looking at all in Mr Bramley's direction. No, she wouldn't marry him. She'd made up her mind to do what she should have done long before. She would tell Mr Patmore about Jack. He might not wish to marry her, but he'd keep her secret, and that was all that mattered. She could still find a way to direct his future. She'd not be another of those shamed women, and there were so many of them in society, who wilted into lonely graves through lack of love because, once, they'd taken it when they shouldn't have.

Antoinette patted her husband's hand and said brightly, "Well, maybe Mr Patmore will come galloping into our midst on his white charger and whisk Miss Montrose away."

"A man has his pride, my dear. No, Mr Patmore got his answer, did he not, Miss Montrose?" The earl sent her a compassionate look. "He would have been good to you, I think, but if you can't return his feelings, then fault should not be attributed to either side, naturally."

Eliza cast a panicked look towards Mr Bramley, hoping he was out of earshot.

Lady Fenton asked sharply, "What's this, my Lord?" Then with more confidence, "Of course Mr Patmore isn't going to do anything rash when it's clear Miss Montrose needs more time following the death of her aunt to know her own heart."

The earl raised an effete hand to brush away a fly. "That's not my understanding, my dear, and nor does it signify if Miss Montrose doesn't wish to have him."

"Darling Quamby," said his wife, sounding distressed, "of course, Mr Patmore's coming back. He simply had some urgent business to attend to."

"Well, that wasn't my understanding. When I spoke to the gentleman, he said the summons he'd received was timely, as he didn't have the fortitude required to suffer further rejection when Miss Montrose had made clear through her actions and behaviour that continuing to press his suit was pointless." He leaned across and said in a loud whisper, "I, too, know what it's like to yearn for a decade or more for the bright spark of love you once thought was yours forever, but which is now forever beyond your realms."

Dear God, did everyone still think she pined for Mr Perceval? Is that what Mr Patmore thought? She was about to refute what the earl had said when a cry rang out, and everyone leapt to their feet and shaded their eyes to see two horses—a bay and a black— splashing through the marshes five hundred yards away, neck and neck.

"Dear God, it's Kardashian and Devil!" Lord Fenton cried, turning to his wife in disbelief.

Eliza's mouth dropped open. Had he really run the entire course?

With flaring nostrils, the two horses struggled through the

muddy depths, their riders exercising their whips to the accompaniment of threats and encouragement.

Loud cheering and whistling issued from the assembled crowd, which now numbered around one hundred. They all surged as far forward as they were allowed since the view of the first families of the district must not be compromised.

"Devil's lagging!" Lady Fenton shouted, and Eliza was surprised to hear glee in her tone. It certainly echoed hers. She wanted no reason to go through with her ridiculous wager, but tugging at her heartstrings were Lord Quamby's words. Surely they couldn't be true? Mr Patmore had left because he didn't want to be humiliated by her rejection? He'd truly left? Forsaken her?

But then, all she had to do was write and tell him she accepted. Yes, that's all she had to do.

"Come on, Devil!" There was Mr Bramley's voice, hard-edged and gritty, urging on his beast. Yes, that's what Mr Bramley mistakenly believed—that Devil belonged to him because Eliza was so desperate as to have thrown herself upon him, and he now realised the advantages of having a beholden wife.

"Devil's falling behind!" Lady Quamby's joyful cry echoed Eliza's, but in the next moment, a great groan swept through the crowd. Eliza strained to see what had happened. One of the horses had faltered when it reached the final drag of the swamp. It was struggling to gain purchase on the muddy bank to haul itself up while the other horse—the black one! Devil!—was nimbly picking its way through the mud and reeds to break through. Clearly tired, it was trotting towards the finish line.

"Devil! Kardashian!"

The names were shouted with equal enthusiasm and a rising edge of panicked excitement, as Kardashian finally made it onto the flat, his rider urging him forwards, furiously using his crop. The distance between the two horses was narrowing, but still Devil trotted leisurely towards the crowd behind the finish line while Kardashian, foaming at the mouth and with a gleam in his eye, surged forwards.

"Devil!" shrieked Eliza, cupping her cheeks and feeling the world spin. "Devil!" He couldn't win. He mustn't!

"Kardashian!" exclaimed Lord Quamby beside her, dropping his opera glasses as he turned to her, his face the picture of shock. "By God, I was sure he was going to catch him. Why, I never saw such a relaxed win. And it's your Devil, Miss Montrose. Your horse is the winner of the East Anglia Cup!"

CHAPTER 17

Dazed, Eliza suffered the congratulations around her. Hats and coins were thrown in the air; a bugle rang out; excited children wove through the legs of the adults.

A mud-spattered horseman came to a halt nearby, and leant down to say something in Lord Fenton's ear.

"Good Lord! Fair and square, then?" she heard him say before Lady Quamby started squealing.

"You've won yourself a fortune, Miss Montrose! Now you just have to decide what to do with all that money! Why, to think that Devil actually covered the entire course as all the other horses fell by the wayside. It's a miracle."

"And it's another miracle that the heavens have only just decided to open upon us now. Hurry, ladies." Lord Quamby waved his sticks about as a glowering rain cloud suddenly emptied its contents. While most of the villagers scattered, Eliza and her friends huddled beneath the canopy that had earlier protected them from the sun.

"Eliza had a different wager on this race."

Her skin crawled as George Bramley's voice sounded in her ear, and she thought she might gag as he gripped her by the upper arm and pulled her proprietarily towards him. "She has promised to be my bride if Devil won. It was to be a secret, but now that we're all gathered here, and Miss Montrose is looking surprisingly glum, I thought this an opportune moment to apprise you of the happy news and hopefully bring a smile to my betrothed's beautiful face."

How could she have thought for one moment that there was any future being married to this toad of a man? It made a travesty of her future, and Jack's too. She must publicly refute it, and she would feel safer to do it here, though it would bring Mr Bramley's ire upon her head, since he clearly had decided there were distinct advantages to this marriage.

She opened her mouth to speak, but Lady Fenton said brightly, "If you imagined you could keep any such thing secret from us, Cousin George, you're wrong. We'd all planned to surprise you at the church."

"Did you, indeed?" He looked enquiringly at Miss Montrose. "So, no secrets, eh?"

"Oh, Miss Montrose said nothing," said Lady Fenton. "Young Jack made some mention of certain duties he was required to perform involving Devil, and, later, at the church."

"Also, my clever Ambrose took it upon himself to tell Whittlesea that your wishes had changed, and you now wanted Devil to begin the race." Lady Quamby smiled sweetly. And, of course, end it too. So, no secrets, Cousin George. And I'm surprised you imagined you could pull one over us."

His expression had momentarily darkened, noticed Eliza, who felt a jolt of shock at what the ladies were insinuating—Mr Bramley really had intended to rig the horse race, though of course she'd had her own doubts. She supposed they were airing the information publicly so she knew what a blackguard she'd pledged herself to, but they didn't need this as evidence to shore up her newfound determination to get herself as far away from Mr Bramley as she could.

"You ladies are too clever by half, aren't you?" said Mr Bramley with a sneer. "Well, I hope Miss Montrose knows that a wager is a wager. She lost the first one, but won the second, and that means she and I shall be husband and wife before the morning." He brought her hand up and kissed the knuckles. "Funny, but I thought you truly *had* developed a *tendre* for my friend, Rufus. He certainly was dangling after you. It was almost comical to watch. He's gone now, though, and your lover's tiff ain't likely to be resolved. He left a note to say any correspondence was to be forwarded to him at a Paris address, when I told him of our wager."

"You told him?" Eliza gasped.

Mr Bramley smiled. "Indeed, I did. I told him everything, and when he realised how little he truly meant to you, if you were prepared to marry me on the back of a horse, so to speak— though no doubt you thought you had time on your side to win him back—he simply rode off into the sunset. Now," he inclined his head and indicated the house. "Shall we bring forward the wedding a few hours? The legalities have all been attended to. Of course, the vicar will want a bit of time to enjoy his winnings, though I'm sure he'll be relieved not to have to stay up until midnight now we all realise how badly secrets are kept around here."

Stricken, Eliza looked at the faces arrayed about her. Ladies Quamby and Fenton seemed uncertain as to how to respond, which was rather extraordinary. Lord Quamby's bristling brows were knitted together over his small black eyes, and Lord Fenton looked quite doleful. Only young Katherine danced about, squealing, as she played with the new puppy, Minnie, she'd been given.

"Mama, when can I take Minnie to show Jack?"

Jack. That's what this had all been about. Eliza's shoulders slumped. What could she do? She *had* to cry off. Even if she didn't have a penny to her name.

"It might be a while before you see Jack," Lady Fenton said distractedly before turning back to Eliza. "So, congratulations really are in order. You really *do* intend marrying my cousin."

"What did Katherine mean?" Eliza ignored her. "About Jack?"

Her mouth felt dry, and she wanted to shake an answer out of someone as Lady Quamby interrupted.

"But of course we're so delighted you're going to be our cousin-in-law, Miss Montrose," she said.

"Where has Jack gone?" She didn't care if she sounded as panic-stricken as she felt.

"Oh, someone employed him in their household up north," Lady Fenton said dismissively. "Katherine's terribly upset—"

"And so am I," said Antoinette, "for he really was marvellous with Young George but, as Quamby said, it was unfair to give him ideas above his station so better to make the break earlier before the children got too attached."

"Where? Whose household? I...I made a promise to him. A little thing, but I'll want an address to send it." She didn't care that she was gabbling, her words sounding odd and out of place given the nature of the discussion.

"I told Billingsly to take down the details," said Lady Fenton, waving a hand vaguely, before attending to the bow in her daughter's hair. "Katherine made me promise we'd send him a token at Christmas."

Eliza tried to respond accordingly. She suffered Mr Bramley's hand on her arm as he led her to the house, now that the rain had eased. It wasn't the right time, in front of everyone, to cry off.

But when *was* the right time?

"I need time to change and rest," she said as they entered the house and stood for a moment in the hallway.

"Of course, my dear." Mr Bramley kissed her knuckles, then released her with a bow before striding away in the direction of the stables.

"Miss Montrose..." It was Ladies Fenton and Quamby advancing towards her, looking concerned, their husbands hovering in the background.

A loud knock on the front door was immediately attended to by Billingsly. He pulled it open to admit a voluble party of three ladies and one gentleman who surged over the threshold, saying gleefully, "We've come to celebrate this auspicious event. To think that Lord Quamby's own horse has won the coveted East Anglia Cup!"

Eliza remained where she was as she watched the gathering proceed towards the drawing room, drawing in its wake Ladies Quamby and Fenton.

She'd never felt more alone or afraid.

"Billingsly." She turned to the butler who was just closing the door. Her heart was thundering and she felt light-headed. "I believe you have an address I want."

CHAPTER 18

Eliza might be uncertain about her future, but she knew she couldn't marry Mr Bramley, just as she couldn't marry Mr Patmore.

She really didn't have much luck with the men in her life.

Since the household was still celebrating victory in the drawing room, she turned towards the stairs to her bedchamber but upon the first stair, decided that nothing was more calculated to calm her confusion and disordered spirits than to rest her cheek against Devil's flank and breathe in his wonderful horsey smell. This had been the panacea for her childhood angst, and she'd never needed soothing more than now.

When she was certain Mr Bramley was nowhere in sight, she ventured into the lofty stables.

Caleb, the junior groom, had finished rubbing him down and otherwise tending to him after his stupendous efforts this afternoon, and now Devil was indulging himself with a big bowl of oats.

"He's a good horse, isn't he, Caleb?" Eliza said, needing to talk to someone who wasn't part of the close set at Quamby House. She felt alien in their midst. Penniless. Childless. And soon she'd cause ructions with her refusal to marry Mr Bramley. Lord, but she wasn't looking forward to that altercation. The longer she could stay here in the safety of the stables, the better.

"Aye, he is that." The lad ambled over. He was a sweet-faced boy of about fifteen, and Eliza could see he loved the animals he looked after. "You own a champion horse, miss. You're very lucky."

Eliza didn't feel very lucky. She felt very alone. But then, she reminded herself that she had Devil. And she owned a house, though she wasn't sure how she'd maintain it and herself with no annuity. And she had an address burning itself into the skin beneath her bodice where she'd tucked it after Billingsly had written it out on a piece of notepaper for her.

Eliza closed her eyes as she crouched down to stroke Devil's muzzle. "I'm sure Mr Bramley's very pleased with his performance too," she muttered. Oh, but she couldn't bear that man. She'd have to return to the house soon, and find him so she could tell him to inform the vicar his services would no longer be required.

"You'd think so, miss, but he were shouting at Whittlesea the rider, rather than congratulatin' him." Caleb picked up a rake and got back to work.

"Why would he do that?" Then, when the boy hesitated, she added, wheedlingly, "I promise not to say anything to Mr Bramley. He's no friend of mine."

Caleb blinked at this then said obligingly, "He said Whittlesea must take orders only from him not..." he struggled to remember the word, before saying with evident pride, "...*emissaries* of his sisters-in-law, and that he was supposed to meet that boy, Jack, halfway through the course." Caleb dropped his eyes for he'd have been aware it smacked of information of an incriminating nature with regard to the race just run.

Eliza pounced on the only part that was of interest to her. "The boy Jack?" Her senses were on high alert now. "What was his role?"

Caleb shrugged. "Dunno, miss."

"Do you know where he is?"

Caleb shrugged again. "No idea, miss."

Well, it didn't matter. Eliza had the address where he'd be

working, and as soon as Ladies Quamby and Fenton could organise it, she'd make her way there. She was all but certain they'd do whatever necessary to facilitate her departure from Quamby House before she fell into the clutches of Mr Bramley. Or rather, before she had to marry him.

"Ah, Eliza, there you are! Don't you think it's time you readied yourself?" Mr Bramley strode into the stables. It didn't escape Eliza's notice that Caleb scuttled into the far recesses of the building.

Eliza rose. It was time to do what she had to. "Mr Bramley..." She clenched her hands into fists and faced him, squarely. "I've changed my mind."

Even in the shadows, she could see the deep flush that stole over his face. His lips twitched. "Changed your mind?" His tone was low and dangerous.

Eliza took a step backwards. "That's right, Mr Bramley. I thank you for your very kind offer, but just as you saw fit to throw me over a few days ago, and to inform me of the fact by letter, I've chosen to do the same thing, only face to face."

Menacingly, he towered over her and gripped her elbow. "You made a wager, Miss Montrose, and marriage to me was the price."

Eliza tried to see past his bulk for a sign of Caleb, but the boy appeared to have deserted the stables. Mr Bramley had backed her into the corner of Devil's stall, and now he was pushing his face into hers. "A wager is a wager, Miss Montrose, and the vicar will be here in an hour. I really don't see what alternatives you have."

"I have free will," Eliza muttered. "Mr Bramley, you're hurting me." His fingers were digging harder into her arm, and his breath was hot and foetid in her face. She turned her own away.

"You have that much of an aversion to me, my dear?" In that moment, he must have seen the depths of her utter dislike, which triggered something deep and dark within him. Without preamble, he curled one hand about her neck, cupped her chin with the other, and forced her face to meet his kiss—hard, loveless, proprietorial.

Eliza struggled with all her might and, obviously realising the inappropriateness of his behaviour, Mr Bramley released her and stepped backwards.

"My apologies, Miss Montrose; I was overcome by the intensity of my emotions."

Eliza ran the back of her hand across her mouth as she glared at him.

He stuck his chin in the air. "You are a very desirable woman, and I am looking forward to offering all the rewards we discussed that you will enjoy as my wife, not least the shelter of Quamby House, a very great estate, you will agree." He drew a wide arc through the air with his arm. "You will enjoy every comfort here; my cousins-in-law are delighted to welcome you and offer their unprejudiced friendship, and you will be saved from having to eke out a meagre existence in a small cottage in the country with, I believe, no annuity to sustain yourself." He cleared his voice and turned, adding over his shoulder, "Think on all these advantages as you prepare yourself, Miss Montrose. The vicar will be here in precisely one hour, and Ladies Fenton and Quamby are eager to help you prepare."

He strode away, and Eliza sank down onto a pile of straw, put her hands over her face and wept. Devil seemed to sense her distress, for he ceased his dinner and brought his head round to nuzzle Eliza.

"Darling horse, you've worked so hard today, you deserve a good long rest, but..." She stood up with renewed determination, wiping her running nose and eyes with the back of her hand. "I want you to do one more thing for me. Caleb!"

The lad answered her summons almost immediately, but he couldn't meet her eyes. He obviously had witnessed the scene between Eliza and Mr Bramley. "Caleb, will you please saddle Devil."

He looked stricken. "If I put on a sidesaddle, ma'am, Mr Bramley will know I had a hand in wot he'll be most put out about, since it's too heavy for you to put on alone. Please, miss, don't ask me to do that."

Eliza's chest rose with suppressed outrage. She put her hand to her bosom and felt the paper with Jack's address. North, somewhere. A small village she'd never heard of. But that's where she was headed.

Now.

"Then I have one much smaller request. Please give me a leg-up."

He looked scandalised as he took in her attire, as well he might. "That's right. You will be the only one to see me; I promise."

Reluctantly, he interlaced his fingers, and she stepped into the manmade brace as he tossed her high, averting his eyes as she flung her far leg over the horse's back. For the first time all day, Eliza smiled. She felt at home. Safe.

Leaning down, she said, "And if Mr Bramley asks if you have any inkling of where I might have gone, be sure to tell him you heard me mention my desire to return home—taking the westward road. Will you do that, Caleb?"

He nodded, and Eliza flicked the reins. "I'm sorry I don't have something to give you, Caleb. Devil is all I have in the world. Goodbye."

CHAPTER 19

"Where will the lad sleep, Mr Patmore?" Rufus's housekeeper, Mrs Dorley, smiled between Jack and her master. "The attic, or the stables?"

Rufus hesitated. He'd just brought the boy to his home, travelling in the same equipage, which must have struck Mrs Dorley as odd, but her sunny nature overrode any reservations or criticisms she might have had. She continued to smile, patient as always, while Rufus considered the question.

The boy *might* belong to Miss Montrose. He still hadn't quite decided what he felt about that, but here he was, having collected him at Fox's Dell, the halfway point of the race, at Lady Fenton's request.

Rufus had been within yards of asking Miss Montrose for her decision, when Lady Fenton had rushed over to tell him about her wild surmising over Miss Montrose's preoccupation with marrying her cousin-in-law, and about the similarities that had struck her when she'd looked from the boy to Mr Perceval.

"It makes no sense at all that Miss Montrose would turn down a good man like you, Mr Patmore, and choose to wed Cousin George!" she'd cried just before he'd left, declining to stay for the race. "Yes! I've had it on good authority that a secret wedding is planned between Miss Montrose and Mr Bramley if Devil's Run wins the East Anglia Cup."

Rufus hadn't known what to say. Miss Montrose was putting him off because she was hedging her bets on a horse race? If Devil didn't come through, then she'd be writing to accept Mr Patmore?

But worse was the reason, so Lady Fenton surmised—a child? Miss Patmore wanted to remain with Bramley because it meant she'd be near a child she'd borne out of wedlock years before? He tried to fathom it and couldn't. Though Lady Fenton might *now* be a charming woman of poise and intelligence, she and her sister were renowned for their wildness. *This* all smacked of wildness. He'd felt bewildered as she'd pressed her point in her usual forthright manner. "Mr Patmore, the only way to determine if I'm right or not is for you to take the boy with you. Yes, you must pick him up at Fox's Dell and convey him with you to your home."

When he'd started to object, she'd put up her hand in that imperious way she sometimes had—and which she'd used often to good effect on her besotted husband if she was intent on having her way—and said, "I shall not tell Miss Montrose you've taken him. No, only that he has been employed at a comfortable manor house just out of the village of Chisley, two hours' ride away. No names, and certainly not yours, but the address, of course. Ha! That will flush her out! Tomorrow, after Devil has lost his race, and before she can make a new wager with Mr Bramley, whom she obviously believes is how she can remain close to the child, I shall make my carriage available to her the following morning and when she steps out at your home, Beechworth Manor, she'll be astonished to find that *you* are the man who has taken Jack." She'd smiled sweetly, given a little shrug of her shoulders, and added, "Then it's up to you to decide what happens after that."

Rufus had just stood there, trying to take in everything Lady Fenton was saying, surmising, and highly conscious that Miss Montrose was at that moment returning from her ride—because he could see the groom running to greet her—and that he would face her in a very few minutes.

"I know it's a lot for you to digest, Mr Patmore." Lady Fenton had patted his hand with condescending solicitude. "Just, *please*, take Jack home with you. It's the only way to determine if *he* is the reason Miss Montrose wishes to marry Mr Bramley. If he travels in your carriage, it'll also give you time to learn his character and come to terms with what you really feel about the young lady."

She'd only just left when Bramley had sidled up to him to inform him of his impending marriage. Rufus was sure he'd only done that because he'd become jealously aware of the tension between Miss Montrose and Rufus.

Eight hours after the race, Rufus still had no idea how he really felt about the young lady, though he'd been surprisingly engaged by the lad's easy chatter as they'd bowled along country lanes lined with hedgerows, and through woods and over roads of varying condition until they'd reached his home, a charming, four-square manor house atop a hill just outside the town of Chisley.

"The attic or the stables?" he now repeated, wondering what on earth he should do. If the boy were in fact the son of Miss Montrose and Mr Perceval, should he not stay in the house?

"I get a choice? Oh, the stables, please!" the boy begged. "I ain't never slept on warm hay wiv horses for company. I only ever shared a bed with two other boys, and that ain't always the best." Rufus had noticed that the boy's criticisms were generally muted. He'd liked that as they'd talked. For a lad who'd grown up in a foundling home, he was sure there was a great deal to complain about, but Jack seemed to have an ever-optimistic outlook.

Lord, what was he to do about him?

And Miss Montrose? If she should arrive in front of his front door in Lady Fenton's carriage the next afternoon and step out, completely unaware that she'd be seeing Rufus, what would Rufus do? How did he *really* feel?

Of course, Lady Fenton assumed that Rufus was in love with her. She was expecting the happy ending.

But that was too simplistic when it implied so much that was new and not in character with the Miss Montrose he thought he knew. He loved Miss Montrose, the sweet, pure, self-contained young woman who'd been left penniless, and whom he'd wanted to rescue and give the life she deserved and be rewarded with her devotion.

But she'd lied to him, or at least been evasive with the truth, *and* she'd been willing to hedge her bets; promising him an answer, when unbeknownst to Rufus, everything hinged on whether she'd exhausted all other avenues and George Bramley was the only means of delivering to her what she really wanted—access to her child.

Which meant she wasn't really in love with Rufus. She couldn't be if she were capable of such duplicity.

For all the long hours journeyed here, the same interminable questions had gone through his mind.

Miss Montrose wanted security and, perhaps, she wanted her son—if Lady Fenton was right in that wild hunch.

But did she want Rufus? Was she even a *little* bit in love with him since he seemed to be her last consideration? He felt hurt and aggrieved; it had to be admitted. He'd need at least a night to sleep on it, and decide in the morning whether or not he could receive Miss Montrose as she'd no doubt wish to be received.

"The stables it is then, Jack," he said, indicating the general direction with a sweep of his arm. "Mrs Dorley will take you to meet my head groom, Wickens."

The boy nodded, then looked up at him with that impish smile. "It ain't half been an adventure, Mr Patmore, and I'm right grateful you took me wiv you in yer coach an' all." He hesitated. "An' I do love 'orses, even tired, old ones wot jest need a bit of kindness like the ones at the 'ome."

"Good...that's good, Jack." Rufus found it hard to concentrate. Once he'd despatched the boy, he was aware of Mr Dorley, his butler, hovering nearby with a silver salver.

"This was delivered while you were gone, sir."

Rufus took the thick package and sat down in his favourite wing-back chair near the window with a well-deserved brandy.

It had been a fraught few hours, but there was relief in receiving the information he'd sought a few days before. A message had come to him at Quamby House that it had arrived, and he'd used the excuse to leave more abruptly than he'd intended after Miss Montrose had been so hesitant in giving him an answer to his proposal.

He broke the seal, unfolded the letter written as a preface to the information contained within, and experienced a very real jolt of excitement.

So his hunch had been correct. It didn't give him the evidence he sought, but the inference was there. And he'd have a definitive answer within days.

Curious, he put down the single sheet of paper and raised the first of several letters to the light.

⚬❈⚬

THE DARKNESS WAS CLOSING IN, AND ELIZA HAD COVERED MORE than half the distance, according to the farm lad she stopped to ask along the way. His eyes had widened to see her, dressed as she was, and riding astride. Eliza's only fear was that news of such a sight would travel fast to Quamby House, though if Caleb had done as she'd asked and sent everyone in the wrong direction, then she had a few hours' lead.

Dressed only in a simple striped silk round gown, she wished she had something to ward off the cold. The day had been balmy with not even the need for a spencer as they'd sheltered from the sun in anticipation of the race finish. When the rain had come, Eliza had been in such an emotional state she'd given no thought to clothing.

Devil was tired too, now. She felt it in his movements. The moon was sufficient to see the road, but he plodded slowly while Eliza lay along his back, her face buried in his mane. She dreamed of Jack, and she thought wistfully of Mr Patmore, by turns.

So much had happened since she'd come to Quamby House less than a fortnight before and gazed upon the face of her son. She may have lost both, but at least she had seized her last opportunity.

They passed through a deserted village, and when they reached an expanse of cultivated paddocks, it began to rain, increasing in intensity. Eliza was wet through when she took shelter in a small wood. She soon decided there was little point in shivering beneath a large elm when she was already drenched, so she urged Devil into a canter. Only two more hours if they continued at this pace.

But the weather worsened; the road turned from a hard rutted surface into a quagmire and Devil, tired from his long race, began to seriously tire.

Fortuitously, Eliza spied a barn which proved empty but for a number of hay bales, which provided her with warmth and shelter until a large rat woke her several hours later. Screaming, she scrambled onto Devil's back to resume her journey. Surely just another hour. That's all she'd have to endure, and then she'd be at the residence that harboured Jack.

She wasn't sure what the owner would say. She'd have to gauge the nature of the occupants. They'd look askance at her, but she didn't care. She had nothing. Only Jack. Only Devil. What did it matter how they looked at her? All she wanted was to take her boy back to the cottage she'd inherited, and the rest of the world could be damned. She'd grow old as the reclusive and shunned spinster whom the fabulously wealthy Annabelle Montrose had passed over for good reason.

The rain continued as they went slowly through the village of Graymere. Eliza didn't know how she could bear more of the cold, but had no idea how she could change her circumstances. It was perhaps two o' clock in the morning; the world was asleep, and Eliza could hardly beg shelter, now.

From the northern side of the village, the gradient became

quite steep, and the running rivulets had scored deeply into the mud. Devil picked his way carefully through the stony earth, but several times he slid. Each time Eliza closed her eyes, clung to his mane, and shifted position. She ached, but she had to place all her trust in the horse.

At the bottom, she was ready to sigh with relief and give herself up to the next part of the journey. Her destination was only a short ride up a steep hill from the next village to a small but imposing manor house at the end of a tree-lined drive.

She'd be able to see it from the village green in the moonlight, she'd been told.

But on the flat, when the worst should have been behind her, an owl flapped its alarm in a flurry of black feathers, and Devil's easy demeanour deserted him. With a loud whinny he took off, and Eliza had to cling with all her strength to his wet and matted mane as the earth sped beneath her.

She shrieked, trying to bring him under control with her voice, but he was past heeding reason. The horse was tired, and his senses addled. Eliza was tired, but now fear fizzed through her veins. Death was just beneath her, for if she fell, she'd be cut to pieces by his hooves, or trampled.

On he galloped, careening in a wild zigzag pattern. Eliza felt her grip weaken as she was jolted like a rag doll.

"Devil!" she tried once more, and the horse stopped abruptly, sending her through the air. She landed on stony ground, winded, as her head hit the earth. For a long time, she couldn't move, but Devil remained loyally nearby, waiting it seemed until she had the energy to drag herself to her feet. It was difficult to inspect herself in the poor light, but she knew she was bleeding when she wiped a hand across the back of her face and tasted metal.

"There's the village, Devil. Just up the hill; it's all we have to manage," she muttered, but her whole body ached, her head pounded, and she shivered uncontrollably.

"Just along the drive," she whispered, barely clinging on now as Devil negotiated the last stretch of driveway and somehow made a beeline for the stable where he sensed company and smelled the welcome scent of hay.

And as he whinnied in relief at the shelter, and brought his head down to take in a mouthful of hay, Eliza slid gracefully off his back and landed in the soft, welcome warmth of her own bed of straw.

⚜

JACK HAD NEVER SLEPT SO WELL. HE WAS USED TO WRIGGLING, kicking boys—three of them to a bed in the foundling home—but here he could stretch out on what felt like a cloud, but really was a thick layer of hay in the loft. He could look down on the horses in their stalls below and imagine that this is where he'd always stay— in this house with these nice people, tending their horses.

The whicker of an intruding animal made him sit upright. Jack wasn't used to sleeping alone, and while the warmth of the hay was comforting, he was also a little afraid once the head groom had disappeared to his quarters and closed the door, leaving Jack to make himself up a bed in the seemingly cavernous stable, on a plat-form above the stalls.

It had been moonlit earlier, but dark thunderclouds had oblit-erated all the light. The sound of rain made it difficult to hear, also, but Jack was sure that a horse had just found sanctuary in the stable. However, when he put his head over the edge of his bed in the loft and tried to adjust his vision to the gloom, he could see nothing.

Then he heard a strange muttering which nearly scared the daylights out of him until he realised it came from a woman.

A lady, he discovered, when he was brave enough to climb down the ladder to investigate.

A fine lady wearing a striped dress with lace he knew was expensive though she was dirty and bedraggled, with a nasty cut across her forehead.

RUFUS WAS IN THE DEPTHS OF SLUMBER WHEN HE WAS WOKEN BY an insistent knocking at his bedchamber door, then heard his housekeeper's muffled voice.

"Come!" he called to this highly irregular intrusion, realising the cause must be serious and reaching for his banyan as Mrs Dorley entered bearing aloft a candle.

"Young Jack says there's a fine lady in the stables, and she appears to be injured. I wouldn't have disturbed you however the boy is most insistent he wasn't having nightmares. I think you should come, Mr Patmore, just in case there's something in what he says."

Good Lord, was this what he feared?

"Of course, Mrs Dorley. I'm ready." He'd pulled on his boots, anticipating the mud, and now wrapped his banyan more closely around him. "Perhaps you should prepare a room. As you say, there might be something in what the boy says, strange though it sounds."

Unfortunately, Rufus was quite prepared to discover Jack was telling the truth, though he wasn't sure he was ready to receive Miss Montrose in such a manner. Her arrival—if indeed it was her—would confirm the worst, which wasn't only that she was hiding a terrible sin, but that she'd failed to be forthcoming with him.

Today was the day she'd promised she'd notify him by letter of her answer to his marriage proposal. Now she was here but under far different circumstances to those under which he'd proposed to her. She surely couldn't expect to fall into his arms in the belief his offer still stood?

For a moment he could not bring himself to rise. Despite the cheerful chatter of Jack in his carriage the previous day, he'd spent many hours brooding. Miss Montrose had treated him poorly.

But when he saw the sodden, mud-spattered young woman lying on a bed of straw, a bloody gash across her forehead, the assault on his senses was a confusing mix.

Foremost was fear that she was wounded beyond what he could see. He knelt at her side and took her hand. "Miss Montrose," he whispered, putting his head close to her ear. Then again, when she made no response, "Miss Montrose, can you hear me?"

He stood up, his heart beating painfully in his chest as he stared down at her, though he counselled himself that the heart-pounding was from natural fear for her physical condition rather than anything else. What desperation must have compelled her to travel all the way here, alone, and on horseback with no saddle? She'd obviously fallen, and she'd had nothing warmer than the thin dress she was wearing. Had she fled Quamby House? Had George Bramley been the cause of this?

The embers of a slow-burning anger were stoked at the thought. George Bramley had a hold over this innocent young woman. All right, she wasn't so innocent. Perhaps he was black-mailing her—

"Jack...Jack, are you there, Jack?"

She was rambling now, and the eyes in the little boy's head understandably grew large as saucers as he looked at Rufus. "Why's she callin' *me*?" he asked.

Rufus deflected the question. "Did *you* cover her with dry straw?" Then, in response to the boy's nod, "Good thinking. But now, we must get her to the house. Miss Montrose, can you hear me? I'm going to lift you up, and carry you. Jack, you hold the lantern and follow me."

She made no indication she was aware of her surroundings as she tossed and turned on her bed of straw. By the soft light, he could see the sheen of moisture on her forehead, and when he touched her, she was ice cold. It sent a chill of fear through him, even though he was trying hard not to feel anything. Miss Montrose was only here because of the boy. She was only inter-ested in a man if he were the means to her being reunited with her child. Rufus meant nothing to her, and if she tried to pretend otherwise, he'd not believe her.

216

He put his arms around her, and she twined her own round his neck and rested her head against his chest with a soft sigh.

۞

WHEN HE GOT HER TO THE CHEERFUL, NORTH-FACING bedchamber Mrs Dorley had had made up for her, his housekeeper drew back the covers and Rufus gently laid her down.

"She's going to develop a fever, sir, unless I get her out of her wet things. You wait here while I find a nightrail belonging to one of your sisters." Rufus's three sisters, now married, were often visitors, and it was quite likely a garment like that may be lying around. He tried not to imagine gazing upon Eliza wearing a transparent shift.

No! He was a gentleman, not a disappointed suitor seeking to alleviate his frustrated desires through voyeurism. Besides, Mrs Dorley would ensure the proprieties were attended to. He couldn't imagine what she must be thinking of his nocturnal visitor right now, but as usual, she was the epitome of discretion.

She certainly made this clear as she put her hands on her hips and faced him from across the bed once Miss Montrose had been tended to. "Now, you get yourself some rest, Mr Patmore. I'll send a lad to fetch the doctor at dawn, but there's no point in you missing out on some much-needed sleep when there's nothing more you can do here."

He didn't want to tear his eyes from the sleeping girl's face. She looked so very vulnerable and alone; as if she existed in a sphere separate from the rest of the world. He'd thought her distance was a disdain for him and others, but those moments when she'd displayed desire revealed a raw earthiness that was disconcerting. It perhaps explained Jack's existence but still, he couldn't make her out.

Reluctantly, he did as his housekeeper all but directed, but he couldn't sleep when he returned to his own quarters.

Miss Montrose had behaved with cavalier disregard for her

reputation and the proprieties when she'd jumped astride Devil's Run and made her way here. Lady Fenton had said she'd send her in her carriage, but the girl must have been desperate.

Yes, Miss Montrose might seem self-contained, but clearly, when her passions were aroused, she let nothing stand in her way.

CHAPTER 20

Eliza felt the warmth and softness of a strange but welcoming bed long before she opened her eyes.

She was too afraid to find herself staring into the eyes of Mr Bramley, and to learn that she had in fact married him when she'd been insensible, and that now she was beneath the covers beside her bridegroom.

When she sensed the presence of someone in the room, she was even more determined to delay the inevitable and for a long time she lay curled up in a ball, too miserable and terrified to move, her mind racing over what might have happened to her.

Finally, a chair scraped on the wooden floor, and she whispered, "Mr Bramley?"

"No, Miss Montrose. It is I—"

"Mr Patmore!" she exclaimed, sitting up so suddenly that the covers fell away from her chest, revealing far too much exposed bosom in a fine cambric nightgown that was too big for her.

"How—? What are you doing here?"

"This is my house."

He was sitting in a relaxed fashion, one leg crossed over the other, on a chair placed at right angles to the bed. Behind him, the window looked onto a lovely garden in riotous colour. Eliza didn't think she'd ever seen a room as charming. On the right wall was a lineup of charming watercolours of various flowers.

He must have registered her admiration for he said, "My sister, Verena, painted those. As you can see, she loves flowers. This was her room before she was married."

"And this is *your* house?"

He nodded. "And Jack is with the horses. He alerted us of your arrival in the middle of the night, in case you don't recall."

Eliza tried to gauge his feelings from his expression. "Jack. So you know." A tremendous shame overcame her. "You must think—"

He cut her off, his tone level. "It doesn't signify what I think, Miss Montrose. You came here to find your son. Jack is your son, I gather. During your journey, you fell from your horse. We've tended to the cut above your eye. The main thing is that you're well and can soon be on your way."

If he had been a casual acquaintance, his words would have sounded just the right reassuring note. The smile he gave her was one he might have given any female visitor or friend.

She covered her face with her hands and tried not to cry. He didn't want her. She couldn't believe how devastated she was, when for so long she'd been pushing him away. Now she realised the true depth of her feelings. "I'm not going to marry Mr Bramley," she whispered, not looking at him.

He rose. "I gathered not. He was, after all, your conduit for having access to the boy. Not that you mentioned that to anyone, of course. Careful deduction on the part of the Lady Fenton, and then my falling in line with her scheme, established that."

"You're leaving, now?" Eliza couldn't bear it.

"You need to rest, Miss Montrose. I was merely here to ensure that you took your medicine and were reassured as to how matters stood."

She stared at him, not knowing what to say until the words came out in a small voice, "How *do* they stand?"

"Jack is here, and you will come to no harm while you are under my roof."

And you no longer wish to marry me, Eliza thought, sliding beneath the bedclothes and turning her face to the ceiling.

⚜

RUFUS HAD TO TAKE THREE STEADYING BREATHS ONCE HE WAS outside her bedchamber door before he could muster the internal resources to attend the various business items that required his attention.

"Don't forget the young lady's correspondence," Mrs Dorley reminded him. He'd given her a vague story about how Miss Montrose had come to land in his stables. He was sure she didn't believe him, but it didn't matter.

"Of course not. I'll deliver them this afternoon after she's had time to rest."

He didn't want to go back, and yet it was an agony to resist. Let her stew behind those doors, and repent of having so used him so ill. She'd allowed him to fall in love with her; allowed him to believe she'd have him. Yet all she could direct her thoughts towards was the boy.

He sent Jack to visit with a bunch of flowers he picked from the gardens. Walking slowly past the door, he heard their chatter within. Or at least, the boy's chatter. But he didn't intrude.

Much later in the afternoon, he steeled himself to pay another visit, taking the letters addressed to Miss Montrose that had been sent in the envelope together with the response to his own enquiry.

She was slightly feverish, he was concerned to note, and she begged him to close the curtains as the light was hurting her eyes. Rufus thought he should send for the doctor, but she said she didn't need one. Then she asked him to read what her aunt had penned to her. "My eyes are sore, Mr Patmore. Like my heart."

She seemed a little breathless and, concerned, he put his hand to her forehead. "You're hot, Miss Montrose. Here, drink some of this."

When she'd taken a little of the soothing medicine Mrs Dorley had prepared for her, he tore open the seal, surprised to see that the date was seven years prior.

He started to read.

Dear Eliza, (her aunt had written)

I enclose a letter from Mr Perceval, but your dear mama has requested you are to have no contact with the gentleman. I am sure you would not wish to, either, knowing he was responsible for the murder— yes, murder! — of your brother, and indirectly, for the death of your father. However, I cannot bring myself to burn correspondence intended for another. I shall therefore withhold it until you are old enough, or wise enough, to hear from the man who has ruined you."

Yours,

Aunt Annabelle Montrose.

Mr Patmore was conscious as she surely must be by the injustice of withholding anything that had been addressed to her, but he made no comment.

"Please read Orlando's letter, if you would, Mr Patmore."

Rufus clutched the envelope in his hand as he hesitated. This was from the man to whom Miss Montrose had foolishly lost her heart. The father of her child. She'd paid the price, but he couldn't help but feel deeply uncomfortable about reading something that would only highlight the fact that Miss Montrose had been morally derelict in allowing herself such weakness with this man. "Are you certain?"

She nodded. "I cannot see to read. And it's all so long ago, now." She ran a weary hand across her brow.

Rufus unfolded the brittle parchment. Immediately, he could

gauge the frenzied emotional state of its writer from the scrawl and ink spots.

"My most beloved Eliza, (began Mr Perceval)

Forgive me, for it was wrong of me to promise you marriage when I was in no position to do so. I know I have appeared to you as an honest suitor. Indeed, it has been a great injustice that my wife has been confined these last five years to a lunatic asylum, leaving me free to love yet forbidden to follow through in any honourable sense.

Yes, I should be condemned for leading you to believe that all was in order for a marriage before God, but I thought I had the means to give you the happiness you deserve.

Now, I have committed a crime which prevents me from returning to England, and which must surely send your feelings for me from passionate love to revolt.

I do not want to leave you—not ever—but you are young and defenceless, and I, who am so much older and should have known better, have taken advantage of your trusting innocence.

Please, Eliza, if there have been consequences from the love we've shared—the sins I've forced you to commit in order to prove the depth of your feelings for me—please contact me at this address, and I will do whatever I can to atone.

I would run away with you tomorrow if you would have me—"

"Stop!" With a cry of pure agony, Miss Montrose threw up one hand.

Her face was pale and strained. With great effort, she said, "And the other letter. Read that now— provided it is *not* from Orlando."

Rufus was relieved it was not. He thought neither of them were in much of a state to endure another passion-infused missive from Mr Perceval.

"It's another from your aunt," he informed her, adding with surprise, "And the date is three years ago."

"Please, read it, Mr Patmore."

He began:

"My dear Eliza,

Mr Morley asked me if I would consent to allowing him to ask you for your hand in marriage. I have seen him pay his addresses to you at the past two Assembly Balls, and he indeed seems very taken.

When he told me how greatly he admired you for your beauty and virtue, I knew there could be no happiness in such a union. Were he to wed you only to discover the truth of your sinful past, your unhappiness would be beyond knowing.

I therefore took it upon myself to inform him that you had evinced a disinclination for his company, which is why you had not attended the last Assembly Ball.

Now he has left the district.

I know you may think my actions cruel, but you must believe that I did it only out of concern for you and the family's good name.

For you to be allied to any gentleman is to risk revealing your wicked past.

You have not yet atoned for your sins, and you would not be happy with Mr Morley.

Please accept that I have done what is in your best interests and the interests of the family."

Yours,

Aunt Annabelle Montrose

Rufus felt a chill as he folded the letter. He saw Eliza was very pale and wore a look of great shock. For some reason, he felt ridiculously jealous. "Who was Mr Morley?" he asked.

"A gentleman who admired me once." She fiddled with the lace edge of her nightrail. "At least there's some comfort in knowing the real reason he left. Aunt Montrose told me it was because he'd heard whispers I was a trollop." She glanced up. "Her words."

"Please don't cry, Miss Montrose."

She squeezed her eyes shut. "I'm sorry. It's hard not to."

Rufus wished he could comfort her, but he felt a great need for comfort, himself.

Miss Montrose's past was casting as great a shadow upon himself as it was on her.

⚜

STILL SHAKEN BY WHAT THE CONTENTS OF THE LETTERS revealed, Rufus was pacing in the garden when Lady Fenton's barouche drew up beside him on the gravel drive, and the two Brightwell sisters descended, helped out by the dashing liveried footmen they employed.

"Tell me she's here!" begged Lady Fenton, cool and elegant in black-and-white stripes on this warm late summer's afternoon.

"And that you've asked her to marry you!" added Lady Quamby, garbed, by contrast, in light muslin which left little to the imagination in the bright sunlight and looking very flirtatious as she gripped his arm, the feathers of her bonnet swaying in the breeze.

"She arrived on Devil in the middle of the night." Rufus felt very sombre in the face of their delight.

"I was right!" Lady Quamby clapped her hands in glee, then forced herself to look serious. "We were very worried when we discovered her gone. But then we knew she was making her way right here, and that you'd greet her with open arms and beg her to say yes to your marriage offer!"

"I'm afraid that's not quite how it is." Rufus began to walk, and the young women fell into step on either side of him.

"Well, it must be *made* to be how it is," Lady Quamby said with some severity.

Her sister directed a speaking look in her direction before

asking Rufus, "Miss Montrose has refused you again? I'm surprised, for it was quite clear she'd lost her heart to you."

Rufus stopped, turned to look at her, and sighed. "Miss Montrose lost her heart to Mr Perceval seven years ago. And another gentleman three years ago. I just read her first love's letter to her, which her aunt had withheld. If Miss Montrose had had possession of that communication, she'd be with Perceval now. And with Jack."

"Well, she didn't receive it, and more's the tragedy," said Lady Fenton matter-of-factly. "But she's not in love with him all these seven years later. She saw he was a cad when he came here. She wondered how she could have allowed herself to be taken in by him, but then she was only seventeen, and some men will take advantage of a young girl's innocence, only of course it's the girl who pays the price. Please don't make Miss Montrose continue to pay it when she's quite mad about you."

"Just as you are for her!" Lady Quamby cried.

Rufus clenched his fists. "I want to forgive her," he muttered. "I know I should, and perhaps in time—"

"Good Lord, *now* is the time!" cried Lady Quamby, stopping on the gravel path to stare at him as if he'd taken leave of his senses. "When she's still in bed, under your roof, and you've proved that once again you are here for her. You're the only man who ever *has* been so there for her. She'll love you for it for the rest of her life."

"Really, Antoinette, you're embarrassing Mr Patmore. He would never take advantage of Miss Montrose while she's depending on his protection."

"Well, he should!"

The way the ladies were talking made matters sound not nearly so dire as they were. But the fundamental problem remained. "Miss Montrose has an illegitimate child she would wish to put above all considerations—"

"Well, make him your ward and then ask her to marry you." Lady Quamby smiled brightly as she patted him on the arm. "Go and *show* her how much you love her, and she'll respond. You'll very soon know if you can excite her passions as much as that good-for-nothing Mr Perceval did."

"Antoinette, I think you are still making Mr Montrose uncomfortable," said her sister. "As I said, he is not that kind of gentleman."

"But he thinks Miss Montrose is that kind of lady, and that's what makes me so cross. The moral inequities that so damn a woman's reputation unless she's married!" grumbled Lady Quamby. "I'm sure Mr Montrose has made mad passionate love to many a widow or *married* lady for whom he retains the utmost respect, but just because Miss Montrose happened to be a seventeen-year-old ninnyhammer when the man she thought was going to marry her instead took advantage of her, he puts her into the forever unredeemable category. Am I right, Mr Patmore?"

He felt the sting of heat in his cheeks, and Lady Quamby said with a gurgle of irritation, "I rest my case."

They'd reached the steps and were now nearly at the house, when Lady Fenton stopped him again with a hand on his sleeve and said in sombre tones, "Do think on what we've said, Mr Patmore. What *is* more important? Happiness, or clinging to your ideals? So, what does it truly signify, if she's sinned? Antoinette and I were both with child when *we* married. We were just fortunate enough to get a ring on our fingers in time. I think the true state of one's heart is more important than getting the timing right. And I believe in second chances for all."

☙❧

ELIZA WAS SURE SHE WAS WELL ENOUGH TO GET OUT OF BED. Only, what was the point? She'd been abandoned to this pretty bedroom by the man she loved, just as she'd been abandoned in the tower room by the man she'd loved seven years before, following the vicious brawling between him and her brother.

She'd not seen Orlando again. She'd waited for some communication, begged her parents to let her find him. She'd been passionate and hysterical with love and frustrated hope, until they'd sent her away.

And then they'd withheld all communication. That hurt, deeply. She felt more bitter towards her parents and her aunt than anyone.

She longed for Mr Patmore, and more than just his forgiveness. But without his forgiveness, what hope had she of happiness?

When Ladies Fenton and Quamby entered her bedroom chattering and bearing chocolates, she felt a little cheered by their robust admiration for fleeing their cousin in such a dramatic manner. But only marginally.

"And now we must get you up and dressed, my dear! Yes, no lying abed, languishing like a half-drugged princess!" declared Lady Quamby. "I do believe you thought you could just stare at the ceiling until it was time to be sent home."

"But happiness *is* within your grasp, my dear, if you just show once more the courage you've shown so many times before." Lady Fenton's look was very knowing as she sat beside her and took her hand.

"Mr Patmore has no respect for me. Whatever plans you might have are futile." A large tear rolled down her cheek.

"Nonsense, my dear." Lady Fenton shook her head. "Mr Patmore cannot trust his own heart, which has been severely bruised since he realises you had so many more important things to pursue than him. Gentlemen can be very trying when their pride is dented, as his is."

"What about this one?" Lady Quamby had suddenly appeared beside her sister bearing aloft a very translucent gown, which must surely need two robust petticoats beneath to be decent.

"No, that's not Miss Montrose's style at all, Antoinette. I've already found just the thing. You don't want to confirm Mr Patmore's sad and very mistaken conclusions."

"That I'm a fallen woman and beyond redemption? Certainly not fit to be his wife," Eliza said sadly.

"Now, just you get dressed in this tonight and do everything we tell you, and you can rest assured all will turn out for the best," said Lady Quamby.

"Or, at least not as badly as it will if you do nothing," her sister added.

⚜

So, now Eliza found herself dressed in a Pomona green satin evening gown with a very low and wide décolletage decorated with appliqued flowers, and a skirt in the latest fuller style falling from a slightly lower bodice.

It was Lady Fenton's, and a few stitches had it fitting as if it were made for her. Once her hair had been arranged on top of her head and threaded through with pearls, she looked a true princess, even if she didn't feel like one.

A few judicious cosmetics: Olympian Dew, tincture of roses in her cheeks, and a light dusting of powder across her bosom, and she was ready for dinner—and very conscious of the furtive looks the two ladies directed at both her and Mr Patmore, who seemed very stiff and barely looked at her.

In fact, he'd barely glanced in her direction until Lady Quamby said gushingly as the syllabub was being served, "I do love those roses edging your gown, Miss Montrose. Mr Patmore, look at the handiwork adorning Miss Montrose's neckline. I'm sure you'd not imagine how many hours of stitching went into them."

Eliza saw his eyes drawn to her décolletage, before he blinked rapidly. "I couldn't imagine," he muttered, studiously returning his attention to his food, which was soon finished and cleared away, leaving Eliza eaten up with mortification.

She had to get away. Mr Patmore would never forgive her, and she was an unwanted imposter in his house. She would leave with Ladies Quamby and Fenton in the morning.

"I do hope you'll let us stay an extra day, Mr Patmore. Apparently, some work needs to be done on the right carriage axle, according to John Coachman." Lady Fenton looked enquiringly at their host. "Miss Montrose will come with us, of course. That's unless she wishes to ride Devil all the way to her home."

"Oh, my dear Miss Montrose, I just can't bear to think of how you will sustain yourself," wailed Lady Quamby. "All alone in that little cottage, and now that you've decided to charitably adopt an orphan boy and keep a horse, I fear you may have to start selling your worldly assets. Mr Patmore, we must find a nice farmer for Miss Montrose to marry." She put down her napkin after delicately wiping her rosebud lips and stood up. "In fact, I think it would be an excellent idea if you took Miss Montrose out for a walk right now as the light is still good. It'll be an excellent opportunity for you to help her decide her future. Two heads are always better than one."

If Eliza had been eaten up with mortification before, it was ten-fold worse now.

For some minutes, they walked in silence until, by the edge of a small stream that ran through the grounds, they stopped, turned, and both started talking at once.

Mr Patmore inclined his head. "Please, go ahead, Miss Montrose."

"I apologise for the inconvenience I've caused you by arriving like this. And the embarrassment." Trembling, she looked at the ground and then up at his face, fine-featured, handsome, crowned with curling brown hair, his eyes grey-blue in this light, and hard to read. "I daresay you'll be glad to see the back of me, and I only wish I were leaving tomorrow."

"Do you, Miss Montrose?"

She wasn't sure what he meant. Was that tone low, enquiring, tinged with...disappointment?

He went on, "I can't help thinking about what the ladies were saying at dinner."

"About finding me a nice farmer?" Eliza smiled.

"Yes, that. But about lost opportunities. I'm thinking about Mr Perceval and also Mr Morley. Both were denied you—wrongly. You should be happily married, now."

"But I'm not. Nor am I the only woman who has a tale of tragedy to tell, Mr Montrose." She raised one shoulder slightly. "I am fortunate, though, to have known love. I can't imagine what it must be to have lived like Aunt Montrose—so bereft of human kindness. She was never loved. She can't have been, else she'd not have treated me as she did. That's why I can't regret my past. I did know love. I took the love that was offered to me, not knowing it was forbidden. I've paid a high price, but how can I wish the past undone? I have Jack."

"And what is more important than one's child?"

She frowned. "You do understand, Mr Patmore, that there is more than one kind of love? The love I feel for Jack is very different from the love I feel for you."

He shifted, uncomfortably. "I was going to get to that. I know how deeply you love your son. I understand it's different from the love you felt for Mr Perceval. And for Mr Morley. I've thought long and hard about it, and my marriage offer stands."

"That's romantic," she remarked with heavy sarcasm, feeling dragged down by a great weight of disappointment. "A sensible woman would accept, but I have too much pride. So, no. I won't marry you, Mr Patmore. Not when I know your offer is prompted by decency with no doubt some judicious prompting by the Brightwell sisters, and because I'm penniless, and you somehow feel responsible for me. I would ask you to kiss me, though."

What had she to lose? She could never sink her pride to accept his offer of marriage, but since the reason for his hitherto reluctance was because he considered her fallen, she would take what she could.

He hesitated, though she saw the longing in his eyes and revelled in that small power she had over him. "I couldn't take advantage like that, Miss Montrose. Not if there is to be...nothing more between us."

"I would say there was a great deal between us still, Mr Patmore." She stepped closer and twined her hands about his neck. "You were in love with the idea of marrying a virtuous woman. But just because I failed to live up to your imaginings doesn't mean you don't desire me."

"Are you taunting me?"

"Not at all. I just would like you to kiss me."

His lips parted slightly. In surprise, she thought, as much as anything else, as she drew his head down.

The moment they touched hers, it was like flame to parchment. Followed by instant conflagration. Their last kiss had been consuming; this was incendiary. As his tongue breached the seam of her lips to explore the cavern of her mouth, she felt a tremendous release, then her knees gave way and she was in his arms. She clung to him, sensation fizzing through her veins, her heart on fire.

Eliza moaned at the heat of his wet mouth upon the swell of her breast. A dull, throbbing ache between her legs made her restless for more but here, by the stream, was not the place, and she would have to be satisfied with what he was prepared to offer her—now.

He was hardly about to lay her on the mossy bank and make ardent love to her with no marriage in the offing. Mr Patmore was far too honorable for that.

Arching to meet him, Eliza closed her eyes to better soak in the sweetness of her last encounter with love.

☙❧

"MR PATMORE, ANOTHER LETTER HAS ARRIVED FOR YOU!" MRS Dorley hurried up the passage and entered the breakfast parlour.

"Where is Miss Montrose?" Rufus asked his two breakfast companions as he took the letter. He knew the reason for his housekeeper's excitement, and he felt nervous and a little sick with expectation.

"She went riding very early with Devil," said Lady Fenton. "Long before I was up."

"Do tell us what's in your latest correspondence that's making you so agitated," urged Lady Quamby. "It is, after all, addressed to you."

Rufus slit the seal and unfolded the letter.

"My, momentous news by the look on your face, Mr Patmore," remarked Lady Fenton who was sitting opposite him.

They turned as Miss Montrose entered the room.

"What's momentous news?" she asked, not looking at Mr Patmore, though he was staring very intently at her. With that flush in her cheeks, she looked very lovely indeed.

"I think, perhaps, this should be read in private. It concerns you, Miss Montrose."

"Me!" she exclaimed. "I thought we knew all there was about me!"

Rufus's heart was hammering as he held the missive in hands. He wasn't sure if he would feel over the moon or deeply disappointed in the next few minutes. "It's your aunt's final letter." He cleared his throat and glanced at the three rapt faces now staring at him. "The letter, itself, is obviously addressed to you, Miss Montrose. This, however, is a response from your aunt's solicitor, Mr Cuthbert, regarding some enquiries I made on your behalf— forgive me—regarding what I thought was...suspicious behaviour on the part of your cousin, Susana." He looked down at the writing and a thrill coursed through him. "He has in fact confirmed everything—"

"Confirmed what?" interrupted Lady Quamby.

"Perhaps Miss Montrose should just read her aunt's letter. Mr Cuthbert says everything is detailed within it."

"You're surely not going to read it in private, are you, Miss Montrose?" demanded Lady Quamby. "Not after all we've done to see you as well situated as possible, enjoying our vested interest."

Ignoring them, Miss Montrose took her aunt's letter. As she began to pace up and down the room by the window, she unfolded it, and began to read aloud:

"My dear Eliza,

Your father left me his fortune with the stipulation that when you had served your sentence, you should be free to enjoy the fruits of his labours as you see fit.

For seven years, I have carried out his orders. You were to have no friends, no followers, and no contact with the child you bore, stained as the creature was, with your sin. There have been times when I've questioned whether I've been too harsh, such as in denying you the chance to make up your own mind with regard to Mr Morley's offer.

However, I am sustained by the rightness in such efforts to cleanse you of your wrongdoing. Only by enduring the severest privations can you hope to be redeemed.

You have served me dutifully, if, at times, wilfully.

And so, I make this final Will and Testament that upon my death—and with the exception of a few small bequests, and my cottage which shall go to Susana—the bulk of my fortune and worldly assets will transfer to you."

There was a moment of silence before Lady Fenton said in wonder, "You are a wealthy woman, Miss Montrose."

"And free to follow your heart!" cried Lady Quamby.

Miss Montrose stared around at all of them as if she couldn't believe her eyes.

And then she picked up her skirts and fled into the corridor.

CHAPTER 21

Immediately Eliza left the breakfast room she ran all the way to Devil.

Together they'd ridden as far as the horizon and back.

A great joy filled her, but a great sadness too. Her aunt had stolen seven years from her through a misguided sense of redeeming her.

Lying on the grass in the middle of a paddock, she thought on all she'd felt and witnessed. The Brightwell sisters claimed Mr Patmore's injured pride coupled with his belief that she'd put Jack ahead of him, accounted for his attitude.

Was pride, rather than condemnation of her moral laxness, the real reason he'd not fought for her?

When she returned as the sun was dipping over the horizon, she went straight to her bedchamber. She couldn't face them at dinner. There was too much to think about. She knew the young ladies would be in a fever of impatience to seek her out and learn what she intended to do.

But they'd have to wait until morning.

Mr Patmore, on the other hand, would only have to wait until tonight.

IT WAS WELL AFTER TEN WHEN THE HOUSE BECAME QUIET, AND she heard the guests retiring for the night. With beating heart, Eliza crept out of her bedchamber, in her nightrail covered with a shawl, and softly trod the corridor towards Mr Patmore's room. She was prepared for a rebuttal, but she also knew she couldn't bear not to be given one more chance.

Just one more chance at happiness. She'd been denied that final chance with Orlando, and she'd been denied any chance with Mr Morley.

After a soft knock on Mr Patmore's bedchamber door, and not hearing any response, she quietly pushed open the door, and candle held aloft, tiptoed into his bedchamber.

Her disappointment was acute when she saw his bed empty and no sign of him anywhere.

Putting her candle on the side table, she lowered herself onto the bed and put her face in her hands.

Well, she had been given a chance, she thought. A chance to save herself the embarrassment of another rebuttal.

Rising to her feet, she turned, just as the door opened.

"Mr Patmore!"

"Miss Montrose!"

They spoke at the same time, as he strode towards her, putting his hands on her shoulders and drawing her into the light.

"Is something the matter?" He looked concerned. And very desirable. She wanted to put her lips to the corner of his mouth and run her tongue down the groove that opened up when he smiled.

Slowly pulling the covers back, she patted the crisp linen sheets. "My aunt has given me leave to follow my heart," she whispered. "And that is what I'm doing."

"Following your heart?"

She nodded, just able to make out his smile in the dim light cast by the candle.

"You realise where this will lead if I let you stay?"

"If you let me stay? Oh, yes." She nodded, a little thrill starting at her toes, for his eyes were fixed firmly on hers, and the intensity in his look was growing her confidence by the moment. "You can join me." She patted the mattress again. "In the bed."

"It *is* my bed, Miss Montrose."

"I think you should call me Eliza, Mr Montrose."

"And Rufus is probably appropriate under the circumstances." He moved very slightly forward, but didn't divest himself of his banyan. Instead, he bent over her to cup her face in his hands so as to direct at her a very serious look.

"You have just inherited a very large amount of money, Eliza. You are free to live your life as you choose."

Eliza opened her mouth, disappointment churning in her belly. This wasn't what he was supposed to say. She wanted him to embrace her with a passionate avowal of all she thought he felt. Instead, he went on, "You don't have to rely on any man to keep you, or to enable you to keep your son, or hunger from the door. Think on what that liberty—so long denied you—could feel like."

Hurt, she said, "Not so long ago, you were willing to marry me to enable me to have and do all those things. Does this mean your feelings have changed?"

"Lord, no!" The vehemence with which he said those words was reassuring. "The truth is, I adore you, Eliza. I have from the moment I laid eyes on you. Actually, that's not true," he amended. "I thought, like Ladies Quamby and Fenton, that you were distant and abrasive. The very words *you* used, as I recall. But then I saw a different side to you, and I was lost. But—" He put his hands on her shoulders to draw her closer, "You were not truthful with me, Eliza. I could have borne anything but that."

Tears thickened her throat. She inhaled on a sob. "I know you've been hurt by the fact I didn't confide in you but you must know how much I had to lose? Everything! Including your love for me." She stared over his shoulder a moment before meeting his eye. "I was afraid, I admit it, Rufus. So afraid that I chose to have your love as a memory to treasure my whole life on the basis that at least I could leave you, knowing you thought only the best of me." She swallowed painfully before adding, "Knowing that if you knew the truth, you would condemn and despise me."

He shook his head. "I have thought long and hard, Eliza, and I do not condemn and despise you. Yes, there was a time I felt your love was only for your child and I was your last consideration—"

"No, that was never the case!" she exclaimed. "I always loved you. I remember the very moment I fell in love with you, Rufus." Gathering herself, Eliza took a deep breath as she guided his hands from her face. "You can lift me onto the bed and join me there." She smiled, embarrassed. "I know exactly where this will lead, and I'm feeling very anxious to...feel your arms about me, instead of making me sit in the cold when you're wearing a cosy banyan while I'm shivery in the finest cambric."

He laughed softly, then leaned over and slipped his hands beneath her knees to lay her on the bed, joining her hurriedly there once he'd removed his banyan.

"Oh! You're not wearing a nightshift!" she squeaked.

"That accounted for part of my reluctance to remove my banyan before I'd established on what basis you were here."

"Because I love you, of course. As I've already told you." She snuggled into his side.

"But that's not enough for me, Eliza." He rolled onto his stomach and stared into her eyes. "I don't want you to leave me after loving me. I want to know you'll stay. That you'll be my wife. But that'll mean you'd have to give up a great deal."

"What do you mean?" she asked in sudden alarm, all the pleasant sensations evaporating upon the instant to be replaced by the familiar angst and uncertainty that had dogged her since she'd known him. "Not Jack!"

"Lord, no!" He looked horrified at the idea. "I know that you love your child above all, and I would never countenance such a thing. He's a very special lad, besides, and we can make a plausible story about him being my ward. I meant your independence, Eliza.

Money confers independence. You could live in great comfort, start afresh, introduce Jack as a legitimate member of your household. You could have anyone you chose—or no one."

"But I want you, Rufus." She took his hand and moved it slightly lower. "Please stroke me there. You almost did before, and I was in a fever of anticipation that you would, until you got distracted and started telling how much I'd enjoy my independence with all that money, and that I wouldn't need you."

"That's not what I said. Or what I meant."

"And loving Jack above all is to entirely misrepresent what love is. Oh yes, that's just perfect." He'd found her nipple, and the warmth of his palm as he stroked her breast, in between rolling her nipple around his palm, caused an utterly delicious warmth to travel up her legs all the way to her groin. She forced herself to blink open her eyes so she could read his expression. "I love Jack with a mother's fierce protective instinct. You'll feel that when you have children of your own, I hope, Rufus."

"Of *our* own, Eliza."

She liked the fact he suddenly looked so happy at the prospect. "Children of our own? Oh yes, that's a perfectly wonderful sounding idea," she said on a sigh, that was both contemplative at what he'd said, but tinged with a growing bodily appreciation of what he was doing, ending on a squeak as he put his mouth to her breast and began to suckle. She put out her hands intending to wrap them round his back, and along the way encountered his very large manhood as he'd now caged her body with her own.

Wrapping her hand around him, she murmured, "You really are the perfect gentleman and my utter ideal of the manliest man, too, Rufus. Ever since I fell in love with you literally two seconds before I found myself face to face with Jack, I thought you the kindest, most *honourable* of gentlemen. And I'm so glad you want to have children with me." Increasing the pressure of her hand at the same time as wriggling and arching a little to meet him, she added, "Can you please ask me that question again. Starting from the beginning, and properly. You know, the question that comes before the talk about having children."

He laughed, raising his face to look at her. "Oh my goodness, Eliza, you are quite delightful! I didn't know you had such a playful side when I was perfectly happy to be in love with you for all your other good qualities." Clearing his voice, he squeezed his eyes closed, briefly, as if enduring a great test, then said, "Just for a second, though, would you mind not putting so much pressure on me down there. I want to gather my thoughts and say this as you'd want to hear it."

"As I want to hear it? But I want you to say it as *you* want to say it."

"Yes, but it's the same thing." He swooped to kiss her briefly on the lips, then rose above her so he could look her in the eye once more. "You'll want to remember the words I use to tell you how much adore you, and how being with you makes me feel complete for the first time in my life. I need to have my wits about me, not addled by the utterly sinfully and wickedly pleasure I'm feeling right now."

"I don't mind if your wits are addled, or if mine are, either. This truly is the most sinfully wicked pleasure I've felt in my life. You can move your hand down a bit while you're telling me."

"You mean here? Oh, my, Eliza, you really are feeling the same as me."

Eliza gasped and hunched her shoulders as he felt the slick desire between her legs. Shivers of anticipation ran through her, and she moaned softly as he began to stroke her.

"That is quite the most beautiful sensation, and you are quite the most beautiful man," she whispered.

"Eliza, before I go any further, I want to know—will you marry me?" His voice was strained. "I promise to ask you again on bended knee in the conservatory. In fact, I was going to do that tomorrow morning so that it would all be beautiful for you and conventional, and then we could emerge, beaming, with you on my arm, while Lady Fenton and Lady Quamby clapped and looked tearful, and exclaimed that it was only due to their intervention that finally you'd accepted my proposal."

Eliza had increased the pressure on his manhood as he spoke, and was now massaging it in a way that was clearly quite distracting for him. As for her, she was drowning in bliss.

"A perfect idea!" she whispered, wriggling some more, then arching, and finally wrapping her legs around his waist. "My answer is an unqualified yes in this instance." She was vaguely aware of how addled her own wits were becoming as she tried to push out the words before pure pleasure took over. Taking a few quick breaths and feeling the heat build within her, she gasped, "Yes! We'll pretend for everyone else that you're making your proposal in just the gentlemanly fashion everyone would expect. That sounds just perfect, don't you think?"

"Just perfect," he managed as he breached her entrance on a groan of pure satisfaction, moving his head down to meet her lips. "Like you."

EPILOGUE

T*wo years later*

Dawn was breaking, and the night had been a long one. At first, Eliza's labour had progressed well, but from midnight, one complication, then another, had soured what was supposed to be a gloriously happy event for their little family.

Rufus stopped his pacing to stare through the window at the lovely garden outside. It was summer, and Eliza had chosen to give birth in the room next door. It's where she'd first slept when she arrived at his house, nearly two years before.

"Uncle?" The door opened and Jack's little face appeared, crumpled with sleep and concern. "Is everything going to be all right, Uncle?" He padded across the room, dragging the quilt he had wrapped around his shoulders, and stood next to Rufus to stare across the dew-covered lawn, glistening in the breaking dawn.

"Your Aunt Eliza should be enjoying this view right now, with the new baby," Rufus murmured, as he ruffled the boy's soft curls. Despite his terrible fears, he had to be calm.

Jack yawned. "I thought the baby would be here by now. I listened all night for the knock. Nurse Mabel said you'd find it under the mulberry tree over there, but it's too cold out for a baby. Don't worry, Uncle. It's just late." He gave another great yawn as he rested his head against Rufus's side and Rufus felt a surge of affection for this joyful, clever child who'd brought Eliza such happiness and him a greater appreciation of life's important nuances. Nothing could ever be regarded in terms of black and white.

"Thank you for the reassurance, Jack. You're quite right, of course," he said, smiling down at the child. "But you should go to bed, now."

Jack yawned again. "I'd really like to answer the door, if I might. I've got so much to show my new cousin. Did you order a boy or a girl? Nurse said you weren't going to tell anyone. She said surprises are nice. Personally, I'm not too fond of surprises, but I'll be happy whether it's a girl or a boy."

"Easy to please, aren't you, Jack?" Despite his growing concern for Eliza, Rufus found himself smiling again. Jack did that to a person, he'd discovered. The boy was a delight to have around, and there'd been no raised eyebrows when he'd been introduced into the household as his ward, even though he'd spoken like an urchin. The assumption was, of course, that Jack was the result of one of Rufus's liaisons, and being the honourable fellow Rufus was, he'd taken responsibility. His sisters had viewed Eliza in an even rosier light as they'd remarked upon how accepting she was. They believed she must love Rufus a great deal to treat Jack as her own, engaging a highly recommended tutor and ensuring the child was as finely dressed as any of the gentleman's sons with whom she seemed to want him to associate.

Rufus had been very happy at the way events had turned out.

Not now, though. Not with tonight's unfolding drama that made his gut churn and only served to highlight how essential Eliza was to his happiness.

"Mr Patmore!" The urgency of the midwife's voice cut through the silence and Rufus's reflections.

"I think you should go back to your room, Jack," Rufus said, trying to hide his fear. "I'll let you know if—when—our little visitor arrives." He patted the boy on the back, and gently propelled him towards the door as he hurried towards the anxious-looking woman.

"Mr Patmore, the doctor wants to know your decision now in case..." The midwife hesitated and wiped her hands on her apron as she looked down, avoiding his eye. "In case he can only save one of them." She cleared her throat. "Would you prefer the doctor to save your son or your wife?"

He looked at her as if she were mad. There was no question about it; Eliza would come first every time. It was only now he registered that the child was a boy. He bit down on the brief flare of excitement. Nothing mattered except Eliza's welbeing.

"Mr Patmore, before you answer, you must know that there's a possibility your wife will be unable to have more children." She sent him an almost challenging look. "You need to know that before you decide."

"No, I don't." He shook his head, closing his eyes as he digested this piece of news. "As long as Eliza makes it through this, that's all that matters." He gripped the curtain, wanting to wrench it from its position as a mark of his rage.

Every day for the last two years, he'd been lucky enough to cherish Eliza. She'd made the days warmer, his life happier, his world brighter.

"I can't bear to lose her."

"Yes, sir," the woman said, returning to the birthing chamber.

With his eyes still closed, he slumped down on the window seat by the half-open door that separated the two bedrooms. He could hear the sounds within as the doctor issued orders to the midwife. Rufus had insisted on a London physician rather than a local midwife, although his sisters had been critical. Eliza had smiled and said she'd do whatever made him happy.

It's how she was. Full of joy, always kind, ready to make so many little concessions to add peace and comfort to Rufus's life, yet not being afraid of telling him when she thought he was wrong. God, he loved her!

And now he feared that his insistence on having his own way might have cost Eliza her life. The Princess Charlotte had died in childbed not long before, under the care of a male physician.

He put his head in his hands and tried to stay strong. Something was happening in the next room, and the increasing urgency transmitted right throughout his body.

"Eliza, my dear one, I don't know if I can go on without you," he whispered to himself. He was unaware of time.

Perhaps hours had passed, perhaps only minutes, when he jerked his head up at the sound of his name being called softly by the midwife, standing on the threshold.

"Mr Patmore, Mr Patmore, would you like to come in now?"

"Eliza...?" he began, his voice breaking.

"Your wife is fine, Mr Patmore. And so is your son." Discreetly, the midwife produced a cloth so he could wipe his streaming eyes. "You may go in and see them now."

"Eliza!" Rufus hurried into the room, unwilling to believe what only his eyes could tell him.

"Rufus!" Pale, and with dark shadows under her eyes, but serene as ever, Eliza was lying in the bed, propped up on pillows. She lowered her voice which was full of pride. "Darling Rufus, look at our new visitor." Smiling, she gently pulled back the soft cloth that was swaddling their new baby.

Rufus went down on his knees and put his arm around them both, resting his head for a moment on Eliza's breast before he raised his eyes to look at her. A love so great it was almost unbearable filled his heart. "You are so brave. I heard it all. I haven't left that room. Eliza—" his voice broke— "I don't think I would have wanted to go on if anything happened to you."

"I wasn't going anywhere, dearest," she told him, leaning over to kiss the top of his head. "Not when there's so much more happiness to be had." She stroked his face and he gripped her hand, not trusting himself to speak as she went on, "So I just followed the doctor's instructions until this little fellow arrived. And now we're a family." Her smile was like the breaking dawn of a new and wonderful day. "You, and our baby son."

"And Jack," murmured Rufus without pausing to think as he kissed her gently on the lips.

THE END

ABOUT THE AUTHOR

Beverley was seventeen when she bundled up her first 500+ page romance and sent it to a publisher. Rejection followed swiftly. Drowning one's heroine on the last page, she was informed, was not in line with the expectations of romance readers.

So Beverley became a journalist.

After a whirlwind romance with a handsome Norwegian bush pilot she met in Botswana's beautiful Okavango Delta, Beverley discovered what real romance was all about, saved her heroine from a watery grave in her next manuscript and published her first romance in 2009.

Since then, she's written more than fifteen sizzling historical romances laced with mystery and intrigue under the name Beverley Oakley.

She also writes psychological historical mysteries, and Colonial-Africa-set romantic suspense, as Beverley Eikli.

With an inspiring view of a Gothic nineteenth-century insane asylum across the road, Beverley lives north of Melbourne with her gorgeous husband, two lovely daughters and a rambunctious Rhodesian Ridgeback called Mombo, named after the safari lodge where she and her husband met.

You can read more at www.beverleyoakley.com

www.beverleyoakley.com/
beverley.oakley@gmail.com

ROGUE'S KISS (BOOK 2)

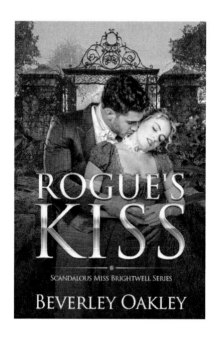

If you'd like to read where Eliza's story begins, seven years earlier, you can meet her on the first page of **Rogue's Kiss**.

Here's an extract.

Rogue's Kiss

Would a potential suitor be bolder if he were told the object of his desire had only six months to live?

Sweet, pretty Thea Brightwell's dull, quiet life with her crotchety aunt is about to be turned upside down by a visit to Bath and a chance encounter with handsome Mr Grayling.

However, the fledgeling affair is quickly nipped in the bud by Thea's aunt who has no intention of losing her unpaid nurse and companion, while Mr Grayling regretfully acknowledges he needs to marry an heiress to restore his family's crumbling fortunes.

Unbeknownst to penniless Thea, she has an unlikely champion in her well-meaning but 'not-too-bright' Cousin Bertram who has decided to play matchmaker.

If the lack of a dowry is the only impediment to Mr Grayling making an offer of marriage, Bertram reasons the gentleman would play a riskier hand if he were told that the damsel he covets were destined for her deathbed within six months?

Crotchety maiden aunts, love letters gone astray, and 'old flames' appearing from the woodwork lead to a most disconcerting outcome!

What Readers are Saying about the series:

"I LOVED beautiful Thea's story and couldn't put it down losing hours of sleep!"

"The unexpected twist at the end made me smile and think...yes that's perfect."

"Nicely written and enjoyable Historical romance with a little steam."

*Note: Due to the respective natures of the various Brightwell heroines, Rogue's Kiss is sensual rather than steamy while Rake's Honour is hot and steamy.

EXTRACT

Sylvester stared after lovely Miss Thea Brightwell in genuine bemusement and, to avoid looking like a fool, half-heartedly speared a slice of nearly transparent ham from the sad looking display before him and deposited it on his plate. This was not the way he'd expected matters to proceed.

Surely the scorching looks Miss Brightwell had sent him could not have been misconstrued? Yet no sooner had he contrived to present himself once more to her when she was no longer in company with the oyster-velvet-clad gorgon, than she'd run off like a frightened rabbit...or a coquette. Which was it? Could she really have been playing games?

"Charming chit, ain't she?" Bertram Brightwell's bluff laugh cut into Sylvester's musings and he turned to raise an eyebrow at the young man who was accompanied by his beautiful sister, the youngest, blonde—not to mention, scandalous—Miss Antoinette, who'd snared an earl and whose supposed antics behind closed doors titillated society.

He'd met Lady Quamby—though he could only think of her as Miss Antoinette—at the earl's birthday celebration earlier that year, just weeks after she'd given birth, in fact. Not that one could tell. The girl was exquisite in pale pink silk with silver trimmings, and her bearing was confident, almost conspiratorial, yet when he glanced over her creamy bared shoulder towards the far corner of the room, where her lovely, chestnut-haired but less flamboyant cousin had just jilted him by the food table, she paled into insignificance.

"More of a charming enigma," Sylvester responded.

"Pray enlarge?" Miss Antoinette's blue eyes danced with mischief. There was nothing maternal about her, he thought. She was as flirtatious as he imagined she must have been before she'd become Lord Quamby's countess. Forcing his gaze away from the more sober but more enticing—to his eyes, at least—Miss Thea Brightwell he tried not to stare, but the stories he'd heard about Quamby's wife were incredible; that the earl gave her complete licence to seek out pleasure discreetly as her reward for silence regarding his own peccadilloes. Dangerous ones, he understood, that courted the death penalty.

Before he had a chance to respond, Bertram said, with an intense frown, "No telling what a gel will do if she's only got six months to live."

"What?"

It tumbled from Miss Antoinette's lips with an expletive and Sylvester's own as a gasp of dismay. "Six months?"

Miss Antoinette looked shocked. "What are you saying, Bertram?" she demanded.

Bertram sighed heavily. "I overheard Dr Horne telling Cousin Thea the terrible news. Don't you wonder why she looks so sad and won't dance? Her heart cannot be exposed to sudden shocks... although," he looked contemplative, "I did also hear the doctor say that gentle pleasures and mild, controlled excitement might well prolong her life." He cleared his throat, adding, "That is, by a couple of months or so only."

Sylvester shook his head, his horror echoing Miss Antoinette's, who clearly had not been privy to the news of her lovely cousin's imminent demise. "Poor young woman," he murmured. "So lovely and so..."

"Doomed," Bertram supplied with a sigh. "Still," he brightened, "she is to be commended on her stoic acceptance of her miserable lot. Her aunt has brought her to Bath to take the waters but sadly is so concerned for her niece's health, she will allow Miss Brightwell no pleasure whatsoever."

"She would not allow me to even dance with her," Sylvester recalled, the rejection taking on a different hue. "Is she...so reduced in health?"

"Oh, Miss Brightwell would dance a jig if she were allowed. She simply craves something that will draw her out of the unhappy final few months she's been allotted." He shrugged before fixing Sylvester with a long and meaningful stare. "But what chance is there of that?"

Buy Rogue's Kiss here.

ALSO BY BEVERLEY OAKLEY

The Daughters of Sin series follows the intertwining lives and sibling rivalry of Lord Partington's two nobly born - and two illegitimate - daughters as they compete for love during several London Seasons.

With Hetty and Araminta both falling for men on opposing sides of a dastardly plot that is being investigated by Stephen Cranbourne, now a secret agent in the Foreign Office, there's lashings of skullduggery and intrigue bound up in the central romance.

And, just in case you're ever worried that someone doesn't get their happy ending, or just desserts – rest assured that they will do, either in their book, or by the end of the series.

What Readers are Saying About the Series:

"...lies, misdeeds, treachery, and romance. What an impressive story! Ms. Oakley has a unique way of telling her stories, bringing unknown heroes/ heroines into the spotlight, as they navigate a world of espionage, and intrigue, all while trying to survive and find their HEA. Magnificent and mesmerizing!" ~ **Amazon reader**

"Full of secrets, murders, intrigues and you feel you know the characters and want to strangle some of them, especially Araminta!!! I have since read all in the series and can't wait for Book 5... This is a series I will read again and again." ~ **Amazon reader**

Below is the order of the books:

Book 1: Her Gilded Prison
  Book 2: Dangerous Gentlemen
  Book 3: The Mysterious Governess Book 4: Beyond Rubies
  Book 5: Lady Unveiled: The Cuckold Conspiracy

Here's a bit about them:

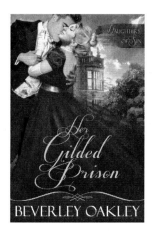

She was determined to secure the succession, he was in it for the pleasure. Falling in love was not part of the arrangement.
*** *When dashing twenty-five-year-old Stephen Cranbourne arrives at the estate he will one day inherit, it's expected he will make a match with his beautiful second cousin, Araminta. But while proud, fiery Araminta and her shy, plain sister, Hetty, parade their very different charms before him, it's their mother, Sybil, a lonely and discarded wife, who evokes first his sympathy and then stokes his lustful fires.*

Shy, plain Hetty was the wallflower beneath his notice...until a terrible mistake has one dangerous, delicious rake believing she's the "fair Cyprian" ordered for his pleasure. *** Shy, self-effacing Henrietta knows her place—in her dazzling older sister's shadow. She's a little brown peahen to Araminta's bird of paradise. But when Hetty mistakenly becomes embroiled in the Regency underworld, the innocent debutante finds herself shockingly compromised by the dashing, dangerous Sir Aubrey, the very gentleman her heart desires. And the man Araminta has in her cold, calculating sights. Branded an enemy of the Crown, bitter over the loss of his wife, Sir Aubrey wants only to lose himself in the warm, willing body of the young "prostitute" Hetty. As he tutors her in the art of lovemaking, Aubrey is pleased to find Hetty not only an ardent student, but a bright, witty and charming companion. Despite a spoiled Araminta plotting for a marriage offer and a powerful political enemy damaging his reputation, Aubrey may suffer the greatest betrayal at the hands of the little "concubine" who's managed to breach the stony exterior of his heart.

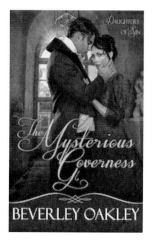

Lissa Hazlett lives life in the shadows. The beautiful, illegitimate daughter of Viscount Partington earns her living as an overworked governess while her vain and spoiled half sister, Araminta, enjoys London's social whirl as its most feted debutante. When Lissa's rare talent as a portraitist brings her unexpectedly into the bosom of society – and into the midst of a scandal involving Araminta and suspected English traitor Lord Debenham – she finds an unlikely ally: charming and besotted Ralph Tunley, Lord Debenham's underpaid, enterprising secretary.

*Fame. Fortune. And finally a marriage proposal! Book 4 of
the Daughters of Sin series introduces Miss Kitty La Bijou,
celebrated London actress, mistress to handsome Lord Nash and the
unacknowledged illegitimate daughter of Viscount Partington.
Having escaped her humble beginnings, Kitty has found fame, fortune
and love, but the respectability she craves eludes her. When she
stumbles across Araminta, her legitimate half-sister, on the verge of
giving birth just seven months after marrying dangerous Viscount
Debenham, Kitty realises respectability is no guarantee of character
or happiness. But helping Araminta has unwittingly embroiled Kitty
in a scandalous deception involving a ruthless brothel madam, a
priceless ruby necklace and the future heir to a dazzling fortune. And
when Kitty finally receives an offer of marriage she must choose.
Respectability or love?*

Kitty has the love of the man of her dreams but as London's most acclaimed actress and a member of the demimondaine, she accepts she can never be kind and handsome Lord Silverton's lawful wedded wife. When Kitty comes to the aid of shy, accident-prone and kind-hearted Octavia Mandelton, her sense of justice leads to her making the most difficult decision of her life: Give up the man she loves for the sake of honour. For Octavia is still betrothed to Lord Silverton who'd rescued Kitty in dramatic circumstances only weeks before. Cast adrift, Kitty joins forces with her sister, Lissa, a talented artist posing as a governess in order to bring to justice a dangerous spy, villainous Lord Debenham. Complicating matters is the fact Debenham is married to their half-sister, vain and beautiful Araminta. However, Araminta has a dark secret which only Kitty knows and which she realizes she is duty-bound to expose if she's to achieve justice and win happiness for deserving Lissa and Lissa's enterprising sweetheart, Ralph Tunley, long-suffering secretary to Lord Debenham. All seems set for a happy ending when Kitty tumbles into mortal danger. A danger from which only a truly honorable man can save her. A man like Silverton who must now make the hardest choice of his life if he's to live with his conscience.

Buy the complete series as a Box set and save.

Four very different sisters compete for love during an exciting London season: a celebrated actress with a heart of gold, a shy yet daring wallflower, and the artistic, illegitimate daughter of a nobleman. Caught up in a high-stakes game of intrigue and deceit orchestrated by their sister, the ton's reigning beauty, each must play their part to bring a dangerous traitor to justice while finding a man deserving of their love and special talents.

SCANDALOUS MISS BRIGHTWELLS BOX SET

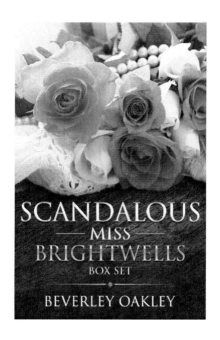

Wicked and lively Fanny and Antoinette Brightwell have made spectacular marriages—despite scandals and the treachery of a disappointed suitor determined to derail their plans and besmirch their reputations.

So, who better to play matchmaker when a deserving candidate waltzes into their orbit?

Here are the first three stories in the series. Each can be read as a stand-alone.

1. Rake's Honour (Totally sizzling. Insatiable Fanny is a wild child!)

2. Rogue's Kiss (Sensual - not sizzling at all. Sweet and innocent Thea follows the rules.)

3. Devil's Run (A bit more sensual than **Rogue's Kiss** but not sizzling like **Rake's Honour**. Eliza has a 'past' and although she's sworn off falling in love, she knows what love is when she stumbles upon it.)

Save when you buy the Scandalous Miss Brightwells Box Set here.

WHAT'S NEXT?

I was going to write the next story about the gypsy girl in *Rogue's Kiss* who had to give up her child, but after writing *Devil's Run*, my fingers were itching to give Jack and Katherine their own story.

Easy-going Jack and spirited Katherine really grew on me as their characters developed and I thought they'd be a great match, so began to write about them the moment I'd finished *Devil's Run*.

Unfortunately, when Jack and Katherine meet each other again at eighteen years old—and fall passionately in love—Jack's about to start a brilliant career and is on the verge of setting sail for the West Indies.

Though the star-crossed lovers try every ingenious way to remain together, they're forced apart by treachery (you'll never guess where from!) and it's another five years before they meet again.

By this time, their respective circumstances are very different.

I haven't thought of a title for this story yet, but I hope to have it available in early 2018.

And if there are any other characters whose stories you'd like to hear, you can let me know at www.beverleyoakley.com or https://www.facebook.com/AuthorBeverleyOakley/

If you enjoyed the *Devil's Ride*, I'd really appreciate an honest review at www.amazon.com.au, www.amazon.com and www.-goodreads.com. Authors rely on readers' reviews to stand out (hopefully in a good way).

Warmest regards,

Beverley Oakley

Manufactured by Amazon.ca
Acheson, AB